FROM THE GRAVE

FROM THE GRAVE

Jay Brandon

This first world edition published 2019
in Great Britain and 2020 in the USA by
SEVERN HOUSE PUBLISHERS LTD of
Eardley House, 4 Uxbridge Street, London W8 7SY.
Trade paperback edition first published
in Great Britain and the USA 2020 by
SEVERN HOUSE PUBLISHERS LTD.

British Library Cataloguing in Publication Data
A CIP catalogue record for this title is available from the British Library.

ISBN-13: 978-0-7278-8900-3 (cased)
ISBN-13: 978-1-78029-644-9 (trade paper)
ISBN-13: 978-1-4483-0343-4 (e-book)

All Severn House titles are printed on acid-free paper.

Severn House Publishers support the Forest Stewardship Council™ [FSC™],
the leading international forest certification organisation.
All our titles that are printed on FSC certified paper carry the FSC logo.

Typeset by Palimpsest Book Production Ltd.,
Falkirk, Stirlingshire, Scotland.
Printed and bound in Great Britain by
TJ International, Padstow, Cornwall.

Long-time friends are the best friends.
This is dedicated to Marina Sifuentes and Barbara Hervey.

ONE

A wall-wide window across from Edward afforded a gorgeous view of downtown Houston from this twenty-fourth-floor vantage. It was a clear day, the blue Texas sky as innocent as a virgin's whisper, and the skyscrapers seemed to give each other breathing room rather than jostling together as they appeared from a distance. It looked like the Emerald City. Around the conference table of this international construction company were several executives, but the important one was the fortyish young woman to Edward's left, the COO. In her two years with the company she had managed to extend its contacts into agreements with the heads of some Middle Eastern partner companies. This firm was now putting up their first office building in Dubai. Their security concerns had grown more complex, which was why Edward was here.

He had impressed Vivian Long with his seriousness and quiet attention to details in the proposal he'd shown her last time. Around the conference table now were five of their highest-level officers. They didn't talk details of computer systems, intranet versus internet, or any of that techie minutiae. They hired people for that. At this meeting these people did most of the talking and Edward mostly nodded. They noticed that he didn't take notes, and approved, especially after he quoted back from memory a sentence the COO had said five minutes earlier. Nothing in writing. Security.

What Edward had missed was this high level of negotiation, so high that no one treated it like a negotiation. The officers acted as if Edward were already working for them, and he in turn acted as if he were already their partner. While in fact they hadn't told him one thing he could use against them if they booted him out the door in the next two minutes. And they all knew he understood that. They didn't have to bullshit each other. Which meant they were all operating at a very refined level of bullshit.

'Our people will never see anything inside your system,' Edward said. 'They will only build walls around them. Your secrets are safe with us because we won't know them.'

'Like the slaves who built the pyramids,' one of the partners said, and Edward chuckled along with the rest of them.

'Exactly. And every few months we kill them and hire new ones.'

That got an even bigger laugh. Buried bodies was an apt subject matter for a security consultant.

A few minutes later Vivian extended her hand. She had given him twenty-three minutes, a huge chunk of her day. After murmured exchanges of respect, Vivian said, 'Do you feel up to meeting with our Mr Windsor, our attorney, to discuss details?'

'Absolutely.'

'Good. Mr Windsor?' Her hand was still in Edward's, and she didn't break their gaze as she spoke to one of the other men at the table. Neither did Edward, until Ms Long intensified the gaze one last time and abruptly turned away.

'This way, please,' said Bill Windsor, who looked as if he might actually be a member of the British royal family, at the grey-at-the-temple stage. As he led Edward to his office he glanced back over his shoulder and said, 'We're not going to talk details, just broad parameters, OK?'

A few minutes later they were Bill and Ed. None of the very few people who knew Edward well called him anything except Edward, but the world beyond those few was littered with his nicknames.

A few minutes later still, Bill leaned back, looked at him more closely, and said, 'Your name sounds awfully familiar to me. Ed Hall. Are you a lawyer?'

A more complicated question than it might seem. 'No. I was. I got bored with it.'

A lie. Sort of the secret handshake of the legal fraternity.

'I know what you mean. So many of us do. Awfully high burnout rate.'

'Awfully high.'

'Want to know my theory on that?'

Less than anything. Hear this mid-six-figures sellout who hadn't really practiced law in years explain why people got tired of it? As if this asshole even knew what practicing law really was? Less than anything.

'Sure, Bill.'

So Edward sat and listened to the blowhard explain why lawyers got tired of solving other people's problems, Edward sitting with a slight smile because he was imagining the silence of his team burrowing through the firm's firewalls into all their secrets, the lies they'd told to judges, the clients they'd overbilled, the mistakes they'd covered up. He was going to keep his promise to Vivian the COO to stay out of this firm's confidential information, with one exception. He was going to know this guy's ugliest secrets. Edward was going to take whatever he could get, like a thief in a bank vault at midnight.

'That's interesting,' he finally applauded the lawyer's smug, quiet rant.

'Right? That's what happened to you, right? Just reached a point of saying, Look, solve your own problems, idiots. It's not that tough. Right?'

Edward closed his briefcase. 'That's it exactly.'

At the same time, down there on the ground in a very different part of town, a SWAT team of police assembled around a little wooden house in the Third Ward, a building little more than a shack. The cops could shoot it full of holes and not change its essential appearance all that much.

But they wouldn't do that, at least not yet. This wasn't just an arrest, it was a rescue.

The negotiator, not part of the team, was closest to the house, unarmed, talking in an only slightly raised tone of voice. The negotiator, a thin African-American of middle height, dressed like a civilian, glanced back over his shoulder like he didn't trust these mostly white cops either. 'Listen, man,' he said, back to the house, 'you need to let her go. That's your only good move now. That'll show some good will on your part. That'll help you in court. 'Cause unless you're digging a tunnel in there, you got no escape route.'

Amazingly, in that cluster with all its potential for din, a silence began, at first a newborn absence of talk, then growing swiftly into a bubble engulfing the whole scene like tear gas. Then a voice emerged from the house. A deep voice but jagged with a high whine close under the surface. 'She's a free agent, man. I ain't holding her. I don't even know what all you assholes are doing here.'

'If that's true then let her go. You and me'll talk.'

'Yeah, and then your friends will shoot my ass up.'

'No, man, no. Not if you let her go.' The negotiator stepped closer to the house and lowered his voice. 'There's a camera crew here, Donald.'

That silence spawned again, groping for a character. Just before it would die of natural causes there was the scrape of a shoe from inside the house, and the door shot open. The negotiator, in the bravest act of his life, stood his ground and held a hand behind his back with the fingers spread, pushing down. Hold your fire.

A woman screamed, then came running out. Luckily, the SWAT team members had good reflexes, and the scream had alerted them this was probably a civilian. It was. It was *the* civilian they had come to rescue. Mrs Diana Greene, prominent Houston socialite, disheveled, frantic, her fashionable shift twisted at the shoulders.

Her husband Sterling threw off the two officers restraining him, broke through the ranks, and held his arms wide. His wife ran into them. They were the picture of a loving couple happily reunited.

Now the negotiator knew it was going to be OK. He'd talked the kidnapper out of the hostage, his main job. Now his armed colleagues could just shoot up the house.

Except for that camera crew.

'Now you, man.' The negotiator was surprised to hear more than indifference in his own voice. 'No point in doing that unless you surrender . . . Donald?'

Slowly two large hands emerged from the doorway. They hung there for a minute. When nothing happened, arms started emerging too. This took longer than one would think, because they were very long arms. Finally, very hesitantly, a large brown shaven head followed the arms out.

'Get down!'

Immediately the man threw himself face down on the ground, arms outstretched. He clearly knew the drill. Now the silence was dead forever, as the SWAT team screamed orders and ran and jostled equipment, while the news crew shouted questions.

The prostrate man on the ground risked death by raising his head slightly. He just stared at the happy couple, an enormously sad expression on his broad features.

TWO

'Let me get this straight. You want me to represent the most hated man in Houston? Again?'

Edward looked around the room: Julia Lipscomb, the District Attorney of Harris County, which meant Houston. David Galindo, one of her chief assistants. A representative of the State Bar Association, which had not so long ago excluded Edward from its membership for the minor infraction of burglarizing a court chamber in the Justice Center to steal cocaine. She was a young woman of Asian extraction who had said almost nothing so far. Edward looked at her for a long moment before returning his eyes to the DA.

'Since you put it that way,' Julia said. Edward used to call her that, when they were assistant DAs together. 'Yes.'

They were in Julia's office, the biggest one in the Justice Center. Julia had the power seat, of course, behind the big antique table she used as a desk, its surface almost empty except for a blotter and a small desk calendar. Around the room were plaques and certificates and pictures of Julia with other important people. Big windows had views of downtown Houston including the baseball stadium. She could almost see the pitcher's mound from here.

Edward sat in one of the chairs in front of the desk, the supplicants' chairs. He crossed his legs. Edward was well-dressed today, his best pin-striped, charcoal gray suit, because he had been pulled here from another presentation to a huge corporate client in his new role as software salesman. 'Then shall I,' he said, 'be the first to mention the elephant in the room?' He looked at the State Bar rep. 'What with me—'

He and the district attorney finished the sentence together: 'Not being licensed to practice law anymore?'

'That's the beauty part,' Julia continued. She had her arms down on the conference table. She was almost ten years older than Edward, in her mid-forties, attractive and very well-kept. Her blonde hair seemed natural and went with her light blue eyes. They twinkled at the moment. Edward waited breathlessly to hear the beauty part of being outcast from the profession he had loved.

'The State Bar will rescind your disbarment and place you on probation. A condition of the probation will be you can only represent this one client in this one case. But you do a good job and they'll consider extending the probation. Isn't that correct, Ms Swan?'

The young representative of the Bar finally had to speak. 'Yes,' she said. Edward didn't want to inquire further, not at the moment. The young woman extended a slender arm and said, 'I'm Elizabeth Swan, by the way.' Edward took her cool hand briefly.

The DA continued. 'And as you pointed out, Edward, you've already represented Donald Willis once. And did an excellent job for him. He's asking to have you again. At first, of course' – she looked around the room as if rounding up a team – 'we all said no way. But then I thought about it a little more and I said to myself, "Why not?".'

'So you worked out a deal on my behalf,' Edward said. 'Don't you think you should have consulted me on that first?'

'Does that mean you don't want it?' Julia leaned back in her padded chair, giving him a level stare.

Oh, he wanted it. Badly. Maybe it was just a natural contrary streak that made him question her. Or maybe it was that Edward *had* practiced law for quite a while, and knew a strange deal when he heard one.

He glanced at Ms Swan. She appeared completely indifferent to his response. For that matter no one in the room seemed to be waiting with bated breath. So he decided to let the air out of the balloon. 'Sure.'

'What do you know about the case?' Julia asked.

Edward knew nothing about it as a case, just as a news event, which he had naturally noticed because of his former client. When he'd read it he'd shaken his head. Poor Donald.

'Not much. Rich woman went missing, her rich developer husband got a demand for ransom. He dropped it off somewhere, then got a call his wife was in some dangerous block in the Third Ward. He went to find her and took the SWAT team along. According to the paper either the kidnapping victim then escaped or the kidnapper released her. Then the usual ending, with Donald back in jail for the same crime that got him sent to prison the last time.'

He'd left out part of what he knew, but Julia apparently had withheld information too. 'What you don't know is the rich woman is my sister, Diana Greene. Because of that, I'm recusing my office from the prosecution. A district attorney *pro tem* will be appointed. We'll try to get the judge to appoint someone you can work with.'

Edward glanced at David Galindo, who had been his opposing counsel in his previous trial, the one Edward had participated in while technically not allowed to do so. Actually there'd been no technically about it. He'd been a disbarred lawyer who shouldn't have been allowed in the front of the courtroom. But he'd also had a sister accused of murder who'd wanted no one but Edward to represent her, so what was a fellow to do? Edward wondered if David was disappointed not to be involved in a big case like this had the potential to be. But David's expression was impossible to read, as he stared at Edward with lowered brows.

Edward returned his attention to Julia. She was watching him with an almost fond expression, not like someone who'd be defending the man accused of holding her sister hostage and terrifying her in the process. 'I'm sorry I won't be working with you, Julia,' he said politely.

'Oh, I'll be monitoring the case closely, no worries.'

'Is that the beauty part you mentioned?'

Julia leaned toward him. 'The beauty part, Edward, is this is a win-win for everyone. I know the defense will be handled by someone I know to be a good lawyer, and you have the chance, if you do it well, to get your law license back.'

All that sounded accurate. So it was odd Julia was the only one smiling.

THREE

Edward knew exactly why the district attorney was oddly cheerful as she gave him this wonderful opportunity. She had little choice but to recuse her office from this case where she had a very personal interest. But it was a case she still badly wanted to control; she wanted the man who'd terrorized her sister to go to prison for a long time. That much seemed obvious. So she'd hand-picked a lawyer to represent him, a lawyer who'd be particularly vulnerable. Edward knew what Julia Lipscomb had meant when she'd described the terms of his release from purgatory as handling the case well. He was expected to do what criminal defense lawyers nearly always do: talk his client into pleading guilty or go to trial and lose.

Edward sat staring at her for a moment before the meeting broke. Julia had brilliantly used what he'd done recently – come back from the dead legally speaking to represent a client in a courtroom again. Their eyes met briefly, hers slid across his as she stood, and he knew she was counting on that. His trial addiction.

But there was still that conflict of interest. Edward explained all that to his client as soon as he saw him.

Edward was standing when a guard pushed Donald into the other side of the attorney–client booth at the Harris County Detention Center, on the other side of the thick Plexiglas from Edward. The booths were as dingy as Edward remembered, unchanged from the times he'd visited clients here in the past, to more recent times when Edward had seen his sister on the other side of that smeared plastic; when Edward himself had been on that other side for that matter. The walls on both sides were white stucco, or at least what had started out white. A metal tabletop extended across both sides, so the lawyer could write on this side and the client could read and sign things on the other, if the lawyer passed him paper through the thin opening at the bottom. But Edward was empty-handed today. He hadn't brought a briefcase or even a legal pad. He wasn't doing the masquerade today.

Big Donald stood there in his jail orange, hands cuffed in front of him. The prison nickname was no joke. Donald stood six-four or -five, with thick biceps and a gut that stuck out. Even his head was big: medium brown, shaven, thrusting up from his tree-like neck. The man just *intruded* on the world. After the door closed behind him with the guard on the other side, Donald's face split in a huge grin.

'Man, it's good to see you. Good to see a friendly face.'

'It's good to see you too, Donald. I wish it were somewhere else.'

Donald shrugged as he sat on the plastic chair on his side. 'Just like old times. Except you should be on this side. Watching my back.'

Edward remembered their time together in prison very differently. He lowered himself into a chair too.

'I'm really glad to see you, man. Glad you're going to be representing me again. This is some bullshit here. I didn't even—'

Edward held up a hand. 'Don't tell me your story yet, Donald. We've got to get some things straight first.'

'Yeah.' Donald leaned forward and put his forearms on the table, his handcuffs clanking against the metal. 'I asked for you, but I didn't think they'd let you be a lawyer again. Not after, you know . . . When we were inside you always said you'd never go back to it.'

Let me be a lawyer again, Edward thought. Very aptly put. That's exactly what the system was doing, letting him be himself again as long as he played it the way the system wanted.

'It's complicated,' he said. 'But Donald?'

'Yes?' The big man looked so eager to hear what he had to say, child-like.

'As my first advice to you as your attorney—'

'Yeah?'

'You're stupid to have me as your attorney.'

Donald leaned back, looking as if someone had just punched him. Someone Edward's size, for example, so Donald wasn't hurt at all, just surprised and beginning to be annoyed.

You did not want Donald to be annoyed at you.

Edward explained quickly, holding out a hand the whole time as if to hold back a tide. Explained that the district attorney would have a hold over him, Edward, a hold so good neither of them would ever mention it but it was still there. He could only get his law license back by doing a lousy job for his one client.

'So I have a conflict of interest, Donald. You see that, right? You want a lawyer who's only thinking about you, not about what's best for himself. Understand?'

Donald nodded slowly. 'Yeah, man. But you know and I know you'll still do your best for me. You can't help it. And I've seen your best. It's very damned good.'

Six years earlier, Edward as a new defense lawyer freshly out of the DA's office had defended Donald Willis on his previous charge, the one that had made him semi-famous. That one had been a kidnapping charge too. Donald had snatched the young son of Ryan Jennings, the star running back for the Houston Texans football team. It had seemed a crime of impulse. The boy was with his father at a baseball game during Ryan's off-season, the football player had turned his back for a minute to get them both hot dogs, when he'd turned back his son was gone. The city had gone crazy for three days, police and everyone else scouring every neighborhood for the boy while the father waited by his police-tapped phone for a ransom demand that never came. That made the crime look worse, as if the boy had been taken for some reason other than money. The newspaper and radio and television stations issued the parents' frantic pleas to the kidnapper to let the boy go.

Which had apparently worked, because at the end of the three days Donald had dropped the boy off in front of the boy's own house and watched him run up the huge lawn to his parents' arms. Donald had let the boy call ahead so they'd know he was coming. Donald had watched the happy reunion, then made a half-hearted attempt at escape, leaving on foot through the neighborhood, knowing it would be swarming with cops. He'd successfully eluded capture for nearly three minutes.

And Edward had defended him, very well, so that Donald got convicted, which was inevitable, but given a sentence of only eight years. Because the boy had been returned safely, unharmed, nearly untouched, well-fed, with stories of watching television and nothing worse. Donald had been incredibly apologetic, first to the boy's parents, then to the jury, and it had worked.

This time was very different.

'I didn't do this one, Edward. I was just there with that woman. I didn't snatch her, I didn't take her there, I didn't hold onto her. We were just there together. Waiting.'

'Waiting for what?' Edward asked, a hand hiding his mouth. Apparently they were just going to blow through what a bad idea it was for Edward to defend him.

Donald hesitated. That was bad. He usually blurted out whatever he was thinking.

'I wasn't quite clear on that. Mr Sterling hired me. Sterling Greene, her husband. He hired me a few days earlier, not long after I got out.'

'Hired you to do what?'

Donald hesitated again. Shit. 'Sort of bodyguard work. He said he needed protection. Sometimes he carried a lot of cash as part of his business, sometimes his wife went out wearing expensive jewelry. He just wanted someone around. Someone, you know . . .'

Someone Donald's size. Edward got it. Just stand around looking menacing, so bad guys – other bad guys – wouldn't be tempted.

'Did he run an ad for that?'

Donald didn't seem to hear the sarcasm. He shrugged his heavy arms and shoulders. 'I'd been out for a while, trying to find work. You know it ain't easy after you've been inside, especially for somebody like me, who kind of . . .'

'Got famous while committing your crime.'

Donald shrugged again. 'Yeah. You know. Although you didn't seem to have any problem, man, going right back to work as a lawyer.'

Edward declined the opening to give him career advice, if that's what Donald was asking. 'So Mr Greene hired you, the most notorious kidnapper in Houston history, to guard his precious wife.'

'Yeah.'

What a terrible story. If Edward did take on this case, that was the worst defense ever. He sat there looking at Donald's broad, brown, earnest face and for a moment it shimmered into Julia Lipscomb's, grinning at him. She wanted him to defend this?

'What were you doing in that house in the Third Ward?'

The Third Ward was one of the poorest and most crime-ridden neighborhoods in Houston. It might as well have been called the third world.

'Mr Sterling—'

'That's what you called him?'

'Yes, sir.' Donald folded his hands in front of him. 'Mr Sterling and Miz Diana.'

Nice touch, actually, as if he'd known the happy couple long enough to establish pet names.

'Anyway, Mr Sterling called me and asked me to get over there right away, so I—'

Edward sat forward. 'He called you?'

'Yeah.'

'Where's your phone?'

Donald shrugged his massive shoulders, indicating where they were. 'I don't know, lock-up? Evidence locker?'

'OK, continue.'

'He called me and said to hustle over to this, uh, drugstore, somewhere in West U, you know the area?'

Edward nodded. His doctor sister had lived there. Very upscale neighborhood.

'And when I got there I picked up Miz Diana and she told me where to go from there.'

Edward tried to construct all this in his head, knowing what he knew of Houston. The distance from West U (short for University, because of its proximity to Rice University) to the Third Ward was maybe five miles. And a million.

As he sat, silence captured the room. It was as if he and Donald noticed it at the same time. Noticed their crummy surroundings. Noticed that behind Edward was Houston, one of the great cities on earth, evidence of what humans could accomplish given enough will and grit and concrete. Behind Donald was one of those really well-built concrete structures.

For a minute the two looked at each other. They'd had many chats in prison. This was different, because one of them could walk out of here.

Donald leaned forward, his big brown eyes getting bigger, consuming all the space.

'Edward?' he said.

FOUR

Walking out of the jail – walking out of a detention facility, what a wonderful, wonderful experience, it never got old – Edward turned and looked back at it. It towered, like all prisons or jails do, not because they're so gigantic, but just because they're so much bigger than an individual person. From a certain distance it would look like a place a person could step over. But as Edward knew from personal experience, inside they were enormous. A giant boot crushing individuality, personality, whatever it meant to be human.

He turned and walked away with incredibly mixed feelings.

And after one stop Edward drove to the Heights. Not nearly as upscale as West U, but lovely. More of a village within the city. Very close to downtown, it was one of Houston's first suburbs. Edward had lived in the city long enough to have seen the Heights emerge from a rundown period when some houses had been abandoned, to a period of resurgence into what it was now, a genuine neighborhood with its own character, modest but well-kept houses interrupted by an occasional mini-mansion someone had squeezed onto a too-small lot. Houston didn't have zoning restrictions and the city planners didn't care about uniformity of housing.

Linda's house was made of wooden slats painted yellow, with white trim. It was April, the small flower bed in front of the porch was abloom with azaleas and violets and others. On the porch two wicker rocking chairs made the place look like a home.

Edward loved Linda's house. It had been a place of refuge for him from the time she'd first brought him here the day he'd been released from prison a year and a half ago and she'd picked him up, even though they were little more than acquaintances. Her letters and packages had given him something to look forward to during his two years in prison, then she'd saved his afterlife by bringing him here and into her life. It had been amazing, because they had known each other only very slightly before he committed the crime that got him put away.

The door opened before he could knock. Linda beamed at him. She had great cheeks, made for beaming a wide smile, lively green eyes, light brown hair hanging to her shoulders. 'Hi, you,' she said, then stepped back as if suddenly shy.

He walked inside, dropped his suit coat on a chair, and took her into his arms. Linda's lips were luscious, always, and she always brought her full attention to the kiss. After a minute they broke apart, a little breathless.

Houston was already hot in April. Linda wore cut-off shorts and a T-shirt filled with Linda. Edward wanted to start removing clothes so he'd look as casual. But now Linda grew distracted. 'I've been waiting for you.'

He was a little later than usual because of seeing Donald, but he'd left work early to do that, so it was still only a little after five. But Edward knew what she meant. Linda led the way to the kitchen just off the living room. There was a large brown envelope on the wooden table. 'It came,' Linda said.

'I see that.' Linda just stared at the envelope, not making a move to open it. 'Shall we call the bomb squad?' Edward asked.

She punched him lightly in the arm. 'I didn't want to open it until you got here. It's from the examining board.' She was still staring.

'Linda?'

She raised her eyebrows.

'They're not going to use that big an envelope to send you a letter saying, Sorry, you failed.'

'How do you know? Maybe they sent forms to fill out to apply to try again.'

'If only there were some way to find out.' But Edward put his arm around her, understanding her nervousness. It was like when he'd waited for his bar exam results, or the decision from the parole board.

Linda had been taking a course in being a court reporter, the people who make the records of trials in court. It would be a step up in income from her current job as a paralegal. It could also bring her into the courthouse full time. Maybe helping Edward in his recent case representing his sister had inspired her, or maybe she'd already been contemplating this career move. She hadn't said. But she'd finished the course and taken the exam.

They moved together and Linda finally picked up the envelope. She handed it to Edward and he opened the flap for her, then handed it back. Linda took a deep breath, exhaled, and pulled out the contents. Edward had dropped back a little and Linda had her back to him. He couldn't tell anything from her shoulders. But he could when she turned around with an even bigger smile, holding a certificate so he could see it.

'The letter says congratulations.' Her eyes were moist.

His were too all of a sudden as he saw how much this meant to her. 'Babe, that's so great. You so deserve it.' He hugged her again as Linda carefully held the certificate out to the side. When they broke apart Linda looked at it again. 'Can we get pizza or something to celebrate?'

'Sure. Uh, I need to step out for just a minute, OK?'

Linda's lips twisted. 'Going to the store for a cake?' Her tone implied it would have been nice if he'd been prepared for her good news, knowing it was on its way soon.

'Something like that. I'll just be a second.'

Linda stood there as he went out, looking at her certificate as if it would vanish if she took her eyes off it. 'Stop being such a sap,' she finally said aloud. 'It's not that big a deal.'

Her front door opened again. She went into the living room and saw Edward coming back in. In one hand he had a big bouquet of roses, in the other three helium balloons that said Congratulations! One had a banner with her name on it.

'I didn't want to bring them in first in case it wasn't good news.'

'Oh, Edward.' She took the roses, inhaled them deeply, then set them down and grabbed him. The balloons rose to the ceiling.

When they broke apart a long minute later his shirt had somehow started unbuttoning itself. 'We've got a reservation at McCormick and Schmidt's,' he said, naming her favorite restaurant.

Linda grabbed him again, completing her job on his shirt. As it opened they stared into each other's eyes as if this was new territory. 'Maybe the pizza after all,' Linda said. Edward nodded, reaching inside her T-shirt.

FIVE

Much later, at her kitchen table in enough clothing not to have shocked the pizza delivery boy, they ate slowly, occasionally looking at Linda's certificate on the other end of the table. 'I have news too,' Edward said. He didn't want to steal the occasion from her, but he knew Linda would want to know.

'All right, but we already celebrated mine. If yours is good news too I'm going to be exhausted.'

'Mine is more mixed.'

He told her quickly, just the outlines of the deal the district attorney had offered him.

'You're going to represent that guy who kidnapped the socialite? What's her name, something Greene?'

'If you're going to work in the criminal justice world, it's going to be important to remember things like the presumption of innocence.'

'It was on television!'

'There's that.' Like a reality TV show.

'Plus this wasn't his first time. It's more like his career.'

Yes, all the news outlets in town had helpfully informed potential jurors of Donald's infamous past.

Linda slumped back. But then she came forward again, smiling. 'But this is good.'

'Wow. Tell me the good part, Opti-Miss.'

Linda took his hand. 'Julia doesn't want you to win. To get your license back you need to lose, and fairly big time.'

Yes, Linda had grasped the big picture quickly.

'So it's great that your client is so obviously guilty. Because you can do your absolute best, not hold anything back, and you're still going to lose.' At Edward's expression she took both his hands and looked into his eyes with total affection. 'Babe, you know I love you and I think you're brilliant. But there's no way to win this one.'

Edward chuckled. 'You're amazing. You did manage to find the pony in all this shit.'

She came into his arms again, tasting of pepperoni and scented lipstick and woman and love.

The rest of the pizza went cold.

A week later Edward returned to the courtroom. It had been a hell of a struggle to get here. Not just the part about getting out of prison and being given a second chance and all. It had been physically almost impossible to get into the building. Since Edward's last trial Houston had had a visitor named Harvey. The hurricane had been incredibly destructive. It hadn't levelled the city, not even close, Houston was too strong for that, but it had ruined hundreds of homes, knocked out factories, landed many, many people stranded on their roofs, left large parts of the city without power and food and drinking water for weeks. One of its victims had been the Criminal Justice Center, the twenty-plus-story downtown tower where Edward had spent his legal career. The building still stood. From even a near distance it looked untouched now, but inside it had been rendered non-functional. The heart of the electrical system in the basement had been flooded, ceilings had burst throughout the building, carpets, of course, ruined. A sewer pipe had burst in the district attorney's offices, leading to very obvious jokes.

The inhabitants of those offices, the assistant DAs, had been dispersed throughout the city to 'temporary' offices that were threatening to become permanent.

Houston's justice system was a complex. The old courthouse, the Criminal Justice Center, a family and probate courthouse, a juvenile courthouse, and a giant civil courthouse all stood within a few blocks of each other. The busiest of these by far had been the Criminal Justice Center, where trials were always going on, and in courtrooms that didn't have a trial in progress dockets were being called every day, plea bargains made, the steady influx of prisoners accused of crimes either released or, much more commonly, sent on their way to prison. When the building could no longer hold all that activity, it had to go somewhere. The most

obvious somewhere was right next door, the gleaming and newer
civil courthouse that was equally imposing against the skyline.
The two buildings were near twins, of similar height and similar
appearances of steel and glass. But the difference in the atmospheres
of the two courthouses was the same as between an auto repair
shop and a cathedral. The Criminal Justice Center was a working
courthouse, every day, so swarming with business it took forever
to get an elevator to one of the upper floors. In the civil courthouse
many fewer cases were called and many fewer still actually went
to trial. The busiest area of civil law was family law – divorces,
child custody, and so forth – and it had its own courthouse. The
civil courthouse was for people or companies suing each other.
The great majority of those cases were settled or dismissed, and
most of the bargaining that led to those results took place elsewhere.
So the civil courthouse was a quiet, serene place where impeccably
dressed lawyers answered respectfully to judges in nearly empty
courtrooms, making their arguments in measured tones.

Then the criminal world had come swarming in. Barbarians
at the gates, then inside the gates. Then taking over the courtrooms themselves. That's what county commissioners had worked
out, again on a 'temporary' basis. Civil judges shared their courtrooms with their criminal law counterparts on a rotating basis,
week on and week off. The once pristine courtrooms were defiled
by criminals and criminal lawyers – the latter almost as bad as
the former in the eyes of civil practitioners.

So when Edward returned to a courtroom it was to one of
those, on the sixteenth floor of the civil courthouse and again, it
had taken forever to get the elevator up here. He'd arrived early,
but it was still after nine a.m. when he rushed in, heard Donald's
name called by the judge, and immediately called, 'Here, Your
Honor.' The judge didn't even glance up, just went on down the
docket, and Edward had a moment to catch his breath.

There were prisoners in orange jumpsuits in the jury box,
hands handcuffed in front of them, and Donald stood out among
them, his shaven head rising above the rest. He smiled at Edward,
obviously relaxing at the sight of his attorney.

Who wasn't actually an attorney. Edward saw a few heads
turn to look at him. One of them was Ms Swan, from the Bar
Association. He walked down the aisle and stood in front of her,

frowning curiously. She was slender and elegant in a brown suit. 'Are you going to be here monitoring me every time I come to court?'

'Do you have a problem with that?'

'It just seems weird. Do you need to record every move I make?'

'What if I do?'

'Are you going to answer every question with a question?'

'Why should that bother you?' She had a hint of a smile with that one. Edward turned away.

One of the other people who'd watched his entrance with interest was Julia Lipscomb, the District Attorney. Oddly, she was sitting in the audience. When she caught Edward's eye, she smiled.

Julia Lipscomb, the two-term District Attorney, was edging gracefully into middle age, a little more padded but much better made up and dressed than when she and Edward had first known each other. Julia had been his supervisor in the DA's office at one time. She had thought him overly independent to the point of insubordination, which unfortunately for their relationship Edward had taken as a compliment. Julia had achieved the administrative level of the office very quickly because she was good at that sort of thing, the paperwork, budgets, moving personnel around. She had even spent time in Law Nerdland: appeals. Trial work was different. No matter how well one prepared a case, trial work required being fast on your feet, flexible, making up what to say as you were saying it; being a good judge of character of prospective jurors, witnesses, opposing counsel, judges. Its main requirement was a feel for people, achieving rapport with a smile and a quip. Trial work had not been Julia's specialty.

As Edward stood there Julia retained her seat, just smiling. He finally said, 'You do know that recusing your office means you're not involved any more, right?'

'Oddly enough, Edward, it doesn't. It just means I have the rights of any other citizen, including observing court.'

Edward pivoted and sat in the seat beside Julia. 'Julia?'

'Yes, Edward?'

'There are two people, a couple, next to you, a few seats down. They seem to be glaring at my client. Would they be your sister and her husband?'

'Yes.'

'What the hell, Julia? First appearance? Are they going to be here for every setting?'

Julia glanced to the side. 'I doubt it. But possibly. My poor sister, Diana, said she wouldn't feel safe until she saw him in jail coveralls.'

'OK.' Edward stretched out the word. Abruptly he decided there was no more to be gained from conversation with Julia at this point, so he stood and strode down the aisle, going inside the bar. He went to the State's counsel table, said hello, and asked for the file. At that point it was very thin, but contained a police report and a complaint. Edward used it as a cover for looking back into the spectator seats from under his brows.

Sterling and Diana Greene stood out in the sparsely-filled seats. They seemed to be dressed for a very different occasion, he in a three-piece suit, she as if on her way for lunch with the ladies who lunch, the ones who notice the state of everyone else's nails and hair and clothes and marriage. But their expressions were those of typical victims. Mr Greene glared into the jury box, occasionally shifting that glare from the criminal to his lawyer. When the glare passed across Edward, he could actually feel it.

Diana Greene, on the other hand, was sunk in her chair looking fearful even of being there. Wearing a dress of a shade of blue that made her stand out in the courtroom, she had it buttoned almost to her neck, but Edward saw it could look very stylish with only a few changes. Mrs Greene shot him a glance as if afraid of Edward too. She clung to her husband's arm.

Edward sighed internally, suspecting he was going to have to contend with that sight every day if this case went to trial, which seemed unlikely. Still riffling the State's file, he walked over to the jury box and, with a look at the bailiff to make sure it was OK, sat beside his client. The chairs were hard, with thin cushions. Donald filled his like ice cream in a generously-scooped cone.

'Edward. Man, I'm glad to see you. Those folks been starin' at me like they got laser eyes. And that other one's her sister, right? The district attorney herself?'

Edward kept his eyes lowered, and pointed at something in the police report as if showing his client. 'Donald? Just listen.

I'm sitting here beside you to show someone cares about you and you're not a dangerous man at all. You're a big puppy dog. Nod your head like you agree.'

Donald nodded, mimicking Edward's gesture of pointing at the police report. At least he took direction well.

'Yes, that's the DA. And yes, that's the Greenes, your new best friends. Want to wave to them?'

Donald glanced that way. 'They wasn't like this, Edward. It wasn't like this at all.'

'Had he paid you, Donald? When Mr Greene hired you, had he paid you yet?'

Donald nodded. 'Eight hundred dollars in advance for that first week.'

That was good. A connection. 'How? Did you deposit it?'

'Cash. He took it right out of his wallet, in hundreds and fifties. First money I'd seen since I got out, Edward. I'd just been living off family handouts. So I—'

'Didn't have a bank account,' Edward finished for him. Damn. Donald's story continued to be unverifiable. In Edward's experience, there was usually a good reason why a story couldn't be confirmed by other sources.

Donald was actually reading the police report now. 'This says I called him to bring the ransom to that little house in the Ward and I'd let her go. Says I gave him a few hours to get five hundred thousand dollars in cash.'

'So?'

Donald frowned into his lawyer's face. They'd want to stay away from that expression in future court appearances. It made Donald look fearsome even when he was only frowning in perplexity.

'It don't work that way, Edward. You don't have the victim and the ransom in the same place. You have the guy with the ransom money drop it off some place where you can pick it up, then later you release the victim from some place far away. You don't bring 'em together. Too much can go wrong, just like happened this time.'

Edward gave his client a look. Donald shrugged. 'Yeah, man, I know how to do this. And you gotta give a guy more than a couple of hours to get that much cash together. I know that. You make it short, sure, but not that short.'

So Sterling Greene had called the cops instead. Edward risked a glance out into the audience. Mr Greene still glared at him, his shoulders straining the sleeves of his suit coat. Had he brought the money to the kidnapping, or only the SWAT team?

'Edward?' Donald tugged at his sleeve. 'You've got to get me out of the jail, man. I can help you investigate this thing. Besides, I don't like the way some of the guys are looking at me inside.' Edward looked at him skeptically. 'I know, man. You know and I know I can take care of myself. But I got nobody watchin' my back now, and some of these guys . . .'

Edward shrugged. 'Maybe I can get your bond lowered, but . . . What's it set at right now?'

'Eight hundred thousand.'

That sounded about right, for a two-time kidnapper who'd committed the second one within a few weeks of being released from prison. Edward was surprised it wasn't higher. A bail bondsman would charge ten percent of that to put up the bond. Edward strongly doubted Donald could raise anything in the vicinity of eighty thousand dollars.

'I'll see what I can do. Do you have any source of funds?'

'Maybe.'

That surprised Edward. He gave his client a long look. Donald, as big and tough as he was, had a childlike appearance at times. Edward was afraid only he could see that. Donald had done his time in prison for his previous crime, but he was still widely loathed when he came out. So he and Edward had something in common.

'Let me ask you something, Donald.'

'Sure.'

'Why the hell did you come back to Houston?'

Donald shrugged. 'It's home.'

Edward just watched him. There had to be more to it than that.

Donald felt his stare and turned to take it on his shoulder, mumbling something.

'What?'

'I said people know me here.'

Edward laughed harshly. 'Yeah, like Dallas knew Lee Harvey Oswald, but that didn't mean he'd want to go back there to live afterwards.'

Donald just shrugged. Edward thought he understood. After all, Edward had come back to Houston too, even though it had been the scene of his disgrace, and sights reminded him of that almost daily, especially if he came anywhere near the courthouse. But he'd returned. There was a guilty knowledge he and Donald shared: notoriety was almost as good as fame. Being known, even for something bad, gave a person substance. It made you somebody.

'I'll see what I can do,' Edward repeated. 'Try to stay out of trouble.'

Edward left the jury box and went and sat in one of the lawyer chairs inside the railing. As he crossed the room he saw Julia and her sister and brother-in-law were gone. They'd apparently achieved whatever they wanted with their appearance. Edward sat and read the police report. Nothing jumped out at him like it had for Donald. Distraught husband had called police head-quarters, been transferred to a detective, and the team had been assembled quickly. This early in the case there was nothing else, no lab reports or crime scene photos. There was one picture of the victim, a full-face shot of Diana Greene looking disheveled and distraught but unharmed. Edward stared at her face for a long minute.

He returned the thin file to the young prosecutor. 'Your office is off the case, so I can't negotiate with you. Who do I talk to?'

'Him, I guess.'

Edward turned to see David Galindo standing behind him. David had been Edward's chief rival when they were both pros-ecutors, but that just meant they competed for promotions, not that they were enemies. In fact David had been strangely helpful when they'd opposed each other in Edward's first trial since getting out of prison, when Edward had defended his sister against a charge of murder.

'Hello, David.'

'Edward.'

'Why were you in the room yesterday when they pushed this assignment on me?'

David ignored the question, pulling Edward aside. David was tall and lanky, wore suits well. He had a long, earnest face with expressive eyebrows. 'You need an opposing counsel,' he said.

'The office hasn't decided yet whom to recommend as district attorney *pro tem*.' That was the legal term for a special prosecutor appointed as the prosecutor for only one case when the DA's office had removed itself.

'I don't think the office gets to make a recommendation.'

David shrugged. 'Then you want to ask the judge right now to appoint someone? I'll just stand there. We've already filed the motion to recuse the office and appoint someone else.'

Edward looked at the woman on the high bench for the first time. A Hispanic woman of about fifty. Edward vaguely remembered her as a former prosecutor, but he'd never dealt with her. As much as he liked David, Edward suspected a trap. At this preliminary hearing this wasn't the judge who'd eventually hear the case.

So sure, let's take a shot with this one. The odds seemed to favor an unknown quantity doing him a solid. He was asking someone to make a decision that would be huge in the case, who would be prosecuting it. With a reasonable person on the other side, the case might be worked out with a plea bargain. If instead a prosecutor was appointed who wanted to get some publicity, this was the case to do it, especially by taking it to trial.

Indicating the judge with a nod, Edward said, 'Tell me about her.'

David seemed taken by surprise. Then he gave the question honest consideration. 'Judge Valencia? Fair judge,' he said slowly. 'Prosecutor for fifteen years or more, then a few years as a defense lawyer before she decided to run, so she's had experience both ways. I got the impression she didn't like defending people, that's why she ran for judge. But she's fair in her rulings and sentencings. Calls things for both sides.'

It sounded like an honest evaluation, and it coincided with what Edward remembered of this judge. Edward did trust David. He looked around the courtroom for someone else to ask, but didn't see any lawyers he knew. Edward had to make this decision on the spot. Once the case was re-set today it would probably be in another judge's court the next time. Did Edward want to take a shot with her or take his chances on who the next judge would be? He ran through in his head the judges in the criminal justice system. There were so many, and he'd been out of touch for a while. How many liked him and would do him a favor, how many who would really like to screw him over, from his time as a prosecutor, his time as a high-flying defense lawyer (when he may have cut a corner or two), and just the interplay of personalities over the years? Of the ones who he wanted to make this decision and the ones he wouldn't, he figured the over/under was about forty. Thirty/forty, as to whom he'd want to make this decision, with him on the downside of all those, if he waited for the next setting.

'Let's approach,' he said.

'Good morning, Your Honor.' Judge Gloria Valencia looked up at the sound of Edward's voice. For a moment she looked at him blankly, then she glanced at David, which seemed to put things in context. 'Good morning, Mr Hall,' she said.

Edward hesitated. He had to make one of those quick judgments about someone, as good trial lawyers do. He could let this end with the greeting, saying he needed to re-set the case, or he could ask this judge to appoint his opposing counsel, the one who would largely decide the course of the case.

She smiled at him. 'What can I do for you?'

That's what decided Edward. The judge sounded pleasant and helpful, like a butcher behind a meat counter. 'Your Honor, I'm sure you've been told about the special circumstances of this case.'

'Yes, the young lady from the Bar was very informative. I hope it works out for you. And of course for your client.'

'Thank you. All I'd ask the court to do today is appoint a prosecutor *pro tem* so I'll have someone to negotiate with. Mr Galindo of course can't—'

'No. All right. Do you want me to appoint someone this minute, or do you want to take some time? Of course I'm not asking you or the DA's office for recommendations. That wouldn't be proper.'

'No.' Edward nodded deferentially. 'I was thinking Cecilia Long or Kevin Lewis.' One was a hard-core defense lawyer, the other a complete incompetent, either of whom would give Edward a sweetheart deal. The judge laughed along with him, then her expression grew serious. She stared at Edward then glanced at

David, as if picturing someone in the prosecutor's place. Edward suddenly wanted to take back his request.

'I'm thinking Veronica Salazar,' she said slowly.

'Uh,' David said immediately, a sound as if he'd been punched. He recovered quickly and said, 'I think she's barely gotten her feet on the ground in private practice, Your Honor. I'm sure she's too . . .'

Edward glanced back and forth between them, lost. The name sounded familiar, but he didn't know the woman in question.

'I was thinking exactly that,' the judge was responding to David. 'This should help her get started. And of course she knows how to prosecute cases. Where's the order?' The judge found the right file, opened it to the State's motion, and flipped its pages to the attached order with a blank for the name of the DA *pro tem.*

'You know the circumstances of Veronica's leaving the office, Your Honor?' David Galindo said, taking one last shot.

The judge filled in the blank, signed the order, and handed it to her clerk. 'Make a copy for Mr Hall.' Then she turned back to the lawyers. Her face had hardened. 'I don't believe those rumors,' she said flatly. To Edward she smiled. 'Have a nice day.'

That was a dismissal. Edward and David walked away. When Edward thought they were out of earshot Edward said, 'What just happened? Who's this Veronica person?'

'She left our office just last week,' David said. 'I forgot Judge Valencia is friendly with her. She's doing her a favor because Veronica's just getting started in private practice, I'm sure she doesn't have very many cases yet.'

'Why would she leave if she didn't have a good place to land set up?'

David looked at him. 'It wasn't voluntary on her part.'

Oh, shit. She'd been fired from the DA's office. Good, maybe it was for being a lousy trial lawyer, making too many easy plea offers. But from looking at David, Edward didn't think that was it.

'What can you tell me about her?'

David shook his head, looking around the courtroom.

'David?'

'Just watch your back,' David said, and turned and hurried away.

Edward stood there alone, then noticed his client staring at him hopefully. Edward felt lost.

First mistake.

SIX

Edward decided he'd wait a day to put in a call to Veronica Salazar. He wanted to do some asking around about her first. He went back to his real job, the one paying the bills, and ended up making a small sale to a company looking for a new email server and cyber security system. He got a call from his biggest client, their CEO wanting to make another appointment with him. He went about his business as if it were an ordinary day, all the while in the back of his mind thinking, Shit shit shit.

This reflected Edward's still being out of touch with the court-house world. After being in prison for two years, out in the world for one and a half, then trying only one case in the ensuing year, he didn't know all the players any more. He shouldn't have gone to Judge Valencia, not on that particular day. On the other hand, it had been a crapshoot. The next judge might be worse. These are the kinds of thoughts that make lawyers wake up at four a.m. In Edward's case, though, it was something else that did that: his phone ringing at that time of the morning.

'This is a call from the Harris County Detention Center,' said an automated voice.

What the hell? Edward looked at the clock as Linda moaned beside him. They didn't let inmates make calls at this time of the morning. 'Hello?' he said automatically.

'Mr Hall? This is Dr Jones. I'm in the infirmary at the jail. I'm sorry to call you at this time of the morning, but your client is here in the infirmary. He's been asking for you and he's very insistent.'

'Donald's in the infirmary?' Edward was confused. The inmates should all be locked down in their cells. 'Is he sick?'

'The incident happened hours ago,' the doctor said.

'Then why are you just now calling me?'

'Your client just now regained consciousness.'

Edward was at the jail forty-five minutes later. It's not possible to get anywhere in Houston in less than forty-five minutes, even at a lightly-trafficked time of the morning. He didn't have a bar card to show the guard, but they were expecting him, and another guard led him to the jail infirmary.

Bruises don't show up well on African-American skin, but the black eye was spectacular enough to draw attention, accompanied by a gash on the temple showing the eye had probably been hit by an implement. Donald's whole face looked swollen.

'What happened? Did guards attack you?'

Donald shook his head. 'Inmates. Four of them. We were in the dayroom and one of them kind of motioned me over to this corner. I should've known better, but I went over there. Turns out it's the one spot that's out of sight of the guard station and the camera.'

He used to know that kind of thing, Edward thought. But Donald hadn't been in this jail long enough to learn the layout. 'And?'

'I just asked what's going on and that's when he punched me.' Donald stopped to swallow. He was stretched out on a metal cot that he almost hid from view. The other beds around them were mostly filled with sleeping inmates. They kept their voices down. 'He tried to hit me in the throat to cut off my wind but I lowered my chin and blocked that. Then I heard the others coming up behind me.'

'Three others.'

Donald nodded. Clearing his throat sounded like scraping mortar off brick. 'One of 'em is going to be limping for the rest of his life, and another one is probably still nursing his swollen nuts, but the other two jumped me and beat me down pretty good. Got me down on the ground.'

That's all he had to say about that. Edward had witnessed such 'fights' in prison. Never as a target, thanks in part to Donald. But when more than one guy got the victim down on the ground, then they could go to work on him, kicking from various angles while the helpless victim tried and failed to cover all his vitals at once. Donald was lucky to be here rather than the morgue.

'I managed to get to my feet—'

'Really?'

'Well, my knees. And I knocked one back far enough that he was in the guards' line of sight. Still took 'em a hell of a long time to get there.'

Paid off, then, Edward thought. A coordinated attack with the overseers paid to look the other way. Donald was *damned* lucky to be here.

'Who were they? What'd they have against you?'

Donald shook his head. 'Never noticed 'em before. And you know me, Edward, I ain't done nothin' to nobody. Hell, I ain't been here long enough to piss anybody off. I've just been keepin' my head down and shufflin' along.'

Edward did know that about his friend. As much space as Donald took up, he tried his best to keep a low profile. Didn't join a gang, didn't reject them in a way to piss anybody off, just did his time and tried to make each day pass as quickly as possible.

'Somebody hates you because of your last caper?' The kidnapping that had made Donald famous in a bad way.

Donald shook his head then groaned. 'They were hired, Edward, you know that. Somebody wants me dead in here.'

'Somebody from your prison days?'

Donald shrugged. His eyelids were lowering. But his eyes snapped open for him to say, 'You've got to get me out of here. They say they'll put me in ad seg, but if the guards're in on it too . . .' Ad seg, administrative segregation, protective custody inside the jail. But Donald was right, he could be protected from inmates but not the keepers.

Edward shook his head. 'Maybe I could get your bond lowered based on this, but that would take a day or two.'

Donald grinned the most hideous grin ever, with one tooth hanging. 'Then you need to get yourself put in here with me so you can cover me.'

No, let's stick with option A. Edward quickly ran through everyone he knew, with the thought of Donald's eighty-thousand-dollar bond fee the goal. Someone in Edward's family would have the money, but he didn't want to go to them. Didn't really want them to know he was practicing law again. Besides, how could he guarantee Donald wouldn't skip? It seemed his best option at this point.

'There's only one guy,' Donald said, reading his thoughts.

Edward's eyes widened. 'Are you crazy?'

Donald's eyes were closing. Man, even his eyelids were bruised. 'I'll get him to call you.'

'*You* will,' Edward said. 'You two are phone buddies?'

But his client was asleep, probably from the pain meds pumping into his arm.

Edward looked around, hoping Donald would be safe here, hoping these inmates really were sleeping. He went to find the doctor who had called him.

It was only late that same morning when Edward got the call on his cell phone, the number Donald knew. 'Edward Hall?' said a deep voice.

Edward found himself nodding. 'Yes, sir.'

'You can come see me. I'm at home.'

'I can?' But he was speaking to dead air. That had been the whole call.

Forty-five minutes later Edward knocked on the door of a mansion in The Woodlands, a large, beautiful community north of Houston, where one moved after striking an oil well or an NFL contract. His caller had expected Edward could learn his home address, and Edward had with a couple of calls, finding his caller had paved the way for him by giving permission to let him have the information. Edward looked up at the house. It was large but understated, made of stone that looked old even though the house couldn't have been more than five years old. The yard sloped down to the street, where Edward saw a security guard in a golf cart sitting idly, not looking at him.

The heavy wooden door opened and Ryan Jennings himself was standing there, in T-shirt and shorts. This close, the African-American running back was an amazing sight. As tall as Donald at six foot five, but where Donald was bulky Jennings was honed. His T-shirt strained around his biceps. His legs, his source of income, were intricately muscled and huge, but he was light on them. Jennings was handsome, too, his short hair showing off a face with imposing cheekbones and a noble nose. His penetrating brown eyes fixed on Edward, who felt like a member of a lesser species.

'Thank you for seeing me,' he said.

The football player waved him in and closed the door behind Edward. He still hadn't spoken. They stood in an entryway that showed imposing twin staircases at the back, forty feet away. An antique credenza sat beside the door. Jennings just stood there. This was as far into the sanctuary as Edward was getting.

'Did you really agree to do this?'

Jennings poked a finger at him and Edward flinched back. 'That's exactly the sort of question I don't want to be asked by anybody else. Understand?'

'Yes, sir. But why would you put up his bond?'

Jennings looked angry, but it was just concentration, studying Edward. 'He gave me back my boy. You understand? Easiest thing for him would've been to kill him and run. Nobody'd seen him, he would've never been caught. Instead he brought him home. Gave up eight years of his life to do that. People make mistakes. Donald realized his and he made up for it. You never heard me say a word against him, did you?'

That was true. Before and during Donald's trial the Jennings family had kept conspicuously silent, having no comments for the press and testifying only minimally to the facts of the case. The prosecution hadn't called Jennings or his wife in the punishment phase to say how this crime had ruined their lives. They'd kept as much out of sight as possible, for one of the most famous men in town and the object of the best-known crime in years.

A checkbook and pen lay on the credenza. Ryan Jennings leaned over them. 'Here's how we're going to do this,' he said over his shoulder, beginning to write. 'I'm making out the check to you. You pay the bond fee. Keep my name out of this.'

'Listen.' Edward licked his lips, risking further speech. 'Could we have a' – he resisted saying *photo op* – 'a public occasion where you're seen making his bail? It would do a lot to show people Donald's not . . . What's the problem?'

Because Jennings was turned back to him, shaking his head. 'I'll do this, man, but if you let anybody know it's me I'll back right out. I can't have this scene. I'm doing this because I don't think he's a bad guy, but I can't look like the moron who paid the bail for my son's kidnapper.'

'But you are. Not the moron, the good guy who thinks what you just said. Donald's not a bad guy, he just made a mistake and then made up for it.' Suddenly Edward was looking him in the eye, talking to him man to man. Jennings, who could have taken Edward's head between his thumb and fingers and squeezed until his eyes popped out, did him the courtesy of looking him back in the same way. But his eyes were hard as stones. 'You talk a good game, counselor. But that's not happening.'

Edward shrugged, accepting. The football star finished writing the check, tore it carefully out, and handed it to Edward. Jennings' stare said their meeting was concluded.

'OK, thank you. This is amazingly—'

But Edward found himself back on the front porch, wafted there gently. As he turned back toward the house the door was closing in his face.

Edward raised his hand in a salute. 'Big fan!' he called. The door gave him no response.

SEVEN

'Now what?' Linda asked. Linda was so lovely, especially at times like this when they were alone in her house and she wasn't trying. Her light brown hair hung to her shoulders, she wore only a T-shirt and cut-off shorts, her best outfit in Edward's opinion. Barefoot. Sexy toes. 'What does the defense do next?'

He lay back on the white sofa, also in T-shirt and shorts. Interesting to talk about a court case like this. 'Well, obviously meet with my client again, now that he's out of jail, hear his story, tell him what crap that is, beat the truth out of him.'

Linda smiled. 'No, really.'

'Well, some version of that. But also . . . you know.'

She did. 'Research the victim. Or victims, if you count the husband.'

Edward nodded. Linda turned away and he followed her into the second bedroom, the office she had turned into an office for both of them, with two desks, one desktop and a laptop open on the other desk. The room still seemed like a work in progress, but her court reporter certificate was already framed and on the wall. Photos also adorned the walls, some of which now included Edward. One prominently placed on the wall above the desktop was of Linda sitting cross-legged, grinning up at the camera. In her lap lolled a much-adored cat, now gone.

Linda sat at the laptop. 'Reminds me of the shorthand machine,' she said, and got to work. Edward half-heartedly opened Google and put in the Greenes' names, first seeing if there were any articles that mentioned them as a couple. Only two. One mentioned them as attendees of a reception at the River Oaks Country Club. Edward would have guessed they lived in his parents' neighborhood, where he'd grown up, the old-money suburb. But this was Houston, the boom town, so the club was also always ready to welcome new money. He didn't bother to open that one.

The other one was about the opening of a show at an art gallery. He assumed that one would also be the lovely couple beaming at the camera, so he didn't bother with clicking through that link either. Instead he typed in only Sterling Greene and found several articles, mostly Sterling announcing the launch of a new vast construction project. Edward did look at a couple of those, always about grand plans of Greene and his partners. Different partners for each project. Probably smart, to be the only guy with a finger in all the pies.

He didn't find anything about just Diana. Interesting. She kept a very low profile. He wondered whom he could interview to find out about her. River Oaks offered possibilities, starting with his own mother.

'Hey,' Linda said quietly. When Edward went to stand over her shoulder she closed out the page. 'Let's go somewhere,' she said, rising and taking his hand.

*   *   *

Twenty minutes later, dressed a little more formally, they were
in the car heading for Bissonette, a street on the edge of West
U, near the museum district of Houston. Linda had kept her little
secret so far. Whatever it was, she liked it. They talked about
what they had learned about the Greenes, which was very little.

'I don't see any reason why he would have hired Donald,'
Edward was saying. 'Nothing about making it a particular project
of his to rehabilitate ex-cons.'

'No. Their only charitable work was attending the occasional
reception.'

Linda pulled into a strip center with only three stores, one of
them a long white stucco space with wide windows. 'Art?' Edward
asked.

Linda nodded. 'You like art, don't you?'

'Sure. In its place.'

They went in. A receptionist's desk, minimal and chrome, sat
empty. They walked slowly through the rooms. The first featured
works by modern artists, none of whom was familiar to Edward.
Linda took his hand and led him onward.

They discovered the reason the receptionist's desk was empty
was because she, a willowy brunette in a black dress, was earnestly
explaining a sculpture to a middle-aged, well-dressed couple who
kept nodding as if they appreciated it. Linda hurried them through
into the final room. This was different. Portraits, all by the same
artist. This must have been the reception Edward hadn't bothered
to read about. This was where the gallery would have made its
money. The portraits were of well-known Houstonians, a former
mayor, an owner of the Astros, his wife, another of a dignified
woman known for wielding her wealth carefully, building up
certain projects and letting others collapse. They didn't by any
means know all the subjects, but enough of them to get the gist.
These were works on loan, commissioned through the gallery and
already sold to the subjects. That reception must have been something, rich people coming to admire themselves and each other.

The portraits were good, most of them life-sized, placed in
settings that demonstrated the subject's interests, such as a man
leaning back on a desk holding a blueprint. Edward studied the
eminent dowager. 'He's good,' Linda murmured, an art gallery
hushed voice. 'I can see why he gets the big commissions.'

Edward saw what she meant. He happened to know this woman, through his family connections. She wore a simple frock, as if for an afternoon cocktail party. Her hair was carefully coiffed, her faded blue eyes gazing out of the frame with a quietly kind expression. It looked like its subject, very much, but it also looked better than she ever had. The artist had emphasized her eyes and minimized the wrinkles Edward knew encircled those eyes. While she wasn't a mean woman by any means, Edward had never seen her with this kindly an expression.

'The best version of herself she's ever seen,' Linda said. Edward nodded.

'But why—?' he began, when Linda took his hand and led him to the next full-sized portrait. This one showed a younger woman dressed in a simple, elegant, dark-blue dress, standing next to a waist-high column on which her hand rested. It was a youthful hand, unmarked, slender. The woman was turned slightly, as if listening to a nearby conversation. But her eyes were a little slanted, looking out of the frame even as her body inclined away. The eyes were a deep blue intensified by the gown. Edward stepped closer, as the woman's stare invited him to do. She seemed about to say something, something witty and fascinating and designed for his ears only.

'Portrait of Mrs Diana Greene,' Linda read from the small plaque.

Of course. But Edward had seen Mrs Greene in person and this portrait, like the last, was at least slightly more beautiful than the woman looked in life. She had a small smile, no, the beginning of a smile, as if she saw him approaching and knew how charming he was.

'This guy's very good,' he said.

Linda nodded. 'I want him to paint me.'

They looked around and found the artist's name. 'Antonio Alberico,' Edward read. 'Really?'

'No,' said a voice behind him. He and Linda turned to find the woman in black had found them. 'Really his name was Tony, but he adopted a sort of nom de brush he thought suited his subjects better.' She turned to Linda. 'And as for painting you, I'm afraid not. This is a posthumous exhibition.'

'That's terrible. Was it recent?'

'Yes, it was tragic. I think the medical examiner still hasn't decided if it was suicide. May I show you something?'

Of course. She led them to an alcove. Inside was one painting on each of three walls. Edward and Linda stepped closer. The largest painting was a landscape. Somewhere in Appalachia maybe, or possibly east Texas. At any rate a very wooded area, the trees intricately detailed, with the suggestion of an overgrown path through them and the hint of a building in the far, secluded distance.

'This was Tony's real passion,' the woman said. 'The portraits he did for the money, and they became very successful. But that was just to allow him to do this.'

'Beautiful,' Linda murmured.

The receptionist nodded. They all stood lost in admiration for a long moment. Then she said, 'Let me know if I can show you anything else,' and glided away.

After a while they returned to the portrait of Diana Greene. She still seemed to carry that amusing secret.

'Now you need to get to know the real her,' Linda finally said.

'I know. And I sincerely hope she can convince me she was a kidnapping victim. Then I can just talk Donald into pleading guilty.'

'Is there anyone you can ask about her?'

Edward thought for only a few seconds. 'Oh yes. There is.'

EIGHT

The next morning, a Sunday, Edward and Linda went to the Avalon Drug Store, in a small shopping center a block from River Oaks. The Avalon had been an institution for decades. It was indeed a small drug store, but it was better known for its luncheonette, *the* place for Sunday breakfast among those who cared. They had to wait for a table, of course. As they did, Edward looked around. Almost immediately he saw three people he knew, two he'd gone to high school with, one a well-known real estate developer. But Edward was looking for one particular person, and quickly spotted him. 'A minute,' he said to Linda, and strolled into the restaurant space.

Gerald spotted him just as Edward pretended to notice him for the first time. They exchanged names and greetings. Gerald held court here most Sunday mornings, taking up a table for hours, sometimes with company, sometimes not. Today he had a young man across from him who ignored Edward. Gerald leaned his cheek on his hand and said, 'Well, the famous Edward. I heard all about your trial, after of course your prison stay. You must tell me all about that someday.'

'Love to.' Edward widened his eyes. 'Which reminds me. I need to talk to someone who lives in River Oaks and knows everybody.'

Gerald smiled. 'That does sound like me. Today, as you can see, I'm preoccupied. But I'll be receiving at home tomorrow. About noon?'

Edward said fine, didn't need to ask the address, and strolled on into the shelves.

'Who's that?' Linda asked. 'Old friend?'

'Not exactly. But we've known each other a long time. Gerald has known everybody a long time.'

Linda gazed at the man. Gerald didn't turn his head, but he grew a smile that said he was aware of her scrutiny and enjoyed it.

Big Donald called later that day, anxious to see Edward. 'We'll get together very soon,' Edward assured him. 'You just keep a low profile while you heal. And try to figure out who wanted you dead. Four strangers jump you in jail, that wasn't a warning. That was supposed to be a hit.'

'Man, you don't have to tell me.'

'So who wants you dead, man?'

Donald didn't answer. Edward thought he himself would lapse into such a silence if someone put that same question to him.

'Think about it. I'll see you Tuesday, man.'

His week was filling up.

Edward kept his appointment, if that's what it was, with Gerald the next day after a busy day of appointments that made him forget he was a sort of lawyer again these days. Gerald lived in a smaller River Oaks home, two stories in the traditional red brick, with vines trailing up one side wall. A bay window in front looked like an eyeball keeping watch on the neighborhood.

Gerald himself opened the door, no boy toy in evidence today, or anyone else in the house. Gerald, who was maybe ten years older than Edward with a world-weariness older than both of them, gestured him into a sitting room. The home was beautifully furnished in a slightly old-fashioned style of angular furniture and elaborate window treatments. The sitting room could have been called a library, since one wall was floor-to-ceiling shelves filled with individual volumes, no matched sets sold by the foot.

Gerald himself was slim and elegant, with a slightly bulging forehead, languid brown eyes that could turn piercing, long-fingered hands. He had tea for them. Many people thought he must have inherited his wealth, since he never lifted a finger to earn a dime, and Gerald encouraged that perception, but Edward happened to know he was a self-made man. From an early age Gerald had been a traveler, fierce to devour the world. And he had written about his travels, in books that became a series under a pseudonym. In the digital age the series had blossomed into apps and websites, long since sold to some conglomerate for enough to keep Gerald comfortably at home.

'Your girl is lovely, Edward. Are you engaged? Has she left that firm where she's a paralegal now that she's earned her court reporter's certification?'

'Not yet,' Edward said, acknowledging Gerald's research with a smile. 'And why am I here, do you know?'

Gerald's smile turned musing. 'I suppose you want to know about the Greenes, what with you being appointed to represent her kidnapper.'

Well, that was easy, it had been reported in a small story in the paper. Edward just nodded.

Gerald frowned, stopped fussing with the tea things, and looked Edward in the eye. 'They are a toxic couple. He's up from nowhere into supposedly a lot of money doing this and that. She's old school Houston rich, the riches probably faded away by this time. They live about three blocks over in some huge eyesore. Sterling, so called, is a thug in a tux. Or a hardhat some days. Diana, she's more interesting. Her family raised her to be a socialite, which to her distress is a category that no longer exists. So she married money, which is the other thing that term means.'

'And the toxicity?'

'No one wants them around but you can't not invite them to things. So you see them at receptions and parties, either avoiding each other or glaring across the room, her flirting with a few carefully selected targets and him clumsily trying to do the same thing and just making a fool of himself with women who wouldn't be caught dead with him. I mean that literally, they would drag themselves back from hell so their bodies would not be found in bed with him. Meanwhile Diana is just expert. She can flirt with a man while talking to his wife. She can flirt with a man while suggesting a new mistress for him. She can . . .'

'Gerald?'

Gerald stopped his monologue and leaned across the space between them, touching Edward's hand just for a moment. His smile was a work of art.

'Are you sure you're not imagining some of this?'

Gerald leaned back and gave the idea due thought. 'As if she's the perfect incarnation of my love of gossip? Edward, you're brilliant. As I always knew. Yes, I see it now, I've been projecting . . .'

Edward shrugged modestly, waiting to get to the real stuff.

'Nothing!' Gerald suddenly said, leaning back into his face. 'Edward, Edward. Edward. When have you ever known me to be wrong? So shut up and let me give you the deal. Diana is designed for this. I love her from afar.'

'So you have a list of her lovers?' Edward mentally took out a pen and notepad.

Gerald stared at him in a very level way, no longer doing anything arch at all.

'No.'

'No? No confirmed kills?' Gerald shrugged. Edward continued, 'So for all you know she's just a serial flirt? And her husband's just jealous over that?'

Gerald opened his mouth, obviously started to explain, then just shrugged. 'Whatever the Greenes' other failings, they've been very discreet. Or nothing ever happened. Who knows?' He raised his eyebrows.

Edward was exasperated. '*You* should.'

Raising his shoulders and his eyebrows, mad at himself, Gerald said, 'I know.'

They finished their meeting with idle chatter about people they knew, what Edward was doing, nothing about Gerald, who never talked about himself, until Edward rose, saying, 'Well, if you hear anything . . .'

He was walking away when he heard a tone in Gerald's voice. 'Are you recruiting me?'

Edward opened his mouth and Gerald continued, 'As one of your team? As your sort of celebrity gossip consultant?'

Edward almost fell for it, stopped his tongue, and said, 'Yes.'

Gerald grew a slow smile. 'Thank you so much, Eddie, for thinking of me.'

Eddie. Edward knew the joke. He smiled back.

NINE

Almost as soon as he left Gerald's place, he called Diana Greene. Her sister the district attorney had actually given him her phone number.

The worst thing about being a defense lawyer was interviewing the victim. But you had to do it, or try. When Edward had been a prosecutor it had been wonderful, bringing in the victim and the victim's family, laying out just how you were going to achieve justice for them. But talking to the victims as a defense lawyer, the representative of the person who'd victimized them, not nearly so wonderful. He'd sometimes been afraid he was going to be punched.

Of his two choices, Sterling Greene was definitely worse. Besides, he needed more background on the tycoon before he took him on *mano a mano*. So he did the cowardly thing and called the woman instead.

To his surprise, she answered, sounding sleepy at one-thirty in the afternoon. Or was that languor in her voice? 'Oh,' Diana said when he told her his name, and her voice went a little squeaky, Little Red Riding Hood talking to the wolf. 'What can I do for you, Mr Hall?'

'It's Edward. And I just want to talk to you. Half an hour of conversation. Can we do that some time?'

'Of course. I guess. Are we allowed to do that? Do I have to do it?'

For someone whose sister was the district attorney, Mrs Greene seemed strangely ignorant of legal proceedings. He could take advantage of that.

But not yet. 'You have no obligation, Mrs Greene. But it would be nice.'

Her hesitation was very brief. When she spoke again she sounded more decisive. 'You are a lucky man, Mr Hall.'

'Am I?'

'Yes. Partly because you have a voice I trust and partly because I just two minutes ago had a friend cancel. So could you meet me for lunch? At three? Would that be OK?'

Edward thought, three o'clock for lunch? What was that? Very late lunch, very early dinner? Lunner? High tea? This was a fashion Edward had obviously missed. But, 'Sure,' he said quickly. 'Name the spot.'

Without hesitation, she did. A little stand-alone café also River Oaks adjacent. Almost next door, in fact, to the gallery where Diana Greene hung. As it were. He could go look at her while he waited for her.

Diana was only a few minutes late. She wore a lightweight dress that ended somewhere around her knees, it was hard to tell from the swirls, and almost covered her cleavage. She must have been just about to go out, because she was expertly made up, to the extent she didn't look made up at all. But her eyes were bright and her lashes long, her lips very red. Her auburn hair danced around her head. She looked nothing like a woman coming to meet the lawyer representing the man who'd kidnapped her.

And she didn't come alone. Julia Lipscomb was at her side.

That must have been quickly arranged. Julia was dressed like a business person, as she was, the head of the biggest law firm in town, the DA's office, that employed upwards of four hundred lawyers. Her eyes were clear and her hands empty.

Edward stood to meet them, his face neutral, and shook hands with each. After exchanging greetings he looked closely at Diana and she did him the favor of looking back. Really lovely blue eyes. Her handshake was soft and quick, and she glided into the booth across from him. Her sister pulled up a chair – one of those cushioned items with a bent wire back, like from a boulevard in Paris – and placed herself between them on the table's end. Oddly like a chaperone on a first date; literally the big sister. Or like a lawyer with a very important client. She smiled at Edward and placed her hand briefly over his. 'Thank you again, Edward, for handling this case. I very much appreciate it.'

It was odd having her here. He wondered if Julia understood what her office being removed from the case meant. But of course she had a dual role.

'You're very welcome, Julia.' Her thanks were odd too. She needed to keep reminding him he was doing her a favor. A waitress quickly appeared and took their orders, salads for both women, nothing for Edward. He kept his attention on the sister.

Under his scrutiny Diana's shoulders rose and she sank in the booth. 'I don't know how any of this works. I gave a statement to the police.'

'And I'll read it. But I wanted to hear directly from you what happened.'

'So he can see if there are any discrepancies,' Julia said, not unkindly. She and Edward exchanged a pleasant look.

'There always are,' Edward said reassuringly. 'Don't worry about that. So where were you when you first . . . encountered Donald?'

Diana leaned forward. 'All right, Mr Hall, I'll—'

'Edward, please.'

Diana frowned briefly. 'Edward? Always? So formal. Never Ed or Eddie?'

'No,' Julia answered for him. She knew Edward well enough to know he didn't like nicknames. He had a perfectly good name, it didn't need a substitute. Why did people have a hard time with that? Anyone who called him something other than Edward didn't know him well, even if they pretended to do so.

Diana shrugged. 'Anyway, your client. That giant man. I first saw him the day he grabbed me. Actually I didn't see him at all at first. I was about to go into a store, a drug store, when someone grabbed me, put a hand over my mouth, and whispered right into my ear, "If you scream I'll kill you".'

Her eyes widened, reliving the terror. 'Then he put a bag over my head. I was terrified. I dropped my purse and he dragged me like a child. I heard a car door open and he shoved me into the back seat. I lay there face down. He hadn't tied me up, but after what he said I was too scared to make a peep.'

Edward nodded. He felt Julia's stare on the side of his face, but kept his eyes on her sister. 'Where were you when this happened?'

'West Gray, I think, near my home. It was early afternoon, I was supposed to meet a girlfriend for lunch and I was early. Anyway, we drove what seemed like forever. I think we were going in circles sometimes, like he was afraid someone was following us.'

'Were you in your own car?'

'Yes. I wasn't sure of that at first, but when we finally stopped I got a glimpse of it as he dragged me out and I saw it was my own. Then we went into that horrible house. It seemed like a crack house, almost no furniture, trash on the floor. Terrible smell.'

'So he'd taken the bag off your head?'

She shook her head. 'It was one of those cloth bags, you know? Maybe burlap. I was getting to where I could see a little bit between the fibers. Then he – your client – shoved me down into a chair and said to stay there. Told me again he'd kill me if I moved.'

Her hand shook as she reached for her water glass. Edward imagined her telling this story on the stand and winced internally. He hoped she'd have to rehearse her story several more times before trial so its freshness would wear off, but right now she was the perfect witness, obviously reliving the nightmare. He wanted to comfort her; anyone would. At the same time he realized as believable as Diana Greene appeared, his client was a liar in direct proportion.

'How long did you sit there?'

'Hours. When we were still in the car I heard him talking to my husband on a cell phone. He had me say something, then shushed me right away. I wanted to call out to Sterling but I was too afraid. They were talking about money, that's all I could hear. Then at the house I just sat there. I heard him talking to somebody else. Finally I told him I was suffocating and asked if he could raise the bag a little. He said he'd take it off, but not to look at him. So I closed my eyes.'

'Did he tie you up?'

'No. He didn't need to. You've seen him. There was no way I was going to make him mad by trying to get away. Besides, I didn't know where I was. From the glimpse of the neighborhood I'd gotten I could see it was no part of town I was familiar with. He told me he just wanted the money, he wasn't going to hurt me unless I did something stupid.' She picked at her salad.

It sounded like Donald's snatching of Ryan Jennings' son years ago, a crime of sudden opportunity. He hadn't come prepared with rope or much of a plan.

Diana had her head down, looking at Edward with her lips pursed, like an injured child. He wanted to take her hand and say it would be all right. She blinked at him in quick succession.

'Then we just waited. I didn't even know how much money he'd asked for, but I imagined Sterling trying to pull it together, rushing to the bank, taking out an emergency loan, I don't know. I wondered what time it was. When the banks would close.'

'Did you and Donald talk?'

'Very little. Mostly he stayed behind me, looking out the window, I think. When I started to turn my head he told me no. He let me walk around a little a couple of times, but I kept my head down.

'Finally police came. We heard them. They didn't have sirens, but you could hear all the cars. He – your client – ran to the back of the house but then he came back. Then the hostage negotiator started talking to him. I almost felt bad for him. But while he was distracted I ran to the door and ran out.'

'She's lucky police didn't kill her,' Julia said coolly. Edward looked at her. He'd been so immersed in the story he'd almost forgotten the district attorney's presence. They looked at each other for a minute. Julia knew how good the story had been, how sympathetic a witness her sister made. As she'd talked both Edward and Julia could hear the numbers clicking upward in their heads, the number of years a prosecutor would offer Edward's client.

'Did he have a gun?' Edward asked Diana.

'I never saw a gun, but I don't know. He didn't have to hold a gun on me, Edward, I was terrified. I wasn't going to do anything.'

'Did he ever—?'

'That's enough for now,' Julia Lipscomb said. She rose quickly. 'You'll have other opportunities, I'm sure. Right now Diana and I have a family function to attend.'

Diana stood too, more slowly. She looked down at Edward, they both seemed about to speak, then she turned away.

He watched them walk away, thinking how much easier this made his life. The victim was not only sympathetic, she was very convincing. Now it was just a matter of negotiation. That, and talking his client into pleading guilty.

TEN

On his way home Edward made one more stop, at a small apartment complex. Inside one of the units he met the manager. Looking around one more time, he said, 'I'll take it.'

Then he went shopping for furniture.

A week later he sat in court with Donald again. Time to meet the special prosecutor. District attorney *pro tem* was the actual term, but everyone called the person appointed in place of the DA's office the special prosecutor. Edward had hopes for her. Veronica Salazar would have no stake in posting a big win in the case. She wasn't angling for promotion in an office she wasn't part of. They should be able to work something out.

Sitting in the spectator seats beside Donald, who looked uncomfortable and massive in a dark suit without a tie, Edward answered the docket when the case was called and waited for a response. There was none. The judge glanced at a note, said, 'She's running late,' and went on to the next case.

Donald looked better than he had the last time Edward had seen him, in the prison infirmary. The bruises were fading, but the scrape beside his eye still flared. Donald sat sullenly, looking around at everyone with suspicious glances, as if wondering which was the secret hit man with a contract on him. Nothing good had ever happened to Donald in a courthouse.

But last time he'd gotten off relatively easy, and he knew it. He knew he'd screwed up, he'd done his time willingly. This time . . .

'We need to talk,' Edward said. Not words anyone wants to hear in any type of relationship.

'So talk. We seem to have time.' His thunder-rumbling voice sounded strange saying something so mild.

'I met with the victim. I've heard her story. It's going to terrify a jury. She might break down in tears on the witness stand.'

Donald turned to look at him full on. 'You sayin' you believe her?'

'It doesn't matter what I believe, big guy. You know that.'

But Donald continued to look at him. Even his stare seemed to carry weight.

Edward said, 'What I want to do—'

'Mr Hall.'

Edward looked up and remembered Veronica Salazar. He'd tried a case against her as a defense lawyer, when she was a young prosecutor. Edward had done in the trial what defense lawyers usually do, lost, but it had been hard-fought.

He stood and shook the hand she offered. Slender hand, long fingers. She had brown eyes that slanted down a little at the inner corners. Luxuriant dark hair, eyebrows expertly done, a long mouth. Very attractive features. She was as tall as Edward, taller in her heels. Her skirt suit had pinstripes and was very crisp. She kept watching him, without looking at his client. 'Can we talk?'

She meant outside, away from the client. Edward nodded and followed her out, glancing left and right rather than at Ms Salazar's back. They found a bench out in the hall but neither sat. The corridor was bustling with lawyers and citizens.

'Well. Very unusual circumstances for both of us, what?' She suddenly smiled. 'But I'm glad to see you again, Edward. Glad to see you working your way back into the profession.'

'I'm glad to see you too, Veronica. Let me know if I can help with your transition from prosecutor to defense lawyer.' He made it sound like a medical procedure. 'I did it myself a few years ago. It can be fun.'

A mean-spirited person could have pointed out it was excess of fun that had gotten Edward sent to prison, but Veronica didn't take the shot. 'Well. Too soon to start negotiating, don't you think? Have you gotten all the discovery you need?'

'I guess. What there is of it. Couple of police reports. No witness statements except from Mrs and Mr Greene. The only other witnesses seem to have been cops.'

Veronica shrugged. 'Third Ward. Nobody saw nothing. You remember.'

He did. It was a poor neighborhood, predominantly African-American, where few residents would have any love for the police. Maybe Edward, or better yet Donald, would have better luck canvassing the neighborhood for witnesses. Wow. An advantage.

'But I certainly think I have all I need. Very straightforward case. Well. Here's my card. Maybe before our next court date you can come to my office to discuss. Then you can give me that advice on morphing into a defense lawyer.'

Edward didn't have a card to give her in return, not a lawyer card. He only had the one case. 'You know right now, Veronica, I only have a provisional law license, sort of a learner's permit. Here's a business card from my outside job, and here's my cell number.' He wrote on the card quickly.

Veronica set down on the bench a new leather briefcase and opened it. It didn't contain much, only three or four manila folders. She took out the top one. 'We'll be seeing each other soon at any event. I got the case indicted this morning. There'll be an arraignment hearing next week in the court where we'll actually be trying it. In the unlikely event we don't work something out, of course.' She smiled. Then handed him a copy of the indictment. The court was in the top corner. The 439th. The number didn't mean anything to Edward.

'Judge Roberts' court,' Veronica said helpfully.

Edward stared at her. 'How did you manage that?'

She shrugged and smiled. 'Just luck of the draw.'

Edward strongly doubted that. *Watch your back,* David had warned him, but Edward couldn't think of any way he could have dodged this. It was up to the prosecutor to take a case to the grand jury, so she could time that so the case would land in the court she wanted. The system wasn't supposed to work that way, but as a former prosecutor Edward knew there were ways. Veronica obviously knew it too.

'So I'll see you next week? You'll tell the court clerk here?' Veronica waved her hand, brushing away details, or rather brushing them all over Edward.

'Sure,' he said, and watched her walk away, hair swinging. Hips too. Knew she was relishing the moment she'd just had.

And Edward walked back into court with the document in his hand, to explain to his client that his case was going to be heard in the court of the judge whose offices Edward had burglarized, the judge who'd insisted he get prison time rather than probation.

'So tell me about Veronica Salazar, David. How do you get yourself kicked out of the DA's office with a trial record like she had?'

They were in David's office in an office building several blocks from the courthouse. Hurricane Harvey had evicted most of the DA's offices from the Justice Center, and they'd grabbed office space wherever they could. David's office had a makeshift quality. He hadn't hung diplomas or photographs, defiantly suggesting this accommodation was only temporary, more than a year after the big storm.

In answer to Edward's question David raised his eyebrow. 'I'd say too much ambition?'

Edward gave David an ironic look. Both of them had been damned ambitious as young prosecutors, furiously winning cases in order to get promoted to even bigger cases. David acknowledged that with a shrug. 'Maybe I mean too nakedly ambitious. Gunning for the felony chief's job when the felony chief still very much wanted it, thank you. Plus there were other things. Veronica cut corners. Spent all her time right on the ethical line. Maybe over it. She'd dump a load of new discovery on defense lawyers on the first day of trial, including maybe witness statements that had been taken weeks earlier. That sort of thing. Rumors that she'd even withheld evidence in some cases. Nobody listened to the defense bar bitching for a while – what else do defense lawyers ever do? – but after a while it got to be a roar. Then something else happened. I don't know, I wasn't in the loop, but Veronica and Julia had a closed-door meeting and while it was going on one of our investigators was packing up Veronica's office for her. She got escorted out of the building.'

'So you're saying Julia could give me better information?'

'I guess she's the only one who could,' David agreed. 'Except Veronica herself.'

They both laughed briefly at that idea. David sobered up quickly. 'How's your sister?' he asked.

A few months earlier, David had prosecuted Edward's sister Amy for murder, with Edward defending.

'She's fine. Relishing her life. Everything tastes better, she says.'

'Good.'

'So tell me more about Ms Salazar.'

David shrugged. 'Like I said, she cut corners. As a special prosecutor with only one case to prosecute, what's her incentive to follow the rules?'

Edward thought of how she'd gotten the case indicted into the one court she wanted. The two of them looked at each other. David's empathy was palpable, but he was still on the opposite side from Edward. He didn't wish Edward luck when he rose to leave.

ELEVEN

'So now you have another good reason to drop me and get a real lawyer,' Edward said to his client. Donald took up most of the space in the front of Edward's car. They were swooping around the elevated wing of Interstate 45, heading south of downtown.

'But then what about you? They wouldn't let you be a lawyer again.'

'It's not as much fun as I remember. Don't worry about me, think about yourself.'

'I am. I still think you're the best, Edward. Let's just see how the judge reacts to you next week.'

If Donald thought he was that good a judge of character, fine. They drove in silence until Edward turned off the highway and

entered the Third Ward, the neighborhood where the SWAT team
had found Donald with Diana Greene. It immediately felt like
another country. The houses were little wooden frame houses,
most of them needing paint. Some of them were 'shotgun shacks',
a living room facing the street with a bedroom behind it and a
kitchen behind that, three rooms and a bathroom with no hallways,
narrow houses looking defensive. Some gentrification was setting
in; real estate this close to downtown was too valuable not to
change. Many houses were ones on which the homeowner had
lavished attention, with fresh paint, curtains in the windows, a
flower bed near the house or the curb. Those houses looked very
brave.

'You remember which one it was?'

'Sure. Turn right down here.'

Following Donald's instructions, Edward pulled up to one of
the crummier-looking establishments. Of the two front windows,
neither had window treatments and one had cracked glass. The
house didn't look like it had been painted this century. Edward
stared at it. It looked like a haunted house.

'How'd you get here?'

'Mrs Greene's car. She drove. I never saw the place before.'

Edward looked around. At a few of the houses people sat out
on their front porches. At one a few doors down a woman worked
on her flower garden. No one made any pretense of looking
anywhere except at Edward. And every face was black. The house
and the neighborhood looked like the kind of place Donald would
have brought his victim, the kind of neighborhood where Diana
Greene had never been before.

They got out and looked in the windows of the house. What
they could see of the interior was as Diana had described, barely
furnished, dusty, trash on the floor. A strip of yellow crime scene
tape dangled from the front doorknob. Edward rattled the knob
but it was locked, amazingly.

'What were you supposedly doing here?'

'Just waiting.'

'For what? Donald. You have to talk to me. I can't go into
court with nothing.'

Donald looked off across the unappealing landscape. 'Mr
Greene told me his wife was meeting here with a dealer in stolen

jewelry. Emeralds. He said good ones are more valuable than diamonds. He wanted me there as the muscle.'

Edward stared. It was an idiotic story. Rich socialite travels to a neighborhood she'd never turn into of her own accord to wait for some mysterious stranger dealing in hot jewels, taking with her a new friend known for only one thing: kidnapping.

Donald must have felt Edward's stare, but he kept looking away. So he knew how dumb the story was.

'He wanted you here as protection but without a gun?'

Donald shrugged.

'How long did you spend here?'

'Not long. Couple of hours tops.'

Even that part of their stories didn't jibe. Diana said they'd been here for hours, making it sound endless. Edward looked around at some of those staring faces. 'Well, let's see if anybody can corroborate your story.'

Nobody could. The neighbors were probably more receptive to Edward and his large black friend than they'd been to police, but no one had seen much. The man directly across the street, a thin African-American of about seventy, wearing dress pants and a white undershirt, said he'd noticed them pull into the driveway.

'Who was driving?'

'I didn't really notice until they was walkin' into the house. They walked in together.' The man watched Edward closely, ready to cut off the flow of information if Edward looked doubtful.

'Was Donald here holding her? Holding her arm or anything?'

'Nah. He was lookin' around like he didn't know where he was. She marched right up to the front door like she was terrified.'

That was unhelpful. Edward asked a few more questions. The man had left to run an errand after a while, came back to find he couldn't get back into his neighborhood because cops had it cordoned off.

Edward looked at Donald to see if he had questions, but Donald just shrugged. He and the neighbor were watching each other closely, maybe communicating on a level Edward couldn't discern.

'Well thank you, sir. I appreciate your help.' Edward gave the man a card. 'Oh. One more thing. Would you know the woman again if you saw her?'

'Sure. She turned and looked right this way as she was going in the door.'

'But what about the bag over her head?'

The man stared at him. 'She a fine-looking woman. Why would he put a bag over her head?'

Well, that was something. One little chink in the Greenes' story. Edward could tell Donald expected him to fall all over himself in credulity after that. But Edward could picture that neighbor on the witness stand, picture at least half the people in the courtroom, including some on the jury, thinking he was just helping a brother out. Edward thanked him politely and he and Donald returned to the kidnap house. Peering through the windows, Edward had a strong feeling there was someone in there to tell him something. He needed to look at the police scene photos. But he'd prefer to return here with lockpicks and look the place over for himself.

After being shown how by a burglar client Edward had become pretty proficient at breaking and entering. So, he later discovered to his surprise, had his sister Amy, through a different route. The very respectable Dr Amy had her own set of lockpicks, though she was supposedly retired from criminal trespassing.

'I don't know . . .' he began, when he noticed Donald had stiffened beside him. They were on the side of the house. Edward looked around the corner and noticed all the neighbors had disappeared.

'What the . . .'

'Oh, shit,' Donald said. He was staring at a black sedan with very tinted windows coming down the street, picking up speed as it neared them. The driver's window was coming down.

Donald shoved Edward. Hard. They were standing next to a window and Edward went right through it, his shoulder breaking the glass. He landed among the shards on the hard-interior floor. And the window was empty. Donald had vanished.

The gunfire had started now. Edward kept his head down. But the bullets were coming through the walls, stitching their way toward him, heading straight for his legs. Or, if the shooter raised his aim slightly, his heart. Edward stared at that syncopation of murder. It was mesmerizing.

Just before the bullets connected the dots to him, he rolled, skidded backwards on his back, looking back over his shoulder for a door to go deeper into the house. There wasn't any, but there was an opening. The bullets *had* started coming higher now, the shooter apparently realizing he'd laid down enough to kill someone at the front of the room. They were spraying wildly around him. Edward went through that opening into a bedroom. The sound of gunfire diminished a bit. Edward scrambled to his knees and crawled fast through that room and the one at back. He reached up for the back-door knob, opened its simple lock, and the door burst in on him. Edward was flung back.

Donald stood there for only a moment before hurtling in. Not nimble enough to jump in the window, he had run around the house hoping Edward would know to let him in. He fell on the floor and the two lay there panting for a minute. Then their eyes both lit on the open back door. Edward kicked it shut. It was flimsy protection but the sound of it opening would at least give them some warning.

'How many in the car?'

Donald shook his head. 'Wasn't lookin'. I had my head down.'

Edward nodded. Good plan. He cautiously raised his own head. Had the shooting stopped? His ears were still ringing.

They waited in the kitchen a good ten minutes before venturing out. By that time they could hear a siren. The black car was gone. The neighbors were creeping back out of their houses. There was no clue who had been shooting. Edward looked at Donald, who shrugged.

'Somebody really wants you dead,' Edward observed in the kindest possible tone.

'Hey, they were shooting at you too.'

There was a point. Edward looked at the smashed window beside him. 'Well, we managed to get into the crime scene.' Optimist.

He decided not to tell Linda about the drive-by. Edward's other news was going to upset her enough already.

Besides, he had no idea what the drive-by meant. Another attempt at Donald, revenge for some prison or jail slight of a gang leader Donald had done without realizing it. Something from his past he wasn't willing to share with Edward? But as Donald had pointed out, this time Edward had been there too, and the gunfire had followed him when he went through the window into the house.

Neither of them had caught even a glimpse of the interior of the car. The window going down was a signal Donald at least had known instinctively. Edward was going through the window before he could observe anything. Donald was sprinting for the back.

They'd left the scene before police had arrived. There was nothing they could tell the cops, and didn't want to be suspected of anything themselves. Already behaving like good Third Warders, they'd bolted at the sound of the siren.

Edward dropped Donald off at the friend's house where he was staying, urging him to find a new place for a while, but Edward understood the look Donald gave him. He didn't have a lot of options. A recent ex-con with a new charge pending had limited real estate choices.

As Edward neared 'home,' Linda's house, he stopped on the side of the road and made sure he didn't have pieces of glass on his clothes. His face in the rearview mirror looked back at him very palely.

'Babe?' he called as he came in the door, in a bright, high tone that sounded fake even to him. He wanted a second take. And Linda was very intuitive.

She peeked around the corner wearing work clothes, a skirt and blouse and indeed, she was frowning. 'Hi?'

'Hi. How was your day? You look great by the way. Like you lounged around a spa all day. Instead of the hard work I know you did.'

'Edward? What's wrong?'

'Nothing.' He shrugged theatrically, then forced himself to say nothing and calm down. While he just stood there looking at her, he actually did. Sight of Linda always had the weird effect of exciting him and calming him. He walked slowly toward her. 'Where'd you get those dimples?'

She dimpled. 'Like them? I'm just renting them now, trying them out.'

Then they were in each other's arms. After a long kiss he drew back. Linda smiled at him lazily. 'What do you want for dinner? I've got chicken thawed. I've got a new recipe. But, you know—'

'Tastes like chicken,' they said together, then Edward said, 'actually, I've got something to show you. Take a ride?'

She looked at him suspiciously. His winning smile really needed work.

In the car she kept asking where they were going. 'Not far,' he kept saying. They had changed into jeans and more casual shirts. And in fact it wasn't far. A small apartment complex on the edge of the Heights, Linda's neighborhood. Conveniently near downtown, a few miles away (or forty minutes in Houston terms).

'Have you found a new restaurant?' Linda asked.

Damn, that would have been a good idea. Find a new place to take her after this. He nodded. 'Not really.'

When he pulled into the parking lot her suspicion deepened. 'An apartment? Eddie? Why are you bringing me here?'

Linda was one of the very few people from whom he'd accept a nickname. But now it sounded like a weapon. He cleared his throat, first move of guilty men everywhere.

'Here's the thing.'

'Oh God.'

'Just wait. It's not bad.'

She turned toward him, crossing her arms. Crossed arms, always a bad sign. Some women did that in a way that emphasized their secondary sex characteristics. With Linda the pose seemed to bar access.

'It's not bad. Please don't look like that. I've just gotten an apartment.'

'Your apartment.' She was looking straight at him, expressionless.

'Yes. You know, I was living with Mike when you and I first met, then you and I started spending more and more time together—'

'Living together,' Linda said.

'Well, yes. And I didn't want to impose on Mike any more . . .'

'I thought we were living together.' Her lips clamped together, trying not to tremble. 'Are you going to tell me you need your own space? Because I thought I'd made space for you in my . . . my house. Sharing my office, emptying that closet . . .'

'You've been great, Linda. And I love you. I love being with you. I just . . .'

'Is this about prison? Are you going to tell me you need your own space because you didn't have any privacy for two years? I thought . . .' She tightened her lips again.

Edward opened the car door. 'Just come in and look, would you?' He hurried around the car, opened her door, and held out his hand.

'Why do I want to see your crummy bachelor pad? What do you want, decorating tips?' She still had her arms folded, rejecting his hand.

'Partly that. Please?'

She looked up at him. Her look hardened, then changed, ever so slightly. Curiosity had crept into her expression. She got out on her own, ignoring his hand. They walked across the cracked pavement of the parking lot. Edward picked up a shopping ad and tossed it into a trash can. The complex they approached was not very prepossessing. One two-story row of apartments, a dozen in all, looking squat. It was under new ownership, one reason Edward had gotten a good deal, and new paint had been promised. Now the blank windows stared mournfully.

'This is what you're leaving me for?' Linda said.

'I'm not leaving.' He led her upstairs to number eight, took out his keys and found the new one. The lock at least was new. Two of them. Edward opened the door, then stepped aside and waved. Linda shook her head. So Edward stepped in, turned on the light, and reached for her. Linda stepped quickly past him. Then stopped, staring.

'Oh, Eddie.' Her expression changed completely.

In the front room were a desk, two slightly padded client chairs in front of it, a bookcase holding some legal tomes, and a couch, as if a waiting room and office had been squashed together. On the walls were his college diplomas and his law license. As he'd once told her, they didn't physically take the document away when they legally stripped him of his right to practice. No photos, no personal touches.

Edward cleared his throat. 'You know, I'm going to be interviewing witnesses and so forth and I didn't want to bring them
to your house. I don't really have an office for my sales job, and
I don't want to bring those types there either. So I . . .'

Linda squeezed his arm. Her eyes liquefied. 'I understand.'

She understood he missed it. Being a lawyer, having the trap-
pings. A place to meet clients, ones he might never have again.
Being a person of substance. 'I'm sorry I got mad, Edward. I'm
glad you have a place of your own again.'

'I expected you to be mad.'

'Not now that I see. Why would I be mad?'

He shrugged, looked around. 'Because I could, you know,
bring babes here.'

Linda laughed. She rubbed his arm. 'Sure you could, sweetheart.' She sounded like a mother comforting a child who'd lost
the spelling bee.

'Well, I've got one here now.' They both laughed and found
themselves in each other's arms.

Some while later Linda drew back and looked around again.
'Actually I've got news of my own.' She suddenly looked nervous.

'What is it?'

Linda smiled shyly. 'I got a new job. Sort of. A court reporter
job.'

His eyebrows went up. 'That fast?'

'Well, I'd been lining it up before. Just in case. They always
need more at the courthouse.'

'You're going to be working in the courthouse?'

Linda nodded again, still watching him closely, as if for disap-
proval. 'Which court?'

'No specific one. I'm going to be a swing court reporter. A
fill-in. For now.'

'Baby, that's great.' He hugged her again, dipped in for a kiss.
Drawing back, he said, 'So now you swing?'

She laughed. 'Only with you, sweetheart.'

They kissed again. It turned unexpectedly deep.

'We have to celebrate.'

Linda nodded agreement. 'So you got a bed in this joint?'

He did.

TWELVE

He spent the next day getting to know Sterling Greene. In the great tradition of Houston entrepreneurs, he seemed to have appeared out of nowhere with his first big deal, an office building in Katy, a booming suburb. Then he'd moved into the big city in a big way, demolishing an old hotel on the edge of downtown and putting up a luxury shopping destination with condos above. There'd been some irregularity about that one, the old hotel lying in ruins before the demolition permit had actually been issued. But Houston was an out-with-the-old kind of place. City leaders preferred something new and gleaming over something shabby with history. Greene came out shining himself.

Then it was an empire: plans announced, crews at work, Greene appointed to boards of directors. There were several articles about him receiving awards. And the marriage to Diana, a fabulous affair at the River Oaks Country Club eight years ago. Only one article mentioned in one sentence it was a second wedding for the bride, after a youthful starter marriage to a rich boy she'd probably known from high school. Diana was described as a socialite, which Edward took to mean a lovely person inexplicably well off without working. She had been a model a few times, but nothing like a career. Articles about their parties and social engagements followed: not many, the newspaper didn't care about that sort of thing any more, but on-line sources and one of Houston's glossy magazines did. It looked like a wonderful matched life.

Linda, who'd been helping him, said in their shared office at her house, 'No kids.'

'I noticed. Doesn't mean anything.'

She agreed with a shrug. 'You know what else I'm not finding. Anything about him having a program to hire ex-convicts. No reform movements. He's got all these plaques for other things, if he did something like that as a business course you know he would've maneuvered to get himself recognized for it.'

Edward sat back. 'Hmph. You're right.'

'Always.' She smiled.

'I guess I'll have to ask him.'

Linda lost her smile. 'When?'

'When I interview him. This afternoon.'

Linda looked even more worried. 'I'll go with you.'

Edward shook his head. 'I need to do it. Don't look like that, I'll be fine. You know how many angry victims and families I've talked to? Besides, it's at his office.'

That turned out not to be true. Edward had an appointment that afternoon, but when he got there the receptionist acted as if nobody remembered, and said Mr Greene was on a job site. His offices were rather grand, in a building adjacent to Greenway Plaza, but also rather empty. Edward heard no hum of activity, just the receptionist, a near-teenager who kept looking at her phone instead of him. 'I had an appointment,' he repeated hopelessly.

She shrugged without looking up. 'I can't teleport him across town, can I?'

'You could call him.'

She looked up as if it were an outlandish idea. 'He's not going to come in for you. Trust me.'

Edward's foot was tapping hard on the linoleum. 'Where's the job site?'

'Look, I . . .' She saw something in Edward's face and stopped. Or more likely he just annoyed her beyond endurance. She wrote hastily on a slip of paper and held it out to him with an expression that said she sincerely hoped a girder would fall on him as soon as he stepped out of his car.

Meanwhile Linda continued her research. She knew the date Donald had gotten out of prison and the date of his arrest, barely six weeks later. She scoured the Houston *Chronicle* for that time period, looking for an article about the Greenes or Greene Construction, anything that might have drawn Donald's attention to them. Assuming the prosecution's case was sound, what had attracted him to Diana as a kidnap victim? She found no mention of the couple, broadened her search on the theory Donald might have read about them while he was still in prison, planning his crime before he was even released. But she had to go back six months to find an article about a reception for the opening of the art exhibition that included the portrait of Diana, and she doubted Donald would have had access to that information while still in prison.

She returned to the day of Donald's arrest and past it, momentum carrying her forward in time. She stopped at a small item on page four in the summaries of stories with fewer details, usually crimes. 'Hmmph,' she said. And smiled. Not that the item was good news, but now she had something to share with Edward.

The construction site was out the Gulf freeway, just inside the Houston city limits. Here was the bustle of activity Edward had missed at Greene's office. Half a dozen men in hardhats and yellow vests walked around a huge lot, several acres, which had been cleared of whatever had been knocked down here and a hole dug for a foundation. A bulldozer was still working on that, while other guys dug holes to connect to the water, electrical, and sewage systems. There was one girder planted in a corner, looking lonely and possibly symbolic. It had no siblings waiting in stacks to be similarly hammered in.

He had no problem spotting Sterling Greene. He was the one in the tie the others huddled around, while the big man looked at a blueprint and pointed around the lot. Edward studied him as he approached. Except for the tie, Greene fit right in among the burly construction workers. The sleeves of his white shirt were rolled up as if they'd found it impossible to contain those hairy forearms. A hardhat shortened his face so his main feature was a large mouth and square chin. Slight beginning of jowls. He might have been forty, but it looked like they'd been a tough, active forty years. Classic high school athlete grown into successful businessman in one of the manly occupations. Sterling Greene produced things, huge things. Unlike, to pick an example at random, lawyers.

Edward parked on the street behind a big black Mercedes with a man in black pants and white shirt leaning on its bumper. Edward left his briefcase and jacket in the car, walking carefully across the gravel and chunks of concrete. His object didn't look up even when Edward was a few feet away, though Edward got the curious stares of a couple of the others.

'Mr Greene?'

He finally looked up, showing nothing but irritation. Didn't bother to reply.

'I'm Edward Hall, the lawyer. We had an appointment, about half an hour ago.'

Greene handed the blueprint off. 'Ex-lawyer, isn't it? You start off every conversation with a lie?'

His crew laughed. 'On this case I'm a lawyer again,' Edward said calmly. 'Specifically Donald Willis's lawyer. I have a few questions for you.'

'I have a few nothings for you. Diana's sister said neither of us has to talk to you.'

'But Diana did talk to me. Julia was there too.'

'What?' Greene scowled, and he had the face for it. He stepped forward and put a finger in Edward's chest. 'You stay away from my family, understand? Do that again and you'll be sorry.' The finger threatened to turn into a drill. Edward stood his ground.

'You realize it's my job to investigate, right? Among other things, that might help us settle the case so you and your wife don't have to testify at trial.'

Sterling considered his point for a moment. It was a good one. A few minutes right now might spare him and especially his wife being grilled in front of a much bigger audience. But Greene had already staked out his position, and he seemed like a man disinclined to change his course once under way.

'You can talk to me now or on the witness stand,' Edward added.

But Greene sneered. 'I'll take the witness stand. Why should I do any favors for the asshole representing the bastard who snatched my wife?'

Wow. He'd played the asshole–bastard coalition card that quickly. 'Mr Greene, it would be for the best—'

'Charlie!'

A guy detached himself from the gang in the hole and came over slowly, sizing up the situation from the great height of his head. Greene obviously had his own Big Donald. Big Charlie was white, with a stubbled face and small eyes that fixed on

Edward as the piece that didn't fit. He was heavily muscled but Edward thought he could take him. In a race. At chess.

'Charlie, this . . . person . . . is uninvited from my job site. Can you show him the door?'

There was no door in sight, but Charlie got the metaphor. He quickly closed the gap and before Edward could move shoved his shoulder hard enough to spin him around.

'You other guys help,' Greene said.

So Edward walked, quickly but with great dignity, so much so some of them started laughing. Edward got directly into his car and slammed the door, glaring out the window at Charlie, who was obviously going to stand there until he was gone. But Edward took a moment to look across the lot at Sterling Greene, who stared back at him.

And Edward smiled.

As he drove away he thought, *So Mrs Greene didn't tell her husband about our meeting. Interesting.*

And he'd learned something else, too.

Linda had news when he returned. She explained her quest and its futility at finding something that would have drawn Donald's attention to the Greenes. Nonetheless, she had an article pulled up on her screen. 'This is the front-page story about the kidnapping and Donald's arrest.'

It was a big article, above the fold, with an excellent photo of Donald on the ground while the happy couple were reunited across from him. 'I've seen it.'

Linda nodded. 'But here's another one, from three days later. Much smaller.'

It was headlined 'Local Artist Found Dead'. The story was about the Houston portrait and landscape painter Antonio Alberico, a promising young artist who had been found dead of a gunshot wound in his Houston home. Police knew nothing else as yet, not even whether the cause of death was murder or suicide. The gun had been found close to the artist's hand and there was no sign anyone else had been present. But he'd been dead for two days by the time he was found. 'So tragic,' said someone identified as a friend who also exhibited his works. 'Tony was right on the cusp of an amazing career.'

Edward looked up. 'Sad. But so?'

Linda pointed. 'This is the guy who painted that big portrait of Diana Greene. Just a strange coincidence.'

'Sad,' Edward repeated. His lawyer's brain started trying to make some connection. Donald went to the exhibition of portraits looking for a rich victim, then found the artist and interrogated him too vigorously trying to get an address? No, that was ridiculous. First it broke down from the premise of Donald going to an art exhibition.

Linda shrugged. 'I spent a lot of time on this and I wanted something to show you for it.'

'Welcome to the world of investigating a case. Lots of wasted time. But it does point out I need to get an investigator.' He saw Linda's face and added, 'An additional investigator.' One familiar with the criminal milieu in which Donald had moved his whole life.

Linda stood up from the computer desk. 'Anyway, I'm not going to have as much time. I start my new job Monday.'

Edward said, 'I guess I've already started my old one.' Linda had sounded much happier about her new beginning.

'Did you find out anything from Sterling Greene?' she asked.

'Only that he's surrounded by hired muscle, and I get the impression at least one or two of them wouldn't balk at doing something marginally illegal. He wouldn't have needed Donald for that.'

They both stood thinking. Then Edward grinned. 'So I'll see you around the Justice Center.'

Linda smiled back, looking nervous.

THIRTEEN

Who wanted Donald dead? Because those four guys in jail hadn't questioned him or threatened him to stay away from somebody. And you don't interrogate somebody with a drive-by shooting. Somebody had tried to kill Edward's client twice. On the other hand, as Donald had pointed out, Edward could have been the target of the drive-by too. OK, so who wanted either or both of them dead? The attempted murder had been a good development, just objectively speaking. If Edward could make something of it.

Of course, it could have been somebody from Donald's criminal past, but that led nowhere. The obvious suspect was Sterling Greene, in retaliation for the crime against his wife. Or maybe, to get far-fetched, it had been Ryan Jennings, whose son Donald had kidnapped years ago, wanting to make sure he wouldn't be targeted again now that Donald seemed to be up to his old trade. Maybe that's why Jennings had bailed him out, so he'd be less protected.

But the speculation was pointless. Edward started by calling a police detective who wasn't exactly a friend but would chat with him now and again. It seemed, perversely, Edward had actually improved his status in that regard by getting convicted and going to prison. Detective Hayes seemed to feel he'd developed some underworld contacts that might come in useful someday. Edward let her think that.

'Antonio who?' she answered unhelpfully.

For a moment Edward couldn't remember the guy's last name either. 'Antonio the artist,' he said into his phone while driving. 'Surely you don't have that many pending investigations into the deaths of local artists.'

'Oh, him,' said Detective Madison Hayes. Edward could picture her leaning back at her desk, putting her legs up on it. 'Antonio, uh, Alberico. Yeah. Not my case, but I've heard about it. George was pretty excited when he got it. Local celebrity if you're into that kind of thing. But I think the investigation's stalled out. When you can't even get the medical examiner to call it murder it's kind of a poor start. Plus with the body not being found for a couple of days it's hard to pin down the time of death, and neighbors have already started to forget which day was which and whether they noticed anything unusual. Sorry, Edward. If I hear anything I'll let you know.'

'Thanks anyway, Maddie.'

'Hey, by the way, is that client of yours going to plead? I mean, the case was cleared for us as soon as he was arrested in the act, but I'm curious.'

'I don't know,' Edward admitted. 'Says he didn't do it.'

Detective Hayes laughed. 'Well, that sets him apart from every other defendant.'

'Ha ha,' Edward said, and hung up.

But his detective friend was right. Defendants always said they didn't do it, and the vast majority of them were lying. Probably the reason this investigation wasn't going anywhere was because it was exactly what it looked like, a foiled kidnapping.

Edward met with his client again Saturday afternoon. For a moment he thought he was being shaken down, because Donald brought company, and while none of them was wearing a white-and-black striped shirt or a mask, they didn't look like business people or tourists. The four or five guys and one woman looked like they knew their ways around a jail cell or a house from which the owner was absent.

'Friends of yours?' Edward said.

Donald smiled. 'Yeah. You know Bill here, he was inside with us.' The guy did look vaguely familiar, though Edward had tried hard to make no friends in prison. Donald named other names Edward saw no reason to remember as of yet. One guy sank onto Edward's new sofa, looking high on something. Religion, probably.

They were in Edward's new 'office,' which Donald admired extravagantly. 'Already back in business. My man.'

'Yeah, I've rehabilitated myself. Unlike you.'

'Hey!'

'Anyway, nice to meet your friends, but you and I have work to do, Donald. We need to put together a case—'

'That's what they're here for.' Donald waved his arms around the room. 'My friends want to help.' A couple of the gang – probably the right word for this group – nodded and smiled. One was picking up the few objects on Edward's shelves. Edward started to protest, then stopped himself. Think outside the box, he told himself. Maybe some people who knew both sides of the law could actually help. 'OK, here's what we need.' He sat behind the desk and laid out what little he knew. 'So we need to find some connection between Sterling Greene and possibly illegal activity, particularly buying stolen jewelry.' It sounded so stupid even as he was saying it. 'Now as for Donald's defense. He claims Sterling hired him the day of the event, but they actually met a few days before when Donald asked him for a job. Then Sterling called him the day of the so-called kidnapping and hired him to do something else. But there's no proof of that because he got paid in cash.' Donald started to speak, Edward just shook his head. 'So we need to find some connection between Donald and Greene before that day. You're his friends, I assume you were hanging out with him after he got out of the joint. Is there anybody here who can say they saw Donald and Sterling Greene together before the day Donald was arrested?'

Every hand in the room went up. Edward sighed.

'Is there anyone here who can *truthfully* say you saw them?'

All the hands went down, slowly. Except one. It belonged to the woman. She was short, wiry, and dark, of hard to determine ethnicity. Edward cocked his head at her and she looked right back at him. 'Yeah,' she said. 'I was with Donald one day when he went to talk to Greene.'

'You went to Greene's office?'

'Naw. They were at some piece of property Greene was supposedly thinking of buying. Old falling-down house on it.'

'Anybody else with them?'

She shook her head. 'I don't even think Greene saw me. I waited in the car.' She added, 'People tend not to see me.'

She probably made good use of that. Edward stared at her now, though, picturing her as the star witness for the defense. Yep, that was about the caliber of defense this was.

'All right, I'll want to talk to you. The rest of you, if you can help, thanks. Bye now. Try not to get arrested.'

They shuffled out. 'Ms—'

'Marie.'

'Marie. Could you wait outside for a few minutes, please? I need to talk to my client in private.'

She obliged without protest. Edward got Donald to tell his story again. This time Donald told it in greater detail but with no contradictions from his previous tellings. Unfortunately.

'Start with the day you got out of prison,' Edward said from the chair behind his desk, then leaned back, eyes locked on his client.

'Oh, man, nobody knows how that feels better than you, Edward. You walk out that door with your little bag in your hand and the bus ticket and fifty bucks they give you. The door slams shut and you're just standing there. All alone.'

Edward did know that moment very well, when your world suddenly expands hugely, back into the great wide world where once you moved so freely. But now it seemed scary, after the security of the little world inside you'd come to know so well. Even to get the few miles from Huntsville to Houston seemed overwhelming.

'I just stood there, almost wanting to knock on the door and go back in, you know.'

Edward nodded, his hand covering his mouth.

'So I took the bus. Drops you off at the Greyhound station downtown Houston. I just walked out and started walking. Thinking the whole world was mine again. Thinking I should've made a plan before I got out.'

'You hadn't contacted anyone ahead of time?'

Donald shook his head, which was lower than it had been a minute earlier. He was a big strong guy who seemed to be deflating. 'You know the parole board, they tell you not to resume any criminal contacts. That's everybody I know. I got on a local bus and let it take me. The second time around the route I got off back in the Third Ward. Walked to where my mama'd been livin' when I went in, but it was vacant.'

'You didn't have a phone number for her?'

Donald shrugged. 'Didn't have a phone. And no, I didn't know her number. Asked a couple of the neighbors, but they didn't know where she'd gone. I ended up sleeping there in the vacant house, trying to sleep on the floor. Used the money to buy a couple of malt liquors to help me sleep. I thought they'd taste better than they did.'

Edward's getting out experience had been very different. There were many people he could call, starting with his wealthy parents or sister, but he hadn't wanted that. But that sense of being overwhelmed had lasted only a few minutes. Linda had been waiting for him. She took him into Houston, a restaurant, into her home, her bed. Her arms. And all that had been wondrously new, because when he went in they'd only been people who saw each other once in a while in an office or at a party. While he was incarcerated Linda had accelerated quickly from acquaintance to friend. And, when he got out, lover.

Donald shook himself and stirred. 'The next morning things looked better. Breakfast in a diner, saw a guy I used to know, he gave me a ride to the library. Looked at the job listings on-line, got a cheap phone and started calling. Nobody was interested, but I kept trying. Found a few day jobs, a friend to stay with. Working my way down my prospects until I met Sterling Greene. He said he didn't have anything for me, but a few days later he called me back. The rest you know.'

Right there was where the story stopped making sense. Sterling Greene needing Donald for anything. More likely Donald had seen him as an opportunity. But they went through the story again. It hadn't gotten any better. Afterwards Edward talked to Marie in more detail. Except she didn't have any details. Mainly he just wanted to watch her as a potential witness. She didn't quiver and she didn't stutter, but she wasn't what he'd call world class. She spoke in a monotone, looking him in the eye but with heavy lids.

Afterwards Edward sat alone in his new office, which looked like a cheap stage set. He thought, well, the case is shaping up. Into a complete loser.

Early Monday morning, before eight o'clock, Edward was alone in the court offices of the 439th District Court. Around him he felt the building beginning to stir, but for the moment he had complete privacy. He wore his best suit, dark blue, and Linda's favorite tie. The offices were set up with a common area where one first entered, with two clerks' desks, filing cabinets, copy machine. On one side from there, down a short hallway, was first the court reporter's office, then the judge's private chambers. On the other side was the court coordinator's office, now with its door closed.

Just as Edward stepped out of the court reporter's office into the common area he heard a key turning in the door, then it opened suddenly. Edward stood very still. Judge Pershing Roberts entered. Tall, black, and imposing, Judge Roberts had presided in this court for fifteen years. He had features that could be read from the far reaches of the courtroom and a perpetual scowl. Or maybe that was just the only expression Edward had ever encountered on his face. Judge Roberts saw Edward and stopped dead, eyes widening. His hand remained on the doorknob. 'You,' he said. An accusation.

'Well,' said Edward. 'This is awkward.'

'We don't have a drug case going on,' the judge said. 'What are you doing here?'

That was as close as Judge Roberts came to joking. The crime that had sent Edward to prison almost four years earlier had been breaking into these very offices. It had happened during a trial that *was* a drug case. The evidence had featured a large bag of cocaine that had been admitted in evidence against Edward's client that afternoon. Edward had watched it carefully from counsel table. As a high-flying, well-known defense lawyer he had, well, flown high. That included developing the habits that went with making a lot of money and spending time with people who made their money from high-end illegal activity. Looking at the bag of cocaine, Edward had thought, *There's a lot of fun going to waste.* So he had hidden in the jury room until the building cleared out after five o'clock, then crept back to the offices. Edward had certain skills with a lockpick learned from a former client, but he hadn't needed those skills because the door had been unlocked. He'd entered the dark offices to find the prosecutor in his case had had the same idea about the cocaine and had beaten him to it. Edward had startled her, reassured her, then they'd become partners in crime. And more. The evening had turned into a memorable drug and eventually sex binge. But it had come to a terrible end when a security guard had entered the offices. Edward ran like a thief, or rather a burglar, drawing the guard away so his partner in crime made her escape. But Edward had gotten caught and eventually convicted. And sent to prison.

The latter was mainly due to the man in front of him. Judge Roberts had been highly offended by the crime. Normally a first offense like that, especially for a lawyer most of the prosecutors knew and liked, would draw a probated sentence. But from what Edward had heard, Judge Roberts had insisted on prison time, and no one in the system wanted to cross him.

Now he stood in front of Edward in the apparently otherwise empty offices, blocking the only exit. 'This is astounding,' he said. 'I thought you were trying to work your way back into practicing law. Instead you're resuming your—'

'Judge, this isn't—'

'And on top of that you're interrupting me?' Judge Roberts made it sound like a worse crime.

'May I? I didn't break in, Judge. I came here early because—'

'Appearances to the contrary notwithstanding. How did you get in? I make very sure my offices are locked every night. Especially since your escapade. I am always the last to leave and I make very sure of that.'

Edward held out his hand. 'Judge, I came in early because your court reporter is on vacation.'

'So you saw an opportunity?'

'No. Well, yes, actually. What I was doing—'

The court coordinator's door opened and the coordinator stuck his head out. 'Oh. Good morning, Judge. Everything OK?'

The judge looked from his coordinator back to Edward. His stare softened a tiny bit, to a beam that would only drill a hole through a man rather than slice his head off.

'I arranged with Richard to come in early because you're going to have a fill-in court reporter. She's my . . . a good friend of mine and to tell you the truth it's her very first day as a court reporter. So I . . .' Edward waved his hand to the court reporter's office behind him. The judge looked that way and saw a helium balloon and a corner of a banner that said 'Congratulations!' in very large letters.

His stare returned to Edward. 'I'm giving employment to someone who holds you in affection?'

'Weird, isn't it?'

They stood without speaking. Some of the best moments in life are when two people who know and like each other very well share a companionable silence where nothing has to be communicated with words. This was not one of those moments.

'Your own case is on my docket this morning, isn't it?' Judge Roberts finally said.

'Yes, sir. About that. I'm going to be filing a motion asking you to recuse yourself.'

'On what basis?'

Edward stared at him. 'Because you insisted I go to prison and put me there, and had me stripped of my law license?'

Judge Roberts stared back. 'Are you saying because of that I won't be impartial? In the trial of a presumably innocent person you represent? Are you ready to put on evidence of that?'

Edward studied the judge. *Just give me a wink. Some human contact. Lawyers have to make these decisions.* Not even a wink and a nod. A stare, like this one, a long stony look.

'Mr Hall, do you know why I insisted on prison time for you? It wasn't about you. I actually liked you, Edward. You were a very good trial lawyer, always prepared, fast on your feet but not with glib answers, with well-reasoned positions. I was sorry to see such a career end.'

Weirdest compliment Edward had ever received. He kept listening, cocking his head.

'It wasn't you, Edward. It was the crime. It wasn't a crime against me. It was a violation of the foundations of our system. If we condoned an attorney, an officer of the court, breaking into a judge's chambers to steal evidence, what next? Breaking in and altering evidence, switching out a fingerprint card? Your offense wasn't just you having a good time. It was an attack on the system of justice itself.'

'I didn't think of it—'

'And there was no doubt of your guilt. The security guard caught you white-handed, so to speak. *Now*, by contrast, you are back to representing a presumably innocent man. It is my responsibility to afford *him* a fair trial.' *Not you*, the judge's voice seemed to emphasize. 'There is nothing I take more seriously. If you don't believe that, file your motion and I will voluntarily step aside.'

Judge Roberts stopped talking and just stood there, staring at Edward. Edward looked back. Judge Roberts was a large black man who had grown up in Houston. In spite of his success, before that success, he had suffered the same prejudices Donald had. He might harbor the most sympathy for Edward's client of any judge in the building.

And given their history, Judge Roberts would try harder than any other judge to at least appear to be giving Edward a fair trial.

'I appreciate that, sir. I won't be filing that motion.'

It could have been a bonding moment. But now it just felt awkward.

'Um, excuse me?' came a small voice from behind the large judge. Linda edged her way around him.

Edward threw on a huge smile. 'Surprise!'

Linda looked past him at the decorated office, then up at the unsmiling judge who was her temporary boss. Then the judge said hello in a measured voice. Linda told him her name, glancing back and forth between the two of them.

And the judge suddenly smiled.

'Welcome to the criminal justice system, Ms Benson. I hope you'll enjoy your time here. It's very important work and very rewarding.'

He shook her hand, glanced at Edward, and withdrew to his office. Edward raised his eyebrows. 'Surprise,' he said in a smaller voice.

Linda looked after the departed judge. 'Yes. It is.'

Edward had committed the crime that sent him to prison long before he and Linda were a couple. But it was a notorious event. Linda knew about it and would probably hear about it again, here in the Justice Center. But no one knew the orgy part, except Edward and the woman, who'd gotten away scot-free, thanks to him. Edward planned to keep it that way. If not for the judge, it wouldn't even have been on his mind this morning.

Docket call was uneventful. Linda sat there at the court reporter's desk staring straight ahead, already with the concentrated look of her job. Edward answered routinely and Veronica Salazar, who had shown up on time, responded. The judge called them forward to the bench, nodding at Linda to record their conference. 'Has discovery been completed in this case?'

Edward looked at his opponent. 'As far as I know, Your Honor. There isn't much. No physical evidence to speak of, no confession. It will just be eyewitness testimony, unless Ms Salazar knows something I don't.'

'That's the way I see it too, Your Honor.' Ms Salazar stood tall in a well-tailored suit, from which her long, slender neck extended. 'My case is ready.'

The judge's look switched to Edward. 'Uh, mine's not, Judge. I need more time for investigation. There are aspects to this case—'

'How much time?' The judge's expression was very neutral. 'Because I'll tell you, Mr Hall, I don't want this case lingering on my docket. It draws unwanted media attention and just distracts from the court's business. So shall we say a trial date of two weeks from today?'

Edward's stomach dropped. Hell no. He could be ready today with his non-existent defense, but to prepare, really prepare for trial, he needed weeks. Till next year, probably. 'I need considerably longer than that, Your Honor.'

The judge looked down, presumably at a calendar. 'All right. Today is September fifteenth. Shall we say thirty days?' Before Edward could speak he added, 'If you believe your developing defense needs more time at that point, Mr Hall, you can file a motion for continuance. But I hope not.' Edward closed his mouth. 'Very well, then,' Judge Roberts concluded. 'We have a trial date. October fifteenth. Thank you both.'

As if he'd given either of them a choice. Edward walked away, feeling hollow. My God. Thirty days. That was the jet plane of trial schedules.

At counsel table, Veronica turned to him. 'Talk?'

Edward nodded numbly and followed her out to the hall, motioning to Donald to keep his seat in the courtroom. In the hall Veronica took a seat and patted the bench beside her. Edward sat.

'It sounds as if the judge would like this case resolved as quickly as possible,' she began.

'Judges always want cases to go away. Why don't they just do their jobs? But if you're saying you're going to file a motion to dismiss . . .'

Veronica laughed, an honest chuckle that lifted her features. She patted Edward's leg. 'Funny. No, I was thinking of the more traditional conclusion of a case.'

Meaning a guilty plea. 'My client insists he's innocent.'

'Of course he does. He got off easy last time. You've given him false hope, my friend. My case is very straightforward, my victim very believable and she will present well, believe me.'

'You don't have a gun,' Edward began on autopilot. 'How does he hold her hostage for hours without a gun?'

Veronica gave him a *really?* expression. 'Look at him, Edward.'

Fair point. Putting Donald next to Diana Greene would be like a guilty plea in itself. 'What's your offer?'

'It's a life sentence case. We both know that. Enhanced so the minimum is fifteen. Even if you somehow convinced a jury he released the victim in a safe place again, the enhancement would still make it a first-degree felony. Still life. For a serial kidnapper who won't stop, this time just a month after getting out of prison. Next time he's likely to kill someone.'

He had just heard her closing argument in brief. 'What's your offer?' Edward said.

Veronica took a breath, looked at him steadily and said, 'Forty years. That's a gift to you of twenty.'

In Texas, any sentence of sixty years or above was treated as sixty years for parole purposes. In a case like this Donald would be eligible for parole after serving half his sentence. Twenty years. Most of the rest of his life in prison.

'I'll convey your offer. But as a betting man, I can tell you he won't take it.'

'Do your best,' she said, leaning toward him to look into his eyes. Then she stood and walked away, long legs moving efficiently.

Edward remained on the bench, watching scenes that had had everyday familiarity for him years ago: lawyers conferring with their clients and, worse, clients' families, talking to each other trying to make cases go away some way short of trial. It all made Edward wonder whether he even wanted to be a lawyer again. Those conversations with the families were the worst. Every sentence the lawyer said began with, 'Yes, but . . .' The practice of law was an esteemed profession from the outside. People who practiced it at ground level, in the courts, knew what a scramble it was. Always balancing one's own interests against the clients, looking for new clients, wanting to dump the ones you had. Clients all had such problems. By definition. No lawyer has ever gotten a call saying, 'Hey, man, I'm having a great day and I just wanted to share with you.' Thanks. Ten-minute call, round up to a quarter hour, that'll be a hundred and twenty dollars. That was the calculus lawyers made. Do I have to take this call? If so, can I charge for it?

And the work. Edward had some investment in this case because he liked Donald and owed him. Donald had saved his life in prison more than once. Edward did OK inside, inmates always wanted to talk to a lawyer about their cases, but every once in a while there'd be a crazy one who'd take offense at the supposedly stuck-up, rich, white lawyer. Donald was his fallback position for guys like that. But in the vast majority of cases the client meant very little to the lawyer and work itself was repetitive and tedious. Playing with numbers. *I'll give you twelve. I'll take eight.* If you were a civil lawyer those numbers were dollars. In Edward's world they were years, except very quickly they were just numbers. Work one out and move on.

Edward was in a unique position out of all the lawyers in this large building, because he had only one client, one case. He didn't have to race from court to court making multiple court appearances. He could spend all his thoughts on this one grim case.

'Penny,' said a voice just above his head. He looked up to see the district attorney of Harris County. She sat beside him as if fascinated by the show herself. 'Wondering if it's worth it to try to become a lawyer again?'

'You're a mind reader?'

'It's not tough, seeing a former lawyer staring at the other lawyers at work. Same thing happened to me after I first got elected. Being DA, not having any trial cases, it gives you the same kind of time. Step back and see if I still want to do it. How are you leaning?'

Edward just shrugged. Julia patted his knee. 'Just do a good job on this one case, Edward. Then you'll really have the choice to make. How's it going, by the way? I saw Veronica walking away. How on earth did you have the bad luck to draw her?'

'I didn't know much about her. Except that you fired her.' He looked directly at Julia Lipscomb. Her mouth hardened. 'She'd turned into the worst kind of prosecutor, too lazy to do anything right herself, taking credit for what her subordinates did. With just the one case you should be fine with her.'

Interesting. Always good to know your opponent had a lazy streak. But Julia was still looking at him for an answer to her first question. 'It's going the way they always do, Julia. My client insists he's innocent, all the evidence says quite the opposite.' Normally he wouldn't reveal so much of his hand, but Julia would know what the evidence was. And even though she was technically out of the case, she was much more emotionally invested in it than he was.

'It's making Diana a nervous wreck. She just wants it over.'

Edward got the broad hint. If he wanted to do the district attorney a favor, get his client to plead guilty.

'I'm doing everything I can, Julia. I certainly don't want to try the damned thing.'

Julia nodded, smiled at him sympathetically and walked away. Edward saw Donald watching her, then turning his gaze back to Edward. His client had been watching him talk to the enemy. Edward and Donald just looked at each other across the courthouse hall.

FOURTEEN

A day later Edward found himself back at the art gallery, staring at the portrait of Mrs Diana Greene, socialite. It looked dated to him, the pose of a rich woman who gave charity balls and rode a carriage through the streets. Until he looked at the eyes and mouth. Her eyes had a twinkle that the sensuous mouth seemed to deliver on. The dead artist's hand had been subtle, but having met the subject in person and learned about her, Edward thought he could read a great deal into the painted face.

'She was still a victim here,' Linda said from behind him. Edward was meeting her for lunch in the café next door, but Linda had obviously run in here for another peek herself first, just as he had. She was gazing at Diana. 'Just because she's a rich bitch doesn't mean she didn't get kidnapped. In fact it makes it more likely.'

Edward shook his head. For a second he thought another woman had been reading his mind, but said, 'That's not the defense I'm thinking of. I've seen her in person, she'll look too anxious and scared to have plotted something.' Vilifying the victim was always a way for the defense to go, and Linda knew it. But Edward had something else in mind. Diana as victim all right, but not of Donald, of her husband. Cowed by him into doing and saying whatever he told her to do.

'You know we need to sneak into their house and look around.'

Edward darted his eyes all around the room. 'I know no such thing. Man, you really got a taste for burglary in your one time, didn't you?'

Because he and Linda had done the same thing in his last case, Amy's case, lockpicked their way into a potential suspect's house. From the way that had turned out, he hadn't thought Linda would be eager to try it again.

Still staring at the portrayed Diana, Linda said, 'You think they staged the kidnapping for some reason, which means they're hiding something. Or one is. How else are we going to find out? Unless you know how to hack into his computer. And I doubt he left "Notes on Faking a Kidnapping".'

No, Edward's only criminal skill was actual illegal entry. His computer skills stopped at 'Have you tried restarting it?'. Maybe one of Donald's cronies could help with that, but they looked more like smash-and-grab guys than hackers.

'I'll keep your advice in mind,' he said, pulling Linda close and kissing her. 'I love your novice enthusiasm.' Then he put his arm around her waist and led her toward the door. 'So tell me what you've learned in your first time in the courthouse.'

Linda began immediately. 'Did you know some judges have little signals for their court reporters to say "Don't take this down." Like in a pretrial hearing where nobody's explicitly asked for a record? Judge Hanson even—'

'I did always suspect that. But I meant more in the way of courthouse gossip.'

Linda's eyes brightened even more. 'Oh. You know Belinda, the coordinator in the 281st? She's been engaged for about a month but she's still carrying on with that sleazy defense lawyer . . .'

Wow, Edward thought, realizing how quickly his girlfriend was plugged into the Rumor Central that was the small legal world. And how invested. It was as if he had a mole on the inside. Hmm . . .

* * *

'I see you appreciate Tony's work.'

After lunch Linda had left to go back to work. Edward, with a more flexible schedule, had returned to the gallery. He'd looked at other portraits, trying to spot the same kind of little smile or twinkle he'd seen in Diana Greene's likeness. He thought he spotted it in one, a fortyish woman of great style, at least in Alberico's likeness. But he'd returned to Diana. Something about that life-size impression seemed to hold a message for Edward. Not from the subject, from the artist. He'd been trying to convey something, though he couldn't possibly have known Edward would be its recipient.

Edward turned to find a woman in her fifties standing just behind and beside him. She stepped forward. Great profile, dominated by a long nose, with no attempt to hide the frank lines around her eyes that made her look alert and sharp. The eye grew a bit of sparkle when she felt him looking at her.

'It's a great shame. He was on the verge of an amazing career. No, he was already at his peak, but it looked as if it was going to be a long plateau instead. You've seen his landscapes?'

Edward nodded. 'I'm sure he made a good living from the portraits but in a way it's a shame he was concentrating on them. I'm sure the market for them is limited to the subjects.'

She nodded, turning toward him with an appreciative look. 'In a generation they'll be very valuable. Who remembers the Mona Lisa was drawn for the rich merchant who was married to her? But for now you're right.'

They looked at each other for a moment. The woman had blue, very clear eyes, a small mouth, tight skin over her cheekbones. Her graying brown hair was relatively short, framing the face well. Made sense.

'Your gallery?' Edward asked. She nodded.

'You called the artist Tony. You were friends?'

She nodded again. 'Anali Haverty. I didn't befriend all my clients, but Tony was special. And you're the lawyer defending the man who kidnapped Diana. Allegedly,' she added before Edward could.

It was his turn to nod. 'Can I ask you a little about Tony?'

She drew herself up. 'I don't get involved in my clients' personal lives.'

'No, of course not.'

'And I'm not a gossip.'

Edward looked shocked that anyone would even use that word in her presence. 'But,' he said delicately, 'this is probably a murder case. And the police don't seem anywhere close to solving it.'

The gallery owner's face became animated. 'We all knew he was banging that Greene slut.'

'"We"?'

'The art community. It's a very small world and nearly everybody knows everybody.' She took his arm and drew him out of the room to her private office. There was a desk but she sat on a small sofa and pulled Edward down next to her. Anali wore a simple, dark gray skirt, rather tight, showing off her calves. A walker's legs, not a runner's. Long smooth muscles. Her thin yellow sweater had three-quarter sleeves. Her hands moved constantly, describing, briefly touching, expressing.

'Tony was rather notorious once he gained a little bit of notoriety. No, before. He didn't kiss and tell, of course, but he was seen having lunch or a drink with some of his subjects. He said he needed to get to know them in order to find his . . . his take on each one. They seemed to like the attention. The men too.

'But that Diana Greene. As soon as her husband hired him you saw Tony and her together in public once or twice, but then the relationship went subterranean. In more than one sense, we all thought. She has a reputation. Maybe it was just a deep flirtation, but I don't think so. There was the way Tony changed, for example.'

'How so?'

She gave him a flat look as if reappraising his intelligence. Downward. 'Red eyes. Bags. Drinking more, alone.'

'Not the life of the party anymore?'

'Tony would always disappear for spells. All artists do. Sometimes he was taking long drives alone, sometimes painting furiously. I tried to get him to open up, but he just spiraled inward.'

Edward hesitated, then said as delicately as possible, 'I've heard he was killed with his own gun. Is it possible she rejected him and he became depressed?'

Anali reached out to him again. 'That was the strangest thing. Tony buying a gun. He was the farthest from a cowboy you ever met. "Not a real Texan," he used to like to say about himself. Never owned cowboy boots or a pickup truck. Or a gun. He was disdainful of people who did.'

'Maybe he'd been burglarized. He lived in the Heights, didn't he? Parts of it are high-crime areas. He wouldn't be the first liberal to change his ways after being a victim.'

She shrugged. 'Possibly. As I say, he didn't confide in me. Can I offer you coffee?'

He'd bet it was good coffee. He watched her cross the office to an already brewed pot and return with two porcelain cups. Edward took a chance and said, 'Are you French by chance? Or do you just spend a lot of time in Paris?'

She gave him a startled but very pleased smile. 'I've just returned from a visit. What made you guess?'

He waved a hand around. 'Well, art world. But mainly your style. The skirt. You look like you walk a lot. Plus the scarf is a dead giveaway.'

She touched it, a filmy mix of multicolored stripes that perfectly set off her neck. She looked as if he couldn't have paid her a better compliment.

'You have a good eye. Do you paint yourself by any chance, Mr Hall?'

'Edward, please. No, I just look.' He returned to the subject. 'Is there anyone else I can ask about Tony? Any special friends?'

She set down her cup and crossed her hands over her knee. 'I don't get involved in my clients' lives.'

But this time she was smiling. 'No, of course not,' Edward said, preparing to take mental notes.

FIFTEEN

Edward delved as deeply as he could into Diana Greene's life, including a return visit to his River Oaks gossip friend, armed with the news of the possible affair with the late artist. But he didn't mention that. He just asked if his friend had

had any more thoughts about the Greenes. Had they changed lately?

'Well, they threw a big party, about six weeks before the so-called kidnapping. The pretext was unveiling that new portrait of Diana, but it seemed to me Sterling was after something more, some entrée to society that he didn't already enjoy. He had seemed to think courting and marrying the famous Diana Lipscomb would usher him right into high society, but it didn't seem to have worked out so far.'

'Why not?'

'Because he's a lout. Oh, I know it's an old-fashioned word, but it fits Sterling Greene perfectly. He's a clumsy lout. Houston doesn't mind a cowboy millionaire, you know that. We celebrate them. But Sterling isn't flamboyant enough to be interesting or rich enough to be worth courting. He tries very hard to give that impression, but you never see . . . oh, a building at St. Thomas being named for him or him sponsoring the new children's wing of a hospital. There's a strong whiff of fraud about him. Or wannabe. He can throw a big soiree, but he can't make witty banter once you get there. Diana'd be the life of the party, making every man there feel the special object of her attention, the women envious except the two or three she singled out to be friends, while Sterling clumsily tried to flirt and just came off looking lecherous. There's an art to the flirt, you know.'

'The title of your memoir?'

His friend smiled and touched Edward's forearm very lightly but deliberately. Edward wondered if he'd just demonstrated his premise. 'To leave the subject thinking he was the special object of her attention and watching her more closely for the rest of the night. So when he started hitting on her he thought it was his idea.'

'Hmm.' Edward started re-evaluating several social gatherings he'd attended, as he looked around the small café he'd never heard of but that had turned out, as Gerald suggested, to be the perfect place for a light lunch and a heavy talk. 'You're right. Damn.'

'Of course I am. You think I just toss these things off?'

Edward pictured Gerald making mental notes at every social occasion he'd ever attended – many, many more than Edward ever had or ever would – just as he'd done when traveling in Prague, for instance. 'So circling back to the actual subject of my inquiry . . .'

'Oh, Tony was at the party. Standing near the portrait and beaming proudly. Then the photographer would try to take a picture of him and Diana with the portrait as backdrop and Tony was very careful always to draw Sterling into the picture too. In fact I saw him a couple of times apparently deep in fascinating conversation with Sterling. Tony spent more time with him than her. It seemed to be a special friendship starting. I hear they were seen together several times in the next few weeks, Sterling and Tony. Which must have been quite an ordeal for Tony.' He shrugged. 'Of course artists always need patrons. But I've never known Tony to paint a subject twice, so there wasn't much point in cultivating the Greenes anymore. Still, Sterling does throw up buildings. Soulless piles of concrete, the ones I've seen. They could always use art in their lobbies to fake classy.'

This was news, Alberico being close to Mr Greene. 'One hears Mr Alberico was actually closer to *Mrs* Greene.'

His friend made a face. 'I assumed you knew that.'

'I'd heard it put forward as a theory,' Edward said carefully.

Gerald laughed. 'Yeah. They were theorizing the shit out of each other. He must have had to buy new sheets.'

Gerald could be blunt, it was one of the traits that made his conversation so lively, but he was seldom crude. At Edward's look he shrugged, and Edward suddenly realized his friend had been jealous. Of whom he wasn't sure.

Gerald continued. 'Just trust me, it was real.'

'Love, you mean?'

Gerald made a dismissive sound. 'Diana Lipscomb Greene doesn't do love. She married money for money and she has affairs for sex. The sex with Tony must have been particularly good because he'd lasted longer than her other lads. Not on individual occasions, you know, I have no way of knowing, but in the long run, so to speak.'

Edward thought of the nervous, shy-seeming woman he'd spent time with in a similar café and of the terrified-seeming woman in the news accounts. He trusted Gerald's insights but not necessarily his conclusions. The artist had been cultivating both Greenes, apparently. Maybe with an entirely different object than sex.

But so what? Maybe the young artist banged every woman he painted. 'I think you're getting off track,' Linda said, and Edward agreed.

'There's just something off about that Sterling Greene. I've only met him once, but he seemed more like a thug than a businessman. I can picture him . . .'

'Follow the money,' Linda said suddenly.

They were sitting in her temporary office in another court's offices. Linda had become quickly in demand in the courthouse. Apparently there was a shortage of court reporters. Or maybe just a shortage of Lindas in the building. She looked very professional in her skirt suit, her crossed legs showing to good advantage as she sat back in the office chair. Edward had pulled a chair around so they were on the same side of the desk.

'What are you talking about?'

'It's what Deep Throat said to—'

'Yeah, yeah, I know. But . . .?'

'Your gossipy friend seemed to think Sterling Greene is a fake rich guy. Maybe his wife was starting to realize that and wanted to . . .'

'Decided to run off with Donald instead?'

Linda stuck out her tongue at him briefly. 'I don't know, planned some scheme to see how much money her husband really could come up with on short notice.'

Edward sat back. That didn't make much sense, but there was a grain of something there. He looked at Linda. It was always great to talk to her. Her mind took unexpected turns, ones he would never see coming. Plus when he talked to her he got to look at her.

'Stop,' she said, flushing a little.

'Stop what?'

'Undressing me with your eyes.'

'I hadn't even gotten around to undressing you yet. I was admiring your thinking.'

'Sure.'

'But now that you've started me down that path . . .'

He leaned forward. Linda did too, but gave him only a quick, demure peck on the lips. After she leaned back and Edward gave her a *what the hell?* look she waved a hand around the offices and by implication the justice system. 'I work here. I need to be careful.'

'There's that.'

'There is that. I'll see you at home, baby.'

He walked out feeling oddly dismissed. Loved, but dismissed. How did she do that? It was very skillful.

Trial loomed. The next day Edward got together with Donald again. It seemed to him their relationship had chilled a little since Donald had watched Edward deep in conversation with not only the special prosecutor but the actual District Attorney of Harris County. Edward had explained that was part of the job and even given him the Vito Corleone *Keep your friends close and your enemies closer* line, but clients never understood that. Or maybe Donald had just realized Edward was a lawyer, not just his old prison buddy.

'I'm staying with Gearhead. You remember him, he got out about a year before you did.'

Vaguely. Edward hadn't tried to make friends in prison. He'd tried to make strangers. He'd wanted no fond memories of the place, no reunions once they got out. Yet here he was.

'I thought your parole conditions said you're not to associate with felons.'

Donald gave him an ironic look. Everyone seemed to be doing that to Edward lately. Had he started getting stupid? Then he realized Donald's point. He was a black man in Texas. He was an African-American ex-con in the deep south of America. He didn't know any non-felons. Hell, he was associating with one now.

Edward changed the subject. 'I want to recreate your day the day of the kidnapping.'

Donald sighed. 'We've gone over this a hundred times.'

'No. This time I want to actually re-enact it.'

'Oh.' Donald looked startled, then thoughtful. Expressions played out so clearly on his oversized face, like watching a drive-in movie. 'OK.'

'Where'd you wake up? Take us there.'

Edward let Donald drive Edward's car, easier than taking directions. Donald probably didn't have a license, but who cared? Edward wanted to be able to see.

His client drove them back into the Third Ward. Only a few miles from River Oaks, actually, the wealthy neighborhood where Edward had grown up, but a small world unto itself. Unto itself because nobody else wanted it. At least that had been true the last time Edward had driven (quickly) through it, but now he saw it was becoming gentrified. There were nice restaurants and shops nearby, the land was too valuable to remain a tiny ghetto in the heart of the city.

Gearhead appeared to be doing well for himself. Donald stopped in front of a small but neat house with a sagging front porch. 'This is where you've been staying?'

Donald nodded, staring at the house. 'Technically I been staying by my Aunt Cecile, that's where I meet my parole officer, but I don't like her rules. Gearhead's easier to live with, 'specially since he's got a girlfriend he stays with 'bout half the time.'

Donald needed alone time. Edward got it. 'So you woke up here. Then what?'

'Mr Greene called me and said to come see him again. So I headed toward his office.'

'Let's do it.'

They drove toward the Galleria, the old shopping mall that had once been the epicenter of commerce but was now a little matronly. Edward thought Sterling Greene must be doing pretty well for himself after all, because the office buildings in the area were still desirable real estate. But Donald kept going, out the Southwest Freeway. Still a nice part of town, but more residential. Donald exited at Chimney Rock, drove a few blocks, and pulled over into the parking lot of a shuttered strip club. Edward stared.

'This is his office?'

'Nah, man.' Donald chuckled. 'This is where I got a call from him and pulled over.'

'Ah. What time was that?'

'Well, I done a couple other things that morning, so it was maybe one, two o'clock.'

Now Donald's story was diverging from the official version. He'd been arrested late in the afternoon after Diana Greene ran out of the house, where she said she'd been held 'for hours.'

'Why did he call you?'

'Asked me to go pick up his wife and head to the Third Ward, like I told you.'

'Let's go.'

They were getting the complete Houston tour. West Gray, the street where Donald had picked up Diana Greene, was maybe ten miles away, on the other side of downtown, a nice, fairly quaint neighborhood with some homes but mostly retail. Donald pulled into the parking lot of a drug store. 'She was waiting here.'

Edward peered around, told Donald to turn off the car, and got out, motioning to his client to stay put. In some situations Donald was an excellent partner to have when questioning someone. In others, not so much. This was the latter. Edward went into the drug store, looked around, found a manager, and asked her if she'd been working on the day in question just a month ago. Yes, she had. Did she remember an attractive woman, reddish brown hair, good figure, just standing around waiting for someone? The manager just stared at him. Edward realized what a stupid question it was while he was asking it. He needed to come back with a picture of Diana, or better yet send an investigator. But while Diana, he'd been told, could be intensely attractive when she chose, she could also be very nondescript. Edward remembered the rather plain woman he'd talked to in the small café and realized he wouldn't remember her except for her large role in his current life. He thanked the manager, asked her to think about it, and said someone would be back to question her.

He walked around the store and no employee remembered anything. That day hadn't been anything special to them. They vaguely remembered hearing about the kidnapping, but it hadn't held any connection to their lives.

Edward returned thoughtfully to the car. 'We need to get one of your friends to come here and ask around. Maybe some addicts were hanging around that day casing the place, hoping to steal oxycontin or something.'

Donald nodded.

'So you picked her up here and what? Had you met Diana before?'

'No, man. She just saw me and waved me over to her car. She'd obviously gotten a description of me.' Which wasn't tough. Donald knew he was easy to describe. But Edward tried to picture a woman with Diana Greene's background running willingly toward a large African-American man she'd never met before and jumping into his car. It wouldn't play. He'd have a hell of a time selling that to a jury.

'OK. Any chitchat? Nice to meet you, you look nice, cocktail party chatter?'

Donald frowned. 'Nah. I mean, we were polite, but . . .'

Edward looked at him closely. Donald stared back. 'OK, then what?'

'She told me to go to that house in the Third Ward.'

Edward gestured and Donald started the car. Edward said, 'Re-enact it for me. Make me believe it. What were y'all saying?'

'Me not much, just taking directions. She was chattering, though. Seemed nervous. Rattling on about the guy we were going to meet, the jewels, all that stuff. Asking how I'd met her husband, what my life was like, just . . . It was tiring, man.'

Edward would bet Diana hadn't been tiring to look at, though, and Donald hadn't been long out of prison. There'd been some suggestion in the reports of the day that the kidnapping may have been accompanied by some inappropriate touching. Maybe that just made for better newspaper stories. He decided not to go there yet. Instead he used the occasion to convey the special prosecutor's offer of forty years to his client.

'Forty isn't really forty, Donald, you know that. Eligible for parole in half that time. You could do it, we both know that. And now that Veronica and I've started talking, I might get her to come down a little. Although forty is kind of the magic number, actually. Twenty down from the max. That's still a sentence a prosecutor can be proud to get. Below that it's just an ordinary sentence. Like retail. Thirty-nine ninety-five sounds better than forty. It's the opposite for prosecutors.'

Donald was silent. At least he was thinking about the offer, Edward thought hopefully.

Then they were in the Third Ward. It seemed abrupt, as always. Exit from I-45 at Calhoun, past the University of Houston, a school that had never made an effort to look bucolic but was urban to its bones, then boom! The ghetto took them.

Donald parked blocks short of the house where they'd been before and got out.

'What's this?' Edward asked, but followed him. Donald stood by the side of the road staring down it. A long open road with the little shotgun shacks on either side.

'Remind you of anything?' Donald asked quietly.

It absolutely did. The prison yard. A long nondescript strip with cells on either side. Open sky giving an illusion of freedom.

Edward and Donald had by some fluke of prison bureaucracy ended up doing their time in The Walls, the historic old prison thirty miles north of Houston, the original Texas prison. Old, decrepit, crusted with generations of despair.

Just like this street.

Donald could tell from Edward's silence he got it. His shoulders seemed to have expanded. His shaved head gleamed in the weak autumnal sunlight. He started walking. Edward followed.

'People say twenty years in prison. What's that to a black man? Hell, it ain't that different from his regular life, is it? But you know what's different about this here?'

Edward shook his head.

'This. I can walk to that horizon, over it, and keep going. Or turn either direction. Nobody yellin' at me to go back. Nobody to shoot me from a guard tower if I keep goin'. It ain't much, but it's . . .'

Everything. Edward understood. He too knew those first days out of prison, the glory of waking up without the sounds and smells of hundreds of other men pressing in on him. The luxury of thinking *What'll I do today?* Without plan or appointments. It had been like the first days of summer for a schoolboy, but better. Much, much better.

He and Donald walked on. Edward looked around, thinking he needed to talk to every resident of these houses or send someone to do it. They walked all the way to the house and stood looking at it. It now featured bullet holes that hadn't been there the last time they'd arrived. They had bloomed while they were here.

They talked some more, Edward got more details, but nothing case-breaking. Just staring at the scene made the case real for him. But it still made no sense. Edward looked around. There was no way a woman like Diana Greene should have ended up spending a couple of hours with anyone like Donald in this place.

Edward decided he should do something similar with Diana and the artist, see where they'd spent time. Alberico was single, he probably worked out of his home, and if he and Diana were really having the affair people assumed it would have been mostly spent at his place, unless the young artist liked flirting with danger, and Edward hadn't gotten that sense from what little he'd known about him.

He called the gallery owner, the one who didn't involve herself in her clients' personal lives, and she knew Tony's address by heart. When she gave it to him Edward recognized it right away.

It was in the Heights.

SIXTEEN

Veronica Salazar was working out of her house too, for the time being. She claimed she just hadn't had time to find an office. Edward suspected she couldn't afford one yet, just starting a practice. He could have invited her to his own office but somehow didn't want her invading his space. So he went to her. Veronica lived in a nice neighborhood off Westheimer, near-suburban Houston, a garden home with a luxuriant garden. Brick walls made it seem isolated from its neighbors.

Veronica answered the door in a robe.

It wasn't remotely terry cloth – *wet hair, oh, sorry, I just stepped out of the shower*. No, this was a lounging garment, silky, peach-colored, which set off her brown skin well. And showing a good deal of it, particularly some cleavage and a lot of legs. Edward just stood there, waiting for her to look embarrassed, clutch the robe to herself, and say, 'I'm sorry, I thought you were the . . .' None of that happened. Veronica just smiled and held the door wide.

'Sorry, I'm getting a slow start today, hope you don't mind.'

'No. You want me to wait out here while you . . .'

'While I what? No, come on in.' She led the way through a tidy, well-arranged living room featuring white furniture down a short hallway past her bedroom to a second bedroom that was an office. Edward breathed a little easier. An office regularized the meeting even if his counterpart remained in bedclothes. Veronica sat in a desk chair and waved Edward to another chair. Four windows in the room gave a lot of sunlight, which didn't hurt Veronica's appearance at all. Her skin was smooth as the robe. Sitting and crossing her legs made the robe part a little more and she did nothing about that.

'I hope you don't mind if I'm comfortable? One of the joys of working from home.'

'No, that's fine. I didn't notice.'

She smiled. 'So let's talk. I don't guess you're here to accept my offer? You could have done that by phone.'

Edward shrugged apologetically. 'I've got one of those hard-headed clients. You know the deal. Keeps insisting he's innocent.'

Veronica shrugged too, smiling. 'The prisons are full of them. Well here, maybe this will give you leverage with him.'

She picked up a file, found the first couple of pages in it, and tossed them to him. A lab report, Edward saw immediately. The exam of Diana Greene, immediately post-kidnapping. He skimmed the first page, went to the second. He stopped.

'Evidence of sexual activity,' Veronica said. He could hear the smile in her voice. 'Shortly before the arrest.'

Edward kept his head down, composing his face. When he lifted it his expression was bland. 'Surely she would have mentioned in her statement she'd been raped.'

'Women are embarrassed about that sort of thing. Some women. So I understand. "I should have put up more resistance, I should've . . ." That sort of thing.'

He looked for something helpful in the report. 'No DNA match.'

Veronica shrugged, which opened the robe slightly wider. 'Insufficient sample. Used a condom, probably. Thoughtful rapist. Or careful.'

Edward thought quickly about the implications. Veronica would imply to the jury the giant black man had forced himself on the terrified white woman . . . 'Imply', hell, she'd say it outright. He could see it now in her quiet smile.

They were having a conversation without words. None needed. They were experienced enough lawyers to run through how this changed the case. The stakes were so much higher now. Her offer looked better. Edward's case looked . . . well, there was no case at all.

Veronica leaned forward. 'Can I get you something? Cup of tea perhaps?'

Edward shook his head. She remained leaning forward. 'I've heard about you,' she said. 'And now I can see it's true.'

'What?' Had her lips somehow gotten fuller while they'd been sitting here? How could that happen?

'Smart. I can see your mind moving ninety miles an hour while you're not saying a word. I can see you've already played out a dozen angles, hit your head on a wall and moved on. But this is just a box with four sides, Edward, it's not a maze. No way out. Like I said, I'm doing you a favor. You use this for leverage with your client and get him to plead. We're done by next week. Too bad, really. I was looking forward to being in trial with you.'

She made 'trial' sound like bed. Or maybe that was just the effect of her continuing to lean forward, the robe parting, now putting a hand on his knee. Edward looked into her eyes, face blank.

'Can I see the rest of that file?'

She laughed, leaned back, glanced at it. 'I guess that is the State's file, isn't it? So I guess you're entitled to see it. I thought it was just mine.'

Anyone reading a transcript of this conversation would find nothing unusual about it. Two lawyers talking. But Veronica's slightly husky, slightly sleepy voice made everything sound like innuendo. 'Entitled to see . . . mine', for example. Edward looked down at the file she'd tossed him.

'Let me know if you need copies of anything,' she said, just watching him read.

He already had almost all of this. Diana's statement, Donald's booking photo – blank-faced, he still looked guilty – the couple of police reports. As they'd said all along, it was a very straightforward case, very quick trip from A to Guilty.

'No statement from Sterling Greene?'

'He didn't give a formal one. Whatever he said is in the police reports.'

She stood up. Thank God. Maybe she was going to get dressed, like a normal prosecutor. Instead Veronica came and stood very close behind him. Edward was leaning forward over the file, so when she bent and put her arms around him her chest was touching his back. Veronica put her lips close to his ear.

'Too bad this is going to be so quick,' she said.

Edward stood up abruptly. 'I have a girlfriend.'

Veronica shrugged. 'So what? I've got like three boyfriends. If we were in court I'd object to lack of relevance.'

'I have a girlfriend I love,' Edward clarified.

Veronica looked baffled. 'Are we talking about our personal lives now? Why?' She glanced down at her outfit. 'This? My God, Ed, get over yourself. Can a woman not be comfortable without you thinking she's coming on to you? Jeez. You're not that cute. I'm just having fun. Not as much as I expected to be having, but . . .'

She did nothing to tighten the robe. Edward found her speech thoroughly confusing. It veered from A to 18. 'I don't know what you're talking about,' he said, and heard his voice sounding very formal. 'We're just talking. Well. I'll get back to you.'

He walked out of the room. She followed, closely enough he expected her hand on him any moment, but it didn't happen. At the door she moved quickly in front of him, but only to open it and hold it wide, as wide as her smile. 'Court next week,' she said. 'Maybe we can have a cup of coffee afterwards.'

She laughed. Edward had no rejoinder. She was probably reassessing his brilliance.

As he walked away Edward went over everything that just happened. Was it possible a woman in dishabille, leading him to a room with a sofa bed in it, a woman practically rubbing her tits in his face, *hadn't* been coming on to him? He barely remembered that the case against his client had just increased its weight exponentially.

Whatever else Veronica Salazar had been trying to accomplish, she'd definitely fucked with Edward's head.

*   *   *

The gallery owner, Anali Haverty – could that be real? – the one who didn't get involved in her clients' personal lives, let them into the artist's house with the key she had.

Them meaning Edward and Linda. She had insisted on coming with him. With a day off from court, she'd met him at the house a few blocks from her own. When Edward, fresh from Veronica Salazar, saw her, he hugged Linda tightly and kissed her, right in front of the gallery owner. Linda joined in the embrace, but then drew back and gave him a puzzled look. 'Are you OK?'

'Sure. I'm just glad to see you.'

'You just got out of bed with me like three hours ago.'

'Is that all it's been? Anyway, it's always good to see you.'

Giving him another strange look, she moved past him into the house. Telling himself to act less stupid, Edward followed.

He didn't know what he'd expected – immaculate style, works of art everywhere, lavish furnishings, a smoking jacket? – but the house disappointed. It was just a guy's house that had been uninhabited for a while, a little messy, a little dusty, a gray T-shirt hanging over the arm of the couch in the living room. No beer cans on the floor, but dishes in the sink in the kitchen.

Edward and Linda searched the whole house thoroughly, particularly the bedroom, while the gallery owner watched curiously. 'What are you looking for?'

'Nothing,' Edward said.

'Evidence of an affair,' Linda said. They exchanged looks. His: *Why would you tell her that?* Hers: *Why would I not?*

The gallery owner saw them talking without words and clearly didn't get it. But: 'Of course he was having an affair,' she said. 'Probably more than one. He was a young, single, attractive heterosexual man.'

'Are you sure about that last part?' Edward asked.

'Tony? Definitely straight. I know what you're thinking, artist. But Tony was only inclined one direction.'

She sounded like a woman with insider information, which they didn't pursue. They moved on to a back room that was the artist's studio, but still found nothing. Police had already searched this house completely and taken away anything that smacked of evidence. 'Damn it,' he finally said.

Linda looked very frustrated too. The last time they'd searched a house together, the first time, actually, they'd found what they needed right away. 'If he was both painting a woman and having sex with her, you'd think . . .'

'Oh,' the gallery owner said brightly. 'Why didn't you say so? You should check his studio.'

They looked at her blankly. What were they standing in?

'His real studio,' she said. 'Come on.'

They followed Anali's car, and she waited eagerly for them in the front yard. She seemed to be enjoying herself, being part of the mystery-solving team. She was got up like Paris again, tight gray slacks, a black and white striped top, and the giveaway scarf, this one burgundy and gray.

Their destination turned out to be her own house. It was in West U, the very upscale neighborhood not far from the gallery. Two-story brick houses, beautifully kept lawns, a general air of money at leisure. Anali led them around hers, through a small gate into the large backyard. It contained an outbuilding, a miniature replica of the main house, lavish with windows.

The whole inside was one big room, rich in sunlight. Drop cloths and art stands were everywhere. Against one wall was a leather sofa, the only furniture except for one small desk and chair, useful for sketching.

'I let Tony use this, when he was really deep into a project.'

'Did police know about it?'

'I never saw a reason to mention it. He wasn't killed here. Besides, truth to tell, I think they didn't care much about the case, in spite of Tony's slight celebrity. They thought it was a gay thing, or something.'

He hadn't lived here, but he had worked here. The room was redolent with the artist's personality. Suddenly Edward felt he knew him, as he hadn't in Tony's house. Propped around the floor were paintings in progress, both portraits and landscapes. There was one simple canvas with only a few lines on it, different colors intersecting and then faring off into the universe. Had he been taking a stab at an abstract, or was this how his paintings began?

There was little to search. Aside from the main room there was only a small bathroom and a utility room with a large sink.

But Edward and Linda searched the place slowly. Linda turned and looked at him with an expression he'd never seen but recognized. *It's here*, her big eyes said. *Something.*

Far at the back of a drawer in the desk she found it, under a stack of catalogs. Where a man would conceal something but not very carefully, never expecting anyone to search for it. For them, actually: a stack of photographs. Linda drew them out, stared, and didn't have to say anything to alert Edward. He came and stood close behind her as she slowly shuffled through.

Nude photos. Not pornography, short of art, but tastefully done, the subject very cooperatively turning. Graceful, poised, with a Mona Lisa smile in most of them. Sometimes gazing dreamily, sometimes staring aggressively into the camera. In one of them she seemed to be asleep, on that leather sofa across the room.

Twenty nudes, all of one subject: Diana Greene. They weren't porn, they were a portrait, or one waiting to be assembled. But very close-up, very detailed, and some, yes, could have passed for pornography in some quarters. But very high-end.

By the time they'd been staring mutely for minutes, Anali had joined them. 'Studies for a portrait,' she said coolly.

'You've seen them?' Edward asked, surprised.

'No, but I know how Tony worked. He'd take pix of the subject from a variety of angles – not this many angles, usually – then use them to paint the portrait so the subject didn't have to spend hours posing. Of course, this one looks like she enjoyed posing.'

Oh yes, that was the sound of jealousy in the gallery owner's voice. Either she was a past lover herself, or had wanted to be, or just would have loved the loving attention obviously being paid to the subject of those photos. No wonder Diana had that little self-satisfied smile in her official portrait.

They didn't linger after that. Anali let them take the photos. In the car Linda kept her gaze fixed on Edward. 'No,' he said.

'We have to.'

'Why?'

'We know now they were having an affair. These pictures weren't taken by a man who was just interested in the subject as an art object. Look at this one.'

He didn't have to. 'Agreed. So we know they were having an affair. We don't have to break into their house to get more proof of that.'

'No. We know about the affair. What we need to know is what effect it was having on their marriage.'

She was right, and as usual Linda had started him thinking again. Because while this was beyond interesting about the Greenes, it still had nothing to do with Donald's case. That they could prove so far.

SEVENTEEN

One last pre-trial meeting with the client. It was early October, Donald's trial was set for the following week. Edward had had no more private meetings with the special prosecutor. They still had very little in the way of a defense.

Donald brought along one of his friends to the meeting in Edward's office. A thin little man in a watch cap, he looked like the inside man for a burglary ring, as if he could slither through pipes to get in. But now he was doing it electronically. From the sound of things he was planning some sort of white-collar crime, a step up from the burglary that had gotten him sent to prison.

But Jimmy had given up on Sterling Greene as a target of his scheme. 'He doesn't have any money,' he complained. 'Or he's got it so well hid it can't be traced.'

'You mean a safe in his house, something like that?' Edward said. 'Don't you think he'd keep the money—'

'No, in his accounts, dum-dum. His business bank accounts. Oh, he can make payroll every week, he's not on the edge of bankruptcy. But he's got almost no cushion. All his money's working hard to make more money, and not doing so good. A couple of his projects have stalled, and this guy is like a shark. If he doesn't keep moving forward he dies. His projects are profitable, on paper, that's how he makes new deals, but I can't find the profits. And believe me, I've looked everywhere.'

Edward didn't ask how. He'd gotten up from behind his desk and was pacing. Missing cash was good. Had Sterling staged the kidnapping to hide money he'd stolen from his own company?

Follow the money, he remembered. Always sound advice.

'Thanks,' Edward finally said, and Jimmy scurried off to the hard work of relieving people with too much money of their burden.

Which left three of them. Linda stood up from her quiet seat on the couch and joined Edward close in front of the client.

'What?' Donald said, turning to put his shoulder between his face and the two of them.

Edward said slowly, as if addressing a classroom, 'Let's assume Donald's story is true. It's ridiculous, but let's go with it. What would that mean?'

Linda answered immediately. 'It would mean Sterling Greene hired him for no particular reason, just to help out a man newly released from prison. Is that a normal practice for him? No. Never did it before as far as anyone can tell. Thought wouldn't occur to him.'

'And hires not just anybody, but the most notorious kidnapper in Houston history. Why?'

Donald looked up. 'Because he wanted me to kidnap somebody?' They stared at him. He shrugged. 'It is my only known skill.'

'There's something else new, Donald. The DA has evidence that Diana had sexual activity shortly before her rescue.'

'What?' Donald stood up and stared back and forth between the two of them. 'Then she must've gone to the bathroom and pleasured herself. I didn't touch that woman.'

Edward felt trial looming, with him unprepared with any kind of a defense.

'Damn it, Donald, just admit it! You kidnapped her, you raped her, just own up.'

Donald spread his large hands. 'OK. I kidnapped her, I raped her, I asked for ransom. Then why the fuck am I here, Edward? What went wrong with my brilliant plan?'

That brought Edward back. He paced away. 'How did you plan to carry it off?' he mused.

'I told you, man, I didn't.'

Edward turned back to him. 'No, no, I'm playing the part of the prosecutor now. You can't tell because I haven't changed makeup. So you got out of prison, you targeted Mrs Greene because you needed money and as you said just now . . .'

'Kidnapping is my only known skill.'

'So you got a job with her husband so you could get close to both of them – and by the way, so they could identify you easily.'

Linda interjected, 'Which means he'd absolutely have to kill the victim who could identify him. And since he had a record it would be easy for police to track him down.'

'Man, what was your plan? Where were you going to dump her where she wouldn't be found until your DNA degraded, which is about, well, a long time?'

'I keep telling you, I didn't—'

Linda put her hand on his arm. 'Donald, we're role-playing. We're showing the problems with the prosecution case.'

Edward, who had paced away a little and turned back, looked at the tableau. Linda's slender white hand on the enormous brown arm, her eyes getting a little teary as she looked up at him, Donald's eyes going liquid too.

How could he get this picture in front of a jury?

'All right then,' he said. 'Time to get ready.'

Donald looked blank. 'For what?'

Linda looked at him sympathetically. 'Trial,' she said.

EIGHTEEN

Trial. Edward stood near the front of the large courtroom feeling his trial personality descend on him. All trial lawyers have them. A lot get more aggressive than they'd ever be in real life even when playing a competitive sport. Some get folksy, harking back to rural childhoods they hadn't had. Edward's trial personality wasn't that different from his real one. He talked a little more slowly than in everyday life, sat a little more languidly, while his mind moved much faster. His language became more precise. He wasn't ready to be fitted for a white wig, but he was a more formal version of himself.

He'd chosen his favorite gray pinstripe this morning, the first day of testimony. Veronica Salazar favored gray pinstripe too, a skirt suit in which she looked almost as good as she had in the peach-colored robe. It showed off her long legs and neck. They could have been Barbie and Ken Trial Lawyers.

One of the first things to do in preparing for trial is to learn as much as you can about your opponent. In this case Edward didn't know much. He'd never tried a case against Veronica, never even been working in the same building when she was a prosecutor. Her reputation was for charging hard, skirting the line of the rules and sometimes crossing over, for treating juries respectfully rather than courting them, for hiding evidence or dumping it on the defense at the last minute, right before trial.

Prosecutors have a constitutional duty to turn over to the defense any evidence in their possession that tends to prove the defendant's innocence. This includes evidence that could discredit State's witnesses. In Texas, after an innocent man spent twenty-five years in prison for a murder he didn't commit, partly because the prosecutor had kept some evidence from the defense, the legislature had made this protection even stronger, passing laws requiring prosecutors to turn over nearly everything to the defense, without even making a decision as to whether it was relevant.

There'd been no evidence dump in this case. Veronica hadn't given him anything more since the medical report on Diana Greene. Both their trial folders were unusually slim. Veronica had let him go through all of hers. Sometimes it seemed she hadn't worked too hard to get ready for this trial. But then, she didn't have to. It was very straightforward.

They'd picked a jury the first day, Edward trying to keep as many African-Americans on the panel as possible, Veronica trying to get most of them removed for cause: prejudice against the State, for example. She'd been largely successful, but there were still four African-Americans on the final jury. Unfortunately, they'd gotten there by being very conservative in their answers and those might actually reflect their beliefs. Sometimes old prejudices didn't work, such as black people favoring black defendants. Which was a damned shame, those old prejudices not working. They were so easy to use.

The rest of the jury was a mix of ethnicities, genders, and ages. As usual, Edward had been a little surprised to see the twelve take their seats, see the twelve they'd allowed to become the jury. While he'd been going over the jury list they'd become just words to him. The twelve living, breathing human beings were surprising.

Donald sat beside Edward wearing a black suit, white shirt, no tie. He looked fine, but there was still nothing to be done about his size. Veronica had directed the jury's attention to him during her opening statement, and that seemed unfair. Donald looked menacing just by existing.

Edward said to him, 'Not your first rodeo, right? How you feeling, man?'

Donald gave him a straight look. 'Not happy to be back in the rodeo. Man.'

Edward acknowledged all the freight of that short speech with a nod. 'But you know what to do, right?'

Donald nodded. He looked at Edward straight again and beamed, a huge happy smile.

'Jesus. Please don't do that. You have such big shiny teeth.'

The smile fell off Donald's face immediately. It would not reappear in this trial.

Judge Roberts sat on his high bench very watchfully. He knew Edward Hall had been a good trial lawyer, but also knew how long he'd been out of practice. The judge didn't want a conviction from his court being reversed for ineffective assistance of counsel. He'd intervene if necessary.

So he had a dilemma hours later when Edward made a bad blunder before the first day of testimony was over.

But before then: 'State, call your first witness,' the judge said blandly.

Deep breaths all around. The whole courtroom seemed to shrink then expand as everyone inhaled deeply and let it out.

'Sterling Greene,' Veronica said from her feet.

Well, she was following DA protocol so far. The common wisdom was for the prosecution to open with its second-strongest witness and close with its strongest. Diana Greene wasn't even in the room. Nor was she being babysat by her big sister. District Attorney Julia Lipscomb sat on the front row of the audience. Edward looked at her and she gave him a smile, which seemed out of keeping with the occasion.

Sterling Greene came down one of the side aisles and through the swinging wooden gate into the front of the courtroom. In Judge Roberts' courtroom the well of the court was larger than average. It took Greene several seconds crossing it, striding purposefully. He wore a dark blue suit obviously tailored to him, white shirt, yellow tie. He was a big man, an inch or two over six feet, with broad shoulders. But he looked nothing like a laborer. He took the stand and stared mournfully at the prosecutor, with not a glance at the jury or the defense table.

Uh oh, Edward thought. Sterling already looked like a victim. Have to take it easy on him when Edward's turn came.

'Please introduce yourself to the jury.'

Given that instruction, he had no choice but to turn toward them. 'I'm Sterling Greene,' he said evenly, then turned back to Veronica.

'And what do you do for a living, Mr Greene?'

'I started out in banking, then went out on my own. I own three or four companies that do different things. Mostly construction and real estate development.'

'Are they successful?'

He hesitated, then said simply, 'Yes.'

'In fact you've been the subject of media reports about how successful your business enterprises have been, haven't you?'

'A few. I don't court them.'

'Has that made you the target of attempted scams or other crimes?'

Edward stood for the first time. 'Objection, Your Honor. Other crimes not connected to my client are irrelevant.'

'The fact Mr Greene is wealthy enough to be targeted by someone like your client is certainly relevant,' Veronica Salazar replied, looking right at Edward.

'And now she's testifying. I object to that as well.'

'I sustain that objection. Jurors, please disregard that and any remarks the attorneys make. They are not evidence.' The jurors looked at him and about half nodded.

'As for the first objection, I can see the relevance so I'll allow that one question but no more on the subject. And in the future, attorneys, address all remarks to the bench and not to each other.'

'Yes, sir,' they said in unison. Judge Roberts was known for running tight trials. He was not going to let this one get away from him so early.

'Yes, I've been targeted by a few scammers,' Sterling said shortly.

'Tell us about the morning of April sixteenth of this year, Mr Greene. How did your day begin?'

'The usual. I got up about six, got ready, and left my house about an hour later. My wife was still in bed.'

'Do you have servants?'

'Not live-in. We have a maid service that comes once a week, yard man too, but that morning Diana was alone in the house when I left.'

'Where do you live, Mr Greene?'

'River Oaks.' He stared straight ahead.

Veronica let that answer sink in. Residency in the wealthiest neighborhood in Houston certainly qualified him as successful enough to be the target of a kidnap attempt. Edward could hardly say anything. He'd grown up in River Oaks and his parents still lived there.

'Where did you go once you left your house, Mr Greene?'

'Straight to a job site. I didn't go to the office first that morning.'

Veronica stood. 'Do you know the man on the far side of the other counsel table, Mr Greene? The defendant?'

'No.'

'Have you ever seen him before?'

'Very briefly, when police rescued my wife and he was arrested.'

There seemed something objectionable about that, but the answer was already out. Edward felt a little rusty.

'Never before that?' Veronica pressed. 'He hadn't applied to you for a job, anything like that?'

'No.' Sterling Greene was very thrifty with words. He'd obviously been well coached. Edward watched him closely, but Sterling wouldn't make eye contact.

'Tell me the next important thing that happened.'

'I got a call from my wife, Diana, on my cell phone. I was a little surprised because she doesn't usually call me during the day. But of course I'm always glad to hear from her.'

'What did she say?'

'Very little. She said my name in a little high-pitched scream, then I could tell the phone was snatched away from her and a man's voice said, "That was to prove I have your wife. Now here's what you have to do . . ."'

'Did you write down his instructions or anything like that?'

'I didn't even hear them the first time. I was stunned. I just stood there with my mouth hanging open.' Sterling showed emotion for the first time, his eyes widening and his hands clutching each other. 'I had to ask him to repeat himself. That seemed to make him mad.'

'What did he tell you to do?'

Over the course of the next several minutes Sterling recounted hours spent scrambling to try to get the half a million dollars the kidnapper demanded, vainly trying to convince bankers his wife was being held hostage and that the bankers should give a damn about that, making a thousand phone calls, even to friends, rushing around the affluent parts of the city.

'How long had he given you?'

'Till five o'clock. After calling me about two p.m.'

'Did you get the money together?'

'Half a million dollars in that short a time?' Sterling made a small scoffing sound. 'Not even close. Nobody has that kind of—'

This time Edward shot to his feet. 'Objection, Your Honor, speculation. Mr Greene has no way of knowing the access many other people might have to ready cash.'

Judge Roberts did something unusual in a trial judge. He sat and thought for a few seconds before ruling. 'Sustained. Just stick to what's relevant to this witness, counsel.'

Veronica was on her feet too. 'Certainly, Your Honor. As the court could tell, I wasn't trying to elicit that answer.'

'Now I object to counsel testifying, Your Honor.'

This time Judge Roberts only made a little brushing away gesture with his hand, meaning a trial judge's favorite ruling. *Move on.* Edward let it go. It was a very small matter.

'But you managed to get some money together, Mr Greene?'

'Yes. Roughly two hundred thousand dollars. A little more.'

'What did you do?'

'I took it to the house where he'd told me to leave the money, with a note explaining I just couldn't get it all given such short notice, begging him for more time and not to hurt my wife.'

'Were you terrified?'

Edward stood again. 'Objection, Your Honor. Leading and irrelevant.' Edward shook his head as he said it, over what an objectionable question it was.

'Sustained.'

'Did you go inside that house, have any contact with your wife or the defendant at all?'

'No.'

'What did you do then, Mr Greene?'

'I called my wife's cell phone, more than once, but he wouldn't answer. So I called police.'

'Did you want to do that?'

'No. I wanted to do exactly what he'd said. But I hadn't managed to get all the money. Time was going by and I was terrified he was going to hurt Diana. I didn't feel I had any choice.'

So Sterling had managed to insert that he'd been terrified, after Veronica had made that suggestion to him, essentially a stage direction. Neither of them shot Edward a look of triumph. In fact Sterling hadn't looked at Edward at all since he'd taken the witness stand.

'What did you do after that?'

'Just cooperated with police. I insisted on going along when they went to the house where Diana was being held. I stayed there until she finally came running out.'

'Was she injured?'

'Not that I could tell. Just scared to death. I did have to take her for a medical exam right away. Mainly for trying to collect evidence, police said.'

Edward made a note of that. That information would get to the jury one way or another anyway. Edward wanted it to, in fact.

'Mr Greene, did you see the kidnapper come out of the house and get arrested?'

'Yes, I did. I was holding my wife so tight. She was trembling when she saw him again.'

'Could you identify him?'

'Yes.'

'Is he in the courtroom now?'

'Yes, he is. He's the large African-American gentleman sitting at the defense table.'

Edward had come to believe over the last years in America that people who were careful to say 'African-American gentleman' harbored racism in their hearts they were trying to conceal. Someone who could more casually toss off 'black dude' probably didn't give a damn about the guy's race. Sterling Greene had done nothing to contradict Edward's theory.

Veronica Salazar stood up. 'Your Honor, I'd like to ask the defendant be instructed to speak, enough to attempt an identification of his voice.'

Edward rose too, slowly, thinking furiously. There was nothing objectionable about this request. A defendant cannot be forced to testify, contrary to his constitutional right to remain silent. But he could be used as an exhibit, as it were. A defendant could be ordered to give a handwriting sample, fingerprints, DNA. He could be asked to display a tattoo on his ass if it was relevant. Still . . .

'I object to that, Your Honor,' Edward said. 'There's no evidence Mr Greene is an expert in voice identification. By his own testimony he only heard the supposed kidnapper say a few words. There's no way—'

'That's an argument you can make to the jury, Mr Hall. It goes to the weight to be given his testimony. I'll allow it for whatever weight jurors choose to give it.'

Veronica slid a note across to Edward. It turned out to be a short script. *I have your wife*, the note read. *Here's what you have to do if you don't want me to kill her.*

Edward shot her a *Fuck off* look. He'd be damned if he'd have his client re-enact the crime with Veronica as the director. He leaned over and whispered to Donald.

Donald cleared his throat and said, 'Good morning, Mr Greene. I'm sorry to meet you under these circumstances.'

He'd whitened his voice a little but still sounded like himself. Veronica gave her witness a questioning look.

'Yes, that sounds like the voice I heard on the phone,' Sterling said simply, not trying to over-sell it.

'And again, you'd never had any contact with this man before that day?'

'No.'

Interesting how Veronica wanted to emphasize that point.

'Did you ever get your two hundred thousand dollars back, Mr Greene?'

'No. He must have had an accomplice—'

'Object to speculation,' Edward said quickly.

Looking down at her notes instead of the witness, Veronica casually said, 'What did your wife convey to you about her kidnapping, Mr Greene?'

Edward shot up. 'Object to hearsay, Your Honor.' He spread his arms in a *What the hell?* gesture.

'Sustained.'

Veronica stared at her opposing counsel as if amazed. 'Of course I didn't mean to elicit hearsay. Let me rephrase. What did you personally observe about your wife, Mr Greene? Her mental state?'

'She was trembling. Obviously terrified. It took all evening to calm her down. Later she told me he—'

'Objection.' Greene stopped and the judge didn't even bother to rule.

Veronica gave Edward an irritated glance and said, 'I'll pass the witness to "defense counsel".'

Edward heard the air quotes in her voice. He stood and said, 'Your Honor, may we have the jury removed for a minute while I make a motion?'

The judge looked at Edward curiously, obviously hoping for more, but when Edward remained silent the judge simply turned to the jury and said, 'Please excuse us briefly.'

The bailiff took them off to the jury room and the lawyers approached the bench, walking shoulder to shoulder. In front of the judge, Edward said, 'Your Honor, I'd like a motion in limine that the prosecutor not refer in any way in front of the jury to the fact that I'm not – you know . . .'

'A real lawyer?' Veronica said, turning to him with folded arms.

Edward stepped closer, almost nose to nose, and said, 'I am going to lawyer the shit out of this case.'

'Counsel?' Judge Roberts said, like a kindergarten teacher. 'Address the bench, please.'

As Edward started to turn in that direction, he caught a glimpse of something out of the corner of his eye. Then he and Veronica were facing the judge, who said, 'I have no idea what you're talking about, counsel. What has Ms Salazar done . . .'

'The way she said "defense counsel" just then, Your Honor, making it sound ironic. She was doing it during jury selection too, always saying the defendant was represented by me, calling me by name rather than saying "attorney".'

'My God.' Veronica turned back to him. 'Defensive much, Edward? Your Honor, let's settle this now. I won't do anything to suggest to this jury the defendant is being represented by a disgraced former lawyer pretending to be one again for one last trial.' She raised her brows at Edward. 'OK?' Drawing out the word as if speaking to the mentally deficient.

My God, she must have been more pissed than Edward thought at his turning her down the other day in her house. He just stared at her.

'OK?' the judge said simply.

The two lawyers turned, glaring at each other, and walked back to their respective tables. With the jury returned to the room, Edward said to the witness, 'Where was the job site where you received the ransom call, Mr Greene?'

Sterling blinked as if being recalled from a long-ago memory. 'Uh, let me think. I believe it was the one we're doing out the Gulf Freeway. Just the other side of Pasadena.'

'And you said that was about two p.m.?'

'Something like that. I didn't make a note of the time.'

'Wouldn't your phone show?'

Sterling blinked. 'I guess I could find that out, yeah.'

'So you were roughly forty-five miles outside Houston.'

'Something like that.' Sterling looked puzzled.

'So you rushed back to – where? – downtown area?'

A couple of people in the audience snickered, and Edward knew he'd made his point to the jury. 'Rushing' through Houston-area traffic at any time of day was only a theoretical concept, very rarely available in practice. 'So you got back to town about, what, three?'

Sterling shifted his broad shoulders. 'Sooner than that. I was barreling.'

Edward let a pause doubt that. 'In your barreling you didn't encounter any wrecks, road closures, ambulances, funeral processions?'

Veronica finally stood. 'Objection, Your Honor. Relevance?'

'Just establishing a timeline, Your Honor,' Edward said from his seat. 'And testing the witness's memory.'

'Continue,' the judge said. 'Briefly, please, Mr Hall.'

Edward stood as a courtesy. 'Thank you, Your Honor.' He dropped back into his chair. 'So, Mr Greene?'

'No. No traffic problems.' His hands were knotted in front of him, looking as if they wanted to throttle something.

'So you got back shortly after lunch time. Did you go straight to your bank?'

'No, my office. I'd already been on the phone with two or three of my bankers. I had one of my men driving me so I'd be free to be on the phone the whole way back.'

'Smart to think of that in such a crisis. Which man was that?'

Sterling's gaze went to a far corner. 'Who was it?' he murmured.

'You seem to have a firm grasp of the other details.'

'Object to the sidebar,' Veronica said, sounding disgusted.

'Sustained.'

As she sat she directed a sneer at Edward that he refused to acknowledge. He just stared at the witness, trying to will the jury to notice how long it was taking him to respond.

'I believe it was Hugh Ferguson, one of the foremen. Frankly I just said somebody drive me and I didn't pay much attention to who responded. I was already on the phone.'

'All right, so you were getting turned down by your bankers—'

'Not all at once, they were responding gradually.'

Edward nodded. 'No emergency loans, no lines of credit, no payroll account you could tap in an emergency?'

'Well, some, of course. I did come up with two hundred thousand. And about half that I had in an account of my own.'

Edward stood, asked permission to approach the witness, and did, taking along a sheaf of papers. He stopped by the court reporter, got his papers marked, then stood two feet in front of the witness. That close, Sterling Greene was a physical presence, broad and radiating heat. He stared at Edward with a clear gaze that revealed very little.

'Mr Greene, I'm handing you what's marked Defendant's Exhibit One. Do you recognize those papers?'

Sterling leafed through them, then looked up at Edward again, his gaze now hooded and full of heat. 'Where did you get these?'

'Only I get to ask the questions, Mr Greene. But I subpoenaed them.' He stared back, emanating his power, the power of paper. 'What are they?'

'These are my bank records. Records of my three business accounts and one personal account.'

'Yes,' Edward said. 'And they show no large withdrawals on the day in question, do they?'

'No.'

'They don't show any unusual activity at all, do they?'

'Not the business ones. My personal savings account shows I pretty much drained that account.'

'Of about five thousand dollars, right?'

'Roughly.'

Which wouldn't pay the average monthly mortgage payment in River Oaks. 'I move to admit Defendant's Exhibit One, Your Honor.'

Veronica Salazar was already on her feet. 'To prove what, Your Honor? By which I mean, I object to relevance.'

Edward stared at her. *Are you kidding?* She stared back at him with a languid hip cocked.

The silence in the courtroom told Edward he needed to explain. Judge Roberts would want something on the record regardless of how he would rule.

'It tends to discredit the witness's testimony, Your Honor. That he was doing his best to raise a large sum of ransom money.'

Edward handed the papers to Judge Roberts, who looked them over and gave them back. 'Admitted.'

Edward handed the exhibit to one of the jurors to pass among them and started back to his seat.

'I have another account you didn't find,' Sterling Greene said.

Edward turned without having to fake a look of surprise. 'I'm sure you can produce a record of that?'

Beat, beat. 'Of course.'

'Thank you.' Edward sat. 'I'd like to ask you about your marriage, Mr Greene.'

Veronica was on her feet instantly. 'Objection. Relevance. My God.'

Edward stood more casually. 'May we approach, Your Honor?'

They did, Veronica actually bumping Edward's shoulder in her hurry. At the bench, very softly, Edward said, 'Judge, this is going to be the crux of the defense case, the state of' – Edward lowered his voice even further – 'this witness's marriage.'

'I cannot possibly think of how that might be a defense to anything,' Judge Roberts said, frowning at him curiously. 'Unless you mean . . . never mind. We'll take this up later. For now the objection is sustained.'

As they turned back, momentarily facing each other, instead of a look of triumph Veronica was staring at Edward with intense curiosity. He wondered if he should have given that up so early.

As he turned away Edward glanced out into the spectator seats. Sometimes, in a big trial like this one, the lawyers had a sense of all those breathing bodies behind them radiating heat and curiosity. But they weren't the audience. The lawyers' audience was in the jury box. But Edward glanced up at the rows of faces turned to him and saw Linda, sitting rather far back. She was giving him a strange look. Not a crossed-arms glare, but not a look of unalloyed affection either. He shot her a quick wink and she rearranged her expression into an encouraging smile.

OK, nothing to worry about there. Edward sat and gave the witness a long look. Sterling Greene looked straight back at him, eyes as lifeless as a snake's.

'I'll pass the witness, Your Honor.'

Veronica asked a few more questions of her witness, mostly reiterating what he'd already said. Edward could have objected to asked and answered – repeating testimony the jury had already heard – but didn't bother. Let her fill time if she wanted.

When Veronica passed the witness back to him, Edward stood, said, 'No more questions, Your Honor,' but stayed on his feet.

Judge Roberts looked at him curiously. Veronica did the same, looking up. 'I just want to add, Your Honor, I will release this witness from the Rule. Now that he's testified, I'm sure he'll be curious about the rest of the trial.'

Two pairs of lawyer-eyes stared at him, the judge's and his opponent's. Both looked concerned. He could almost hear Veronica's mind clicking.

There is one rule of procedure in trial work known as The Rule. It says simply anyone who is a witness in a case can't remain in the courtroom while other witnesses are testifying. Obviously a potential witness listening to earlier witnesses can tailor his testimony to match theirs, maybe not even consciously. It was a way of testing each witness's credibility. Even police separate witnesses and take their statements in different rooms.

To release a witness from the Rule, even after he had testified, simply wasn't done. Veronica could still re-call Sterling Greene to testify further, after he'd heard every other witness's version of events.

Besides, why would a defense lawyer be nice to the victim's husband, who was essentially one of the lawyer's opponents? It made no sense.

Judge Roberts stared at Edward, who had re-seated himself and was blandly looking at his notes. The judge wondered if he was watching ineffective assistance of counsel right before his eyes. Was that the disbarred lawyer's plan, to be so obviously inept any conviction would be reversed?

But Judge Roberts took his oath to follow the rules seriously, including this one. 'The rule is invoked at the behest of one of the parties,' he said flatly, staring at Edward, who didn't look back. 'And a party can withdraw that invocation. Mr Greene.' The judge turned to the witness. 'You are free to remain in the courtroom and view the rest of the trial if you wish.'

'Thank you, Judge.' Greene rose quickly and walked out into the spectator seats, still not looking at either lawyer or the defendant.

But both the prosecutor and the judge were staring at Edward. So did the woman from the State Bar, sitting in the first row of spectator seats. Even Donald was looking at his lawyer. Edward almost needed armor to deflect all the stares.

NINETEEN

Next Veronica called the police officer who'd gotten Sterling Greene's supposedly frantic phone call and two of the SWAT team members. She tried to use them to convey a sense of dramatic urgency, the horror of the crime scene, but cops weren't good witnesses for that sort of thing. They were too focused on the appearance of just another day on the job, I can handle whatever comes. If police ever formed an acting troupe, their only production ever would be *Waiting for Godot*. Performed in the original Deadpan.

'How did you rescue Mrs Greene, Sergeant Vasquez?'

'She sort of rescued herself,' said the witness. Not very tall, he apparently made up for that by living in the gym. His uniform shirt was tight everywhere. 'Our negotiator had been talking to the suspect for almost an hour, we had men stationed at every angle of the house, and were starting to talk about some going in through the back while we distracted him in front. But of course the safety of the hostage—'

'Object to narrative,' Edward said, just to slow down the rush of drama.

'Yes,' said Judge Roberts. 'Ask questions, please, counsel.'

'Certainly, Your Honor.' Veronica was cool as summer dessert. 'What was your primary imperative, Sergeant?'

'The safety of the hostage,' he said flatly. 'We didn't want to do anything that would jeopardize her.'

'What do you know about the perpetrator generally in that situation?'

The witness shrugged. 'He only has one card to play. That he's got a hostage. And this time he only had the one, so he couldn't start shooting them one at a time. He knew we weren't going anywhere, so like I said, it had been a standoff for an hour or so.'

'You said something about the hostage rescuing herself. What did you mean by that?'

The cop stared off into the recent past. 'Our negotiator was talking, maybe he distracted the suspect, I don't know, but we heard a little scream. I sort of jerked my head, because I thought he was hurting her and we'd have to make a quick decision, but then the front door burst open and she came running out. In her stockinged feet, still screaming, waving her arms. Thank God none of us fired. Our training—'

'What did happen to her?'

'Her husband was there, she ran to him, he grabbed her, and somebody scurried them both out of the line of fire.'

'And then the suspect was alone in the house?' *Then There Were None.*

'As far as we knew.' The sergeant shrugged.

'So did your team open fire?'

He shook his head. 'We still wanted to take him alive if we could. So we waited. Our negotiator started talking to him again. It wasn't long before he came out. We took him down without much fuss.'

After a couple of more questions Veronica passed the witness. She wasn't looking at Edward any more. When she wasn't questioning a witness she had her head down, making furious notes. There must have been more drama on her legal pad than in the courtroom.

Edward said, 'How much fire did you take from the suspect, Sergeant?'

'None.' The witness had his fingers interlaced now. Some police officers seemed to hate defense lawyers, staring at them while answering cross-examination. Sergeant Vasquez appeared indifferent.

'Did you find any gun?'

'No, sir. There were none in the house.'

'Seems like a pretty poorly-planned kidnapping, doesn't it, Sergeant?'

'It may have been spur of the moment, sir, I have no way of knowing. But Mrs Greene is a fairly small woman and she seemed very timid that day. Your client wouldn't have had to do much to control her. Look at him.'

People kept saying that about Donald. Size-ists.

'Nonetheless, over the course of hours, don't people have to go to the bathroom?'

'Most people. Of course.' The cop may have been implying he was Super Bladder, but Edward didn't care.

'And a kidnapper has to look out the window, make phone calls, get, as you say, distracted. Isn't that your experience?'

'Yes. Sure.'

'Did you examine Mrs Greene after she came out of the house, Sergeant?'

'No, sir. Not one of my functions.'

'No more questions, Your Honor.'

Edward turned and watched the witness stroll out of the well of the courtroom and up the aisle. Edward glanced at Sterling Greene, now sitting in the audience looking at him intently. Then Edward looked up higher and saw Linda again. He couldn't smile at her, not in front of the jury, but hoped she could see the gleam in his eye when he spotted her.

If she did, she completely took it in her stride.

They broke for lunch. Veronica turned toward Edward, leaned toward him, in fact, then thought better of whatever she intended to say and went out quickly, through the door that led to the hallway behind the courtroom.

As she exited Linda appeared to take her place, coming into the well. Edward stood and hugged her. She felt very tight. And she had been more responsive to hugs. When Edward stepped back Linda crossed her arms.

'What?'

'What's up with you and the lady prosecutor?'

'What are you talking about? It's enmity. Adversarial relationship.'

'That's not what it looked like when you were in each other's faces in front of the judge when the jury was out.'

Edward started to respond, then just cocked his head to the side. After a moment Linda shook her own head and said, 'I know. What's wrong with me? Well, I know what's wrong. There's something you and I have to do.' She shook off the petty jealousy that fast. But her focus had changed. Now she just looked at him.

After a moment Edward said, 'No.' Irritably.

Linda just shifted her stance a little. She brought her hands up, palms upward.

Edward shook his head firmly.

'What?' Donald said, still seated.

'Nothing. No,' Edward repeated to his lover.

She sighed.

'This is some white people thing, right? You people don't want to say anything in front of the black guy, right?'

It was such a great opening for *Who are you calling 'You people?'*. But Edward didn't take it. 'Not the black guy, the client.' Or any witness, for that matter. He turned back to Linda, raised his eyebrows, giving her the crazy eyes, because that's what she was proposing.

'What?' Donald said again.

Edward turned to him. 'Linda wants us to do something. I think it's a poor idea. It's also illegal, which is why we're not saying it in front of you. OK, Donald? We're protecting you from joining us in crime.' Donald shrugged.

Linda would not let it go. 'What other choice do we have? How's your trial strategy going so far, Edward?'

'It's fine. I discredited some of Sterling Greene's testimony. The rest of the witnesses were inconsequential.'

'Except for proving your client committed the crime he's charged with.'

'You think?' Donald asked. Alarmed.

Linda glanced at him. 'I'm sorry, Donald. Maybe, maybe not.' She returned her gaze to Edward. He sighed and rolled his eyes.

'Donald, will you excuse us, please?'

'Why? Why don't you just go on "talking" right in front of me? I can't understand a word you're not saying anyway.'

'Never mind. We can talk about this later. Let's just go to lunch and get ready for the afternoon.'

Linda also silently agreed to truce. 'I can't,' she said. 'I have to see someone and I'm in another court this afternoon, filling in for their regular reporter.'

'OK.' Edward hugged her again. This one was better, Linda's hands coming up his back. Then she hurried away.

Edward and Donald went to Treebeard's, a Creole restaurant a couple of blocks from the Justice Center. It had been there for decades, minimally decorated and furnished with long picnic-type tables where one grabbed seats catch-as-catch-can, sitting close with strangers, and the noise level was high. But the jambalaya made up for all that. And the hubbub meant conversations were private. When you could barely hear the person sitting across the table, eavesdropping by others was extremely unlikely.

'What about Sterling Greene's testimony was untrue?' Edward asked.

Donald's eyes widened. 'Easier to say what wasn't. Yeah, she called him on her cell a couple of times, but all they talked about was why the guy with the jewelry was late.'

'Did you ever call him on your phone?'

'I *got* a call from him to set the whole thing up, telling me where to go pick her up.'

'Where were you?'

'I showed you. Just around, you know. I didn't know it was going to be important to remember that.'

Edward nodded. 'And you two waited hours in that house for a stolen jewelry guy who wasn't showing.'

'More like a couple of hours. You heard what the neighbor said.'

'Did you have her restrained in any way? Tied to a chair, something like that?'

Donald stared at him. 'Why would I do that, man? You think I'm into that kind of thing?'

Edward sat thinking for a minute. In his head, the uproar around them went silent.

'You got an idea?' Donald asked.

'I hope to God I've got more than one.' Because Linda was right. This trial was going smoothly without any bumps. That kind of trial only ever ended in one verdict.

TWENTY

More cops in the afternoon. They certainly made the scene of the kidnapping sound frantic and frightening. All emphasized Diana Greene's small size and obvious terror. Every time anyone looked at Donald it didn't help discredit the narrative.

'Could you ever see either the suspect or the victim through a window, Officer?' Veronica asked of the commander in charge.

'Only once, personally. I saw Mrs Greene peering out a front window with her hands pressed against the glass, but then something snatched her back.'

'Objection,' Edward said. 'Speculation. He couldn't possibly tell whether she was "snatched" or just jumped back.'

Veronica responded, 'He's just describing what he saw, Your Honor.'

'Overruled,' the judge said after a moment.

Edward decided to make lemonade out of that when the witness was passed to him. 'This time when you saw Mrs Greene at the window. Did she call out? Make any gestures toward you or the other officers?'

'No, sir. Just stared out the window. It looked like she was about to—'

'Objection to speculation,' Edward said quickly.

'That one is sustained,' Judge Roberts said.

Edward just looked at the witness. He couldn't think of anything to be gained from questioning him further. The case was all so straightforward.

'Pass the witness.'

The afternoon wound down. Toward the end Veronica had a problem with an unavailable witness and the judge let them break for the day early. Normally Edward would spend part of that time talking to his opposing counsel, both of them cautiously evaluating the case. When he turned toward Veronica, though, she was closing her thin file, gave him an icy look, and turned away.

So Edward reassured his client for a few minutes and went to find Linda. When he did her courtroom was almost empty, the judge gone from the bench, but Linda sat in the court reporter's station with a man in a suit leaning over her. A lawyer, obviously, talking quickly. Linda threw back her head and laughed. The man looked pleased with himself.

Knock yourself out, pal, Edward thought. *She's going home with me.* He walked closer slowly, until Linda obviously noticed him, but she kept listening to the lawyer's tale. He was older than Edward, mid-forties maybe, and looked prosperous. Linda chuckled again. Then the lawyer saw Edward. 'Need something?'

Edward shook his head. 'Finish your chat. I'll just wait.'

But the guy obviously didn't like the added audience. After a minute he shut up and walked away, giving Edward an irritated glance. Edward just gave Linda a look. He refused to act jealous the way she had a little earlier.

'What?' she said innocently. Then she dimpled. 'How do you think I get all the good courthouse gossip?'

He laughed and they went to find the car.

On the ride home Linda's silence brought up the original topic. Edward said, 'I knew what you were thinking. What do you expect to find by burglarizing the Greenes' home?'

'I don't know. That's why you go looking.'

Edward just rode, but feeling a little itch. His fingers rubbed each other. 'All right, I'll do it. Alone.'

'No.'

'Yes. Damn it, Linda, I've been to prison for this, my sister's been to jail. There's absolutely nothing fun about it.'

'So you're saying I'm the only one of us who's done it and not gotten arrested? Sounds like you need me.'

He laughed. Looked at her across the car seat. She took her eyes off the road for a second to shoot him a glance that combined amusement, excitement, and a kind of longing.

'All right.' He gave in. 'But this time we're not going to do it spur of the moment. We're going to prepare.'

Linda nodded soberly. 'I approve of planning. Starting with?'

'Well, borrowing Amy's lockpicks. That's going to be a conversation.'

'Which I've already had.' Not taking her eyes off the road, Linda reached into her purse and her fingers emerged holding said lockpicks. They actually gleamed. Well, it was Houston. Lots of sunlight, glass, and steel. Everything gleamed.

'How did . . .?' Edward waved his hand. 'Just assume I asked all the questions.'

Linda glanced at him. 'Tired?'

Edward suddenly realized his weariness. You sit in trial poised to respond, or studying a witness for insight, adrenaline pumping all the while, as Edward's just had for hours. 'It has been a long day.'

Linda put her hand on his leg sympathetically.

'Questions?' Edward reminded her.

'I had a strong feeling this would come up, so I went to see Amy a couple of days ago and explained the situation.'

'How so?'

'That you were in trouble and might be rescued by a bit of burglary.'

'So you made me the victim?' Edward thought for a moment, then nodded. 'Good work.'

'Thanks. What else do we need to do to prepare?'

'Just not go in half-assed this time.'

Linda had a small smile of satisfaction, at having convinced him she was right. 'Oh, we're going in fully assed this time, love.'

Edward called on his River Oaks insider friend. 'Gerald? Hi, it's Edward.'

'Yes, I know. You called me.'

'You have me in your contacts.' Edward felt flattered. Then he realized it was Gerald. Probably half of Houston resided in his Contacts. No, not half. One percent.

Silence passed for a sigh. 'What can I help you with, Edward?'

'I was wondering what the hot social calendar is for the next few days, you know, for social RO people.'

'I assume in your world RO stands for River Oaks. And you want to know why?'

'You know, I thought I'd get back in the game, mingle, maybe meet a nice . . .'

The silence stopped him again. It was barely bearable, even over the phone. 'OK, Gerald, here's the truth. I want to get close to the Greenes, I thought maybe meet them socially, they might let something slip that will help me in trial.'

Another silence, finally interrupted by Gerald saying, 'Actually, there's a "hot social event" at the country club tonight. Very exclusive, invitation only. I'm quite sure the Greenes will be there. They have to be seen. They have to play out their private drama in public.'

'Were you invited?'

'That pointed silence is me not saying, "Duh." But I'm attending a much more exclusive gathering elsewhere.'

'Your house?'

Gerald didn't even sigh this time. Edward said, 'Thanks, man, I owe you one.'

'Several, actually, and you always will. And Edward—'

'Yes?'

'If you ever want any more favors from me in the future – and I feel quite sure you will—'

'Yes?'

'Don't ever lie to me again.'

Edward let a few beats of his own pass. 'Noted. Thanks, Gerald, good talk.'

They hung up without the formalities of goodbyes. Per standard protocol.

'Tonight? Damn, Edward, that doesn't give us much time to reconnoiter.'

'Tell me about it. I barely know their address. I say we wait.'

They were at home, on Linda's white sofa. It was October dusk, still light, but that light growing slanted, casting long shadows through the large front window, shades opened to the world. In that light Linda looked lovely, brown hair pulled back, eyes sparkling with thought, the flesh of her arms taut. When they'd come home she'd changed immediately into shorts and a T-shirt, her standard home attire. Her legs were across Edward's lap. Now, at his suggestion, she pulled them back quickly and planted them on the floor.

'We can't wait, Edward. You're already in trial. How many days are left? Do you want to wait until after the guilty verdict?'

'Your confidence in my trial skills is—'

'Please, Edward.' She brought her face close. God, when she was earnest she was even more beautiful. 'You know I think you're great. And I've listened to you all those times you say what the odds are in trial. Stop fishing and stick to the point. You need whatever we can find right now.'

'I could ask for a continuance.'

'Your Honor, I need a few days in order to burglarize the victim's home in hopes of finding something helpful for the defense.'

Edward replayed that in his head. He could come up with something else, but Linda was right. Asking for a continuance after one day of trial would be silly. He could picture Judge Roberts' face as he made the request.

Their discussion was beside the point, anyway. Edward could feel the gathering inside himself. Renewed energy. Resolve. Fending off Linda was just to distract his conscious mind while his subconscious was marshaling forces, already planning. Looking at Linda, it was clear she knew this. She was doing the same thing. Her breathing had deepened, her cheeks were slightly flushed.

'All right, Mrs Peele, get your black turtleneck.'

She smiled. Quickly, because she was already jumping up from the couch.

They had dinner at a little Italian place in the opposite direction from River Oaks, as far away as they could risk. The bill would show them across town from the Greenes' house at the approximate time the burglary occurred. Linda chatted up the waitress, making herself memorable. Edward thought she was babbling a bit, nerves talking. He didn't blame her.

For himself, he was growing calmer by the minute. Knowing he was going to do it, break the law – again – was calming. His hand was steady as he reached for his water. In his mind he was already in their house, learning their secrets, breathing in their discarded cells, absorbing Diana and Sterling Greene into himself.

Without discussing it, he and Linda both ordered a lot of food and a bottle of wine, leaving most of it largely untouched. Their bill would paint a portrait of two people tired at the end of a long day, full, sated, ready to go home and crash. At seven forty-five Edward gave her a steady look and said, 'Ready?'

Linda just smiled.

'What are we going to be looking for?'

'Some sign they planned this "kidnapping",' Linda replied.

'Like handwritten plans? "Honey, pick up bread and milk and some guy we can frame for kidnapping me"?'

Linda shot him a look. 'You're hilarious.'

But Edward was doing his own thinking. He knew what they'd be looking for. Some clue, some sign of the break and renewal in the Greenes' marriage. A diary was too much to hope for, but a social calendar might help. Something showing a falling off of spending time together, followed immediately after the artist's murder with a flurry of social activity. A second honeymoon.

Because he could investigate that. Piece together their lives from available public sources. They couldn't use anything from the upcoming burglary in trial. Not straightforwardly. Nothing they found tonight could be used directly in trial. The constitutional protection against unreasonable, warrantless searches only applied to law enforcement personnel, but in Texas a statute made the results of illegal searches even by private citizens inadmissible in court. The statute had been passed during Prohibition, when roving bands of 'citizen committees' broke up stills and tried to get bootleggers arrested. But Texas legislators apparently liked their moonshine too, and made those searches illegal. So even if Edward and Linda found something, it couldn't be used in court. Not directly. But it might give Edward something else to investigate, another avenue to pursue.

It was full dark when they drove into River Oaks. Stately oaks surrounding stately homes of brick and stone. The most beautiful, placid, old neighborhood in Houston. Edward's stomach tightened. He had grown up here, but the family had moved from a much more modest neighborhood when he was eight, and he'd never felt quite comfortable with the new, fancy lifestyle. It seemed like pretension, these fine old mini-mansions, some of them vine-covered, as if the families had lived here for generations, out in the English countryside, instead of with your neighbor's wall thirty feet away. In some cases the homes were multi-generational, but if you struck a good oil well in west Texas yesterday you could move into River Oaks tomorrow. Houston didn't believe new money was tainted and old money wasn't. Houston believed money was money.

They drove past the Greene home, two stories of stone and shutters and chimneys. It wasn't dark, exactly, but did appear unoccupied. Edward assumed a country club event would start early, eight at the latest. He looked for an inconspicuous place to park the car. Not many cars were parked on the street here.

'I thought we'd park at your parents' place and walk back over here,' Linda said.

Good plan. She *had* thought this through. He put a hand on her leg as a compliment and turned the corner. His parents lived only a couple of blocks away. Edward glided to a stop in front of the grand old place. If his parents noticed his car they'd be curious but not suspicious. Edward and Linda could drop in afterwards and establish an even more solid alibi. They might be panting a bit. *Hi, Mom, Dad. We've been . . . jogging.*

They walked back to the Greenes' house quickly. A crisp fall evening, windy. Hurricane season wasn't over yet. The trees seemed to be waving their limbs in alarm. *Look! Outsiders!* But Edward walked with the confidence of someone who'd ridden his bicycle along here.

They stood for just a moment looking in the Greenes' windows. Nothing moved, no one cast a shadow. No blue flicker of a TV screen. After a moment, without a word, they walked up the driveway and around to the back. They didn't bother to ring the doorbell. That would leave them exposed to neighbors' views even longer. They came to a wooden gate, locked, of course. Edward laced his fingers together and Linda stepped into them, going over. For a moment her ass in tight jeans was all he saw. Then all of her disappeared. She didn't make a sound when she landed.

Edward scrambled over himself and they held hands briefly as they walked around to the back. Then they were at the back door. They looked at each other and Linda nodded, a contract. Edward bent to the lock, a ridiculously simple one in the door-knob, and in seconds it clicked. Edward put his hand on it.

'If there's a security system—'

'We won't have very long to find something. I know, Edward. Go.'

Edward opened the door. It was into a kitchen, and across the room from them, on the wall next to the phone, was indeed the control panel of a home security system. Edward cursed and turned around in the doorway. Linda put a hand on his arm. 'Wait.'

'For what? Getting caught?'

She crossed to the alarm panel and studied it. 'I have one of these, Edward. Not this exact model, but it's supposed to scare off a burglar. It beeps until you feed it the code. I think this one's dead.'

This was a two-story house. Trusting Linda's hunch was an extreme risk. He was the only one of the two of them who'd been arrested. It was no fun.

'This is an expense they'd cut,' Linda said. 'Or maybe they just forgot to turn it on. People are idiots.'

Edward stared at the contraption suspiciously. 'I feel like that's a trap.'

'Then let's get moving.'

They did. Trusting Linda's intuition left them both tingling with nerve endings. The house was well-lighted. The Greenes, like many people, obviously believed a well-lit house would fend off burglaries when in fact having the lights on just made it easier for the burglars. Stealth was barely required. Edward knew as soon as they entered the house it was empty of other people. He had an instinct for that, or maybe just excellent hearing. At any rate, there were no other hearts beating in that house at the moment, only his and Linda's, and those were pretty rapid. But they calmed as they moved through the house and encountered no problems. The living room had the calm, elegant appearance of a couple with a maid service and no children. Magazines spread in a fan on the glass coffee table, for decoration rather than reading.

They stood there for a minute catching their breaths and looking around. Over the elegant fireplace with the white mantelpiece was a large blank space on the brick wall. Clearly waiting for the portrait of Diana to be released from the gallery exhibit and take its place of honor.

Everything in that room was white: white in color and white people in taste. They wouldn't find anything there. There was also a den that looked more lived-in, with a complicated home entertainment system requiring multiple remotes. They went through drawers in there, but moved on quickly. Diana and Sterling wouldn't keep anything incriminating in the public rooms. The burglars needed to go behind the scenes.

The staircase was elegant, curved, with a landing. They went up the carpeted stairs without touching the railing or anything else. Linda's breathing had calmed. It seemed clear no police were coming. But going upstairs took them farther from the exits and the street. They were committed.

The first room they came to was a study. Again, no children. The Greenes had bedrooms they could re-purpose. This one was clearly a man's study. A huge wooden desk, computer, filing cabinet. Edward groaned mentally looking at all those drawers and other spaces. They would need a day to search this thoroughly. Longer than that if they could get into his computer files.

Linda was already rapidly going through the contents of a drawer, finding nothing quickly and moving on to the filing cabinet.

'You already subpoenaed his bank records. He might not have anything else worthwhile here. Anything he'd want to keep secret from his wife he'd have at the office.'

'But I thought we thought they were in on this together.'

'I haven't rejected any theories yet.'

Edward chuckled. God, he loved her. He looked at the windows, picturing jumping through them if cops showed up. Then he calmed down and just walked around the room, imagining himself Sterling Greene. Here at literally the top of the hill, having scrambled his way up from whatever his upbringing was. Wherever that had happened, it wasn't River Oaks. He could look out that window and know he lived among the elite of the richest neighborhood in the richest city in Texas.

But from the top of the hill there was only one direction to go. Sterling might have looked out that window in desperation sometimes.

'Here we go,' Linda said. She had a drawer open. It was apparently filled with documents. 'Bank statements, you've already got those. But here are creditor letters, demands. Man, he's on the edge.'

'But why would he keep them here instead of – oh.'

'Yes.' Linda got there at the same time. 'Wouldn't want that shit at the office in case someone whose paychecks you're writing goes snooping.'

'Yeah, I got it. Let me look at those.'

They exchanged a quick kiss as they switched places. Then Edward pulled her back and gave her a real one, including hand on the ass. Linda joined in enthusiastically.

It was exciting, being in someone else's house, in their lives. It was hot. Probably said something bad about them psychologically, but who cared. They clung to each other like they could come at each other through their clothing.

'OK,' Linda said with little breath. 'I'm going to . . .'

She waved vaguely in the direction of the other room. Some other room. The rest of the house.

'Yeah. Right. I'm just going to go through this stuff for a minute.'

'All right. Good talk.' Linda walked away, gaining purpose with every step. She was through the door almost at a run.

She had come across something, though. Bank statements, creditor letters. These painted a portrait of a man in free fall.

The kind who'd stage a kidnapping to raise some money? Edward tried to picture how that would work. Maybe Sterling hadn't been thinking it through real clearly, but seriously, how could he even . . .

'Here.'

He heard Linda's voice from somewhere nearby. She hadn't raised it, counting on him to hear her. But now she did raise it a little. 'You need to come in here.'

Oh, no. What had she encountered in the bedroom? A video security system? Was she already spotted? Edward hurried across the hall into the master bedroom. Large unmade bed with a frilly white duster. The room was rather feminine, in shades of white and yellow and pastel green. Restful to the eye. A long white dresser, covered with beauty ointments and sprays and lotions. Edward didn't see anything that seemed immediately threatening and wondered what Linda . . .

He took a step toward her and came to a dead stop. They were a matched pair of statues. Linda was staring at a painting on an easel set up at the foot of the bed. The painting wasn't huge, maybe three feet by three. It was a nude. It was *the* nude, the one for which they'd found the photo studies. But this differed completely from the photos. Those had been photographically accurate. But the painting looked more lifelike. Diana Greene lay on her stomach, her ass barely in the frame, overshadowed by her upper half. Diana's face and upper body were turned toward the artist, so one full breast and most of the other were in frame. Her flesh was warm and pink and flushed. But it was her face that arrested his attention. She was looking frankly out of the frame toward the viewer, the tiniest of smiles beginning to blossom, barely starting to shape her full lips. Her eyes looked slightly sleepy. She was the definition of languid. Content but still excited.

'Oh my,' he said.

Linda agreed with a nod.

That the painting existed wasn't a surprise, they'd already found evidence the artist had been working on it. But finding it here, in the Greenes' bedroom, was a bit of a shock. Edward's mind was just starting to work out the logistics of that. But mainly he and Diana just stared, fascinated and repelled. Edward turned to look at the bed. The painting was barely a yard from the foot of it. He turned back to the painting, stepped closer.

Linda noted where he was looking.

'Hmm.'

Linda pointed into the frame. 'That's not the couch in the room behind the gallery owner's house. And do you think that lady gallery owner knows what goes on in there? She's almost . . . Never mind. But look. This painting isn't set in the studio we saw.'

'What are you saying?'

'Take your eyes off her tits and look at the background. That corner of a dresser? The other corner of an unmade bed? That's the artist's house.'

'I wasn't looking at her tits.'

'Then what's wrong with you? They're magnificent.'

But while talking they stared, hands reaching toward the painting. There was some profit, however, from Edward's focus on the naked woman. 'Look,' he said, pointing.

There was something on her neck, a mark, very faint. They both leaned in to it.

'Love bite?' Linda said.

Could be. Edward felt pretty sure Diana didn't have anything permanent on her neck, a mole or birthmark. Had Alberico invented this, or had it actually been there one day? What kind of message had the artist been trying to send?

Edward straightened up to find Linda looking at the bed. He joined her in studying the angles, staring back and forth from the bed to the painting at its foot.

'Do you think this is where they always keep it?' he asked. Linda shrugged.

'God.'

'Eeuw,' she agreed.

'He wants to see it when they're in bed? It's . . . inspiration?'

'Or wants to make her look at it.' Edward turned to Linda. 'Do you think Sterling commissioned it, after the first official portrait? He wanted this portrayal of his wife?'

'Or Diana gave it to him as a present, which is even weirder. She was trying to hold the marriage together,' Linda said.

'But why keep it in here?'

'It's private, it's safe. Maybe they put it in a closet when guests are in the house, but guests don't go into the bedrooms.' Linda moved around the side of the bed, staring at the painting. 'Look.'

Had her perspective changed from that small a change in position? Had Linda spotted something else, some other message? Then Edward saw what she was saying.

Linda said it out loud. 'Both things could be true. Sterling wanted to see it while they were having sex and he wanted her to see it too.'

'Is that flattering to her?' Edward asked.

Linda shrugged. 'It's kind of punishment too. The painting is gorgeous. Diana Greene may look great most of the time, but she can never live up to that.'

He was making her compete with herself. And flesh and blood would always lose out to the perfect image on the canvas.

'Besides that,' Linda continued, 'the painting will never age. It's a reverse portrait of Dorian Gray.'

Linda stood with her arms folded, gooseflesh on those arms, turning away to survey the room. There'd been a very sexy vibe when they first entered the house, intruding into forbidden territory. They'd had that long kiss in the study.

The sexy vibe was dead. Linda gave a little shudder. Edward felt the same way.

'Should we take a picture? For evidence?'

It wouldn't do him any good. They weren't supposed to be here, nothing they found could be admitted in court. Edward still snapped a couple of quick pix with his phone, then they both turned toward the door. 'Should we . . .?' Linda began.

Then they froze as they heard very distinctly a door downstairs open then slam shut.

TWENTY-ONE

Linda stared at Edward, clearly wondering why they hadn't planned a contingency for this. They knew the state of the Greenes' marriage, they could get furious at each other in an instant and go storming out of any social event.

Linda started back into the bedroom. Edward grabbed her arm and shook his head. Never the bed, don't ever hide under the bed. And the bedroom closet wasn't much better. They could be stuck in there all night. He hurried them out and back across the hall to the study.

Crossing the hall, they could hear the couple. Not talking. Indistinct sounds of moaning and mumbling.

Oh, God. They weren't mad at each other. It was worse. Much, much worse.

He turned off the study light as they went through the door, hoping the Greenes wouldn't notice the change in lighting, feeling pretty sure they wouldn't. He and Linda had barely stepped into the gloom of the study, looking around for places to hide, when Mr and Mrs Greene came through the door behind them.

Edward stepped behind the open door of the room. Linda crouched in a small space in an alcove that held the filing cabinet.

Diana Greene was already half undressed, her evening gown to her hips. Sterling, his shirt hanging around his waist, fumbled with the catch of her bra. He was all black hair, some missing from the top of his head but making up for it in body covering. Diana, though, was pristine, all smooth unblemished pink skin, a few extra pounds of it from when she'd been the debutante of the year, but it suited her. She wore it well. She had her head thrown back as her husband nuzzled her, Diana laughing.

Then he had the bra open and it fell to the ground. Sterling feasted. Edward looked at Linda, whose eyes were huge, beacons in the dark. He shook his head at her and she drew back even further into the darkness, barely visible now, if anyone looked.

He continued peeking around the door. Damn it, they had a perfectly good bedroom a few feet across the hall, already decorated for sex. Was this their deal, some weird boss-and-secretary thing?

Or maybe Sterling just liked the angle. He pulled her dress the rest of the way off and lifted her up to sit on the desk, then nuzzled her breasts again. Diana's head was thrown back, showing off her neck. For a moment her rolling eyes crossed Edward's. He ducked back. But she made no outcry, except the continued moaning and sounds of encouragement.

Finally – *finally!* – Sterling had had enough of that. Diana wrapped her legs around his waist and he carried her out of the room, his pants falling to his ankles so they were in danger of capsizing every moment. But finally they staggered out of view.

Linda poked her head out of her inadequate hiding space. Edward shook a cautioning head at her, and she froze.

The couple across the hall left the door open and the light on. Edward wasn't the least curious about what exactly they were doing, just wanted them to be loud about it, preferably with their eyes closed. But they wouldn't be. All four eyes would probably be focused on that painting.

A moment later Linda was standing beside him, holding his hand tightly.

'Window?' she mouthed as Edward turned to her. He looked across the room. They couldn't even be sure those windows opened and weren't painted shut. In any event they might creak, drawing the attention of the pair across the hall. Then they'd have to close the window behind themselves, leaving a sign of their exit.

No, in his experience as a burglar – this was his third time, and he'd gotten caught both of the first two – it was better to go boldly out the way they'd come. The Greenes would think in their lustful haste they'd forgotten to lock the kitchen door behind them when they'd come in. Edward doubted they'd even remember staggering up the stairs.

They could dart out now, when the homeowners were definitively distracted, or wait until they fell asleep afterwards. But what if they engaged in extended pillow talk afterwards, cuddling and murmuring? Sterling didn't seem like the type, but one never knew. And suppose even worse, in the afterglow he remembered something he wanted to see in his study?

Edward risked peeking out again. Damn it, he could see them. They'd left the light on in the hall, too. For people on the edge of bankruptcy, these two didn't seem to give a damn about the electricity bill. Edward and Linda were dressed in matching black, which was great for blending into the darkness, but would make them stand out like cardboard cutouts in that well-lit white hallway.

The window exit was looking better. Edward was studying it when he was yanked to the side. Linda, still holding his hand tightly, was going around the door. He had no choice but to follow her lead.

He risked a glance at the groaning couple in the moment he could and saw they weren't in position to look at the painting. In fact they both had their heads turned away. Had Linda seen that, or just risked it? Then Edward and Linda were hurtling through the open space. As they reached the head of the stairs, the panting stopped and they both distinctly heard Sterling Greene say, 'Did you hear something?'

Diana chuckled and obviously made a sexy rejoinder. Linda tiptoed down the stairs, still tightly clutching Edward's hand. They heard no sounds of pursuit.

The kitchen door opened soundlessly under Linda's touch and closed the same way. Then they were scrambling across the backyard. This time Linda needed no help with the locked gate. She just took it at a run, leaped, grabbed the top, and vaulted over. Sometimes a burglar's most valuable tool was adrenaline.

Later, in the car – they hadn't bothered to stop into his parents' house to establish an alibi, instead just ran like thieves – Linda looked thoughtful. Edward raised an eyebrow and either she saw that in the dark or knew an unspoken question when she heard one.

Linda said, 'You think Sterling actually heard us going across that hall? During *that*?'

Edward shrugged. 'Seems so.'

Linda's thoughtful look remained in place. 'I hope you're more in the moment than that when we make love.'

'We'll never know. Those two have killed sex for me forever.'
Linda put a hand on his thigh. 'I strongly doubt forever.'

And from the way he reacted to her hand and her husky chuckle, she was probably right.

TWENTY-TWO

The next morning Linda woke to find Edward lying beside her staring up into the dimness of early morning. 'Did you sleep?'

'Must have.'

It didn't look like it. She sat up on her elbow. 'What are you thinking?'

'After last night I'm probably going to be cross-examining Diana Greene today or tomorrow.'

Linda laughed. 'Thinking of what you can ask her?'

He answered seriously. 'Yes.' That's what he'd been lying there trying to decide. Go into everything he knew about her private life this early in the trial, during the prosecution's case, trying to wreck that case from near the start, or hold off to use it as the big finish? There was no science to trial work, it was instinct. Art. He was trying to picture this scene as he composed it.

Linda was scrambling out of bed. She was so conscientious these days. 'You'll be brilliant, Eddie, you know that.'

'That's a relief. I was briefly worried.'

Linda chuckled and padded away to start her day. For a minute Edward lay there thinking about that. Their days were remarkably similar now, going off to the Justice Center, coming home together. But Linda would be there in the center of justice after Edward's brief re-emergence was over. She'd helped bring him back to life after prison and then had come completely into his world.

He rose and went after her.

The once-pristine Civil Justice Center now hosted the same grime and smells imported from the nearly defunct criminal courthouse next door. Smells of sweat and fear. And it took as long to get up to the courtroom on the fourteenth floor as it used to take in the criminal courts building. The few civil lawyers and judges one saw in the hallways looked horrified still. Edward popped out of the elevator doors and headed for the court, comparatively on time.

Going down the aisle, he glanced over the crowd. The seats were no longer packed, but it was a much bigger crowd than for an ordinary criminal trial. Sterling Greene was in his place near the front and his glare was in its place too, aimed at Edward. But it was much easier confronting that face in here than it would have been in Greene's hallway. Edward resisted the urge to grin at him.

Then he looked past Sterling and frowned, seeing a face he knew. Edward crossed seats to her and said, 'Melanie?'

She glanced up at him nervously, which was odd. A lawyer shouldn't be nervous in a courtroom. 'Hello, Edward. Is this all right?'

'I'm not the bailiff.' But he did make a slight head gesture, asking her to come out with him. He heard her breathing as they went back up the aisle. Melanie Bass was a family lawyer he'd met while in private practice. While Edward had specialized in criminal defense, there were so many family law cases available – divorce, child custody – that lawyers new to private practice almost inevitably took on a few of them. He and Melanie had also had a brief flirtation, amounting to no more than a couple of lunches and meeting for drinks. Which may have meant more to her than he'd realized, since she was here to watch him perform.

She was a willowy blonde who looked good in a suit. 'Interested in this trial?' he asked without preliminaries, setting his briefcase down on a bench out in the hall.

She shrugged. 'You know, it's gotten a lot of publicity. I've got a temporary orders hearing this afternoon across the street, so I thought I'd look in on this for a while.'

That wasn't how Melanie practiced. Edward knew from his brief experience of her that the morning of a hearing she'd be in her office furiously going over every document again, and on the phone with her client rehearsing again. He just studied her. She actually blushed.

'Melanie, do you know something about this case I should know?'

She looked him in the eye. 'I can't say anything.'

That was carefully worded, demonstrative of the good lawyer she was. 'Can't' meant she was forbidden from saying something she did think he'd want to know. Or thought she was.

Edward could only think of one reason for that. Attorney–client privilege. 'Did Mr or Mrs Sterling Greene hire you for something?'

He could see her thinking. Did acknowledging she had an attorney–client relationship with one of the Greenes violate that privilege? Edward decided to make it easier for her.

'Melanie, the presumption of innocence and the right to present a defense in a criminal trial trumps any attorney–client privileged information.'

She grew a pretty set of lines between her eyes as she tilted her head toward him. 'Is that true?'

He had no idea. 'Absolutely.'

Relief coursed through her. 'Mrs Greene hired me to review a pre-nup she'd signed. Actually a post-nup, signed after they'd been married for several years. Sterling hired a lawyer to draw it up and she didn't consult one before she signed it. She came to me with it to ask if it could be undone somehow.'

'When was this?'

'Maybe a year ago. Sometime around there.'

Well before the kidnapping. 'What did you tell her? Was there a way to undo it?'

Melanie frowned. 'No! I'm not a miracle worker. It was a very standard agreement and she signed it voluntarily. If she'd consulted me beforehand – but she didn't. She's stuck with it.' She was obviously still pissed about the client bringing her an insoluble dilemma.

'What does the agreement provide?'

'In the event of divorce, if he even alleges she's at fault, she gets almost nothing. Six months of spousal support, a small percentage of whatever they have in savings. Much less than a normal divorce agreement would get her. His businesses are all his.'

'Wow.'

Melanie nodded. Now that Edward had released her from her obligation to this client, she had obviously been dying to dish. 'Diana must have been a naughty girl.'

Edward nodded. There was no other way to see it. Sterling must have had something big to hold over her to get her to submit to such a harsh agreement.

'Thanks, Melanie.'

'So I was interested to see her testify in this trial.'

Edward looked back at her and gave her a little self-deprecating smile. 'I can't promise it will be entertaining. I'm a little rusty.'

She ducked her head, giving him a look saying both she didn't believe that and didn't think he did either.

Edward shrugged and returned to the courtroom, this time going down the aisle much more thoughtfully.

'What's up?' Donald asked, already in his place at the defense table.

'Not sure. What about you? Doing all right?'

'You tell me, Edward. *Am* I doing all right?'

'Is that you reminding me of the "I'm an innocent man on trial" thing? Like I'd forget?' Edward relented and put a hand on Donald's forearm. 'I'm doing my best, man. And I think it's going OK.' He turned and looked back out into the spectator seats. Melanie watched him closely with an odd expression, all big eyes and hopefulness. Sterling Greene, on the other hand, was watching him with a stare like a club.

'I am about to do something weird, though,' Edward warned his client.

'Man, why you even tell me that? I'm no lawyer, I wouldn't even know it was weird if you didn't tell me.'

The special prosecutor was watching Edward closely, sensing trouble, or at least drama. Edward smiled at her. Veronica's expression didn't melt. She turned back to her legal pad and started making rapid notes. No one was testifying, so the subject of her notes wasn't apparent.

Judge Roberts took the bench and immediately told the bailiff, 'Bring the jury.'

Edward stood and said, 'I have something preliminary, Your Honor. It will be very brief.'

With a hand gesture the judge told the bailiff to go ahead, and the deputy went out to get the jury. Edward said, 'I just want to inform the court I release Mrs Diana Greene from the Rule. She can come in. I'm sure she'll be testifying very shortly and I'm sure she'd like to have the support of her husband here.'

Veronica Salazar was standing a few feet to his side, staring at him. Edward didn't turn, but he could feel it. Judge Roberts' stare he could see, because it was coming at him full frontal. The judge said slowly, 'That's your prerogative, counsel. If you're sure . . .?'

Edward said casually, 'I am, Your Honor. It's fine. Her husband already testified, and he was her main corroborating witness.'

The judge's face was still willing Edward to take back this pronouncement, but when that didn't work Judge Roberts lifted his gaze to the audience. 'Mr Greene, you may tell your wife she can join us if she wishes.'

'Thank you, Your Honor.' Sterling immediately pulled out a cell phone and started texting.

Edward resumed his seat and started looking over his notes, feeling the center of attention to varying degrees. His client leaned over him. 'OK, even I know that was weird. I haven't seen too many trials, Edward, mainly just my own two, but I know you don't let the victim watch other witnesses testify. What's going on?'

'It's fine, Donald. I know what I'm doing.'

'Everybody knows what you're doing, man, it's right out here in the open. But what's it mean?'

Edward turned his head to look his client in the eye. 'It's fine, Donald. She'll be testifying soon. Let her sit here and watch a couple of cops or something. Let her get comfortable.'

False comfort, Edward hoped. But that wasn't why he'd done what he'd just done.

Veronica didn't call a cop for her next witness. She called a nurse.

They were called SANEs. Sexual Assault Nurse Examiner. Edward had already seen her report, so knew essentially what her testimony would be. Nurse DeShaunte Taylor was a dark-skinned African-American with a strong nose and straightforward eyes difficult to read, at least for Edward. She sat very straight but also apparently at ease in the witness chair. A woman in her profession would have testified many times.

SANEs examined alleged victims of sexual assault specifically to collect evidence for criminal cases. It was a little surprising one had examined Diana Greene. Edward was eager to hear her testimony but also a little terrified the jury was going to hear it.

As Veronica went through the preliminaries of having Ms Taylor elaborate her training and experience, he heard a stir behind him and turned to see Diana Greene coming down the aisle. The steps slanted down toward the well of the courtroom, as in a movie theater, so anyone entering was briefly on display. Diana walked as if aware of that, head ducked and stepping carefully. She looked up, caught Edward's eye, and looked away at once. She was dressed differently from the last time he'd seen her, which was to say she was dressed. In a conservative navy-blue dress with a coral-colored collar. Her hair was pulled back, not into a bun exactly, but held from her face.

Her husband watched her come, not rising to assist her. Diana scooched across the seats and sat quickly beside him, immediately taking his hand and holding it in her lap. Edward kept watching her, his back almost turned to the judge. He felt others at the front of the courtroom gazing in that direction too, as if there were a tiny bit of drama in the audience.

'Nurse Taylor, did you examine one Diana Greene last April?'

'I did.'

'How soon was that after she was rescued from a house in the Third Ward by SWAT team officers?'

'An hour or so later. My understanding is the officers brought her directly to my hospital.'

Why? Had Diana said something to the cops? Probably not. Edward resisted looking at his client, because he didn't want the jurors doing that, glaring at him thinking, What *else* did you do, you bastard?

'How thoroughly did you examine her, Nurse Taylor?'

'Head to toe, plus probing and taking samples, determining whether she had someone else's DNA on her, for example.'

'Tell us your findings, please.' Veronica was all business this morning, staring down at her notes.

'She was a well-developed forty-two-year-old woman in good general health. Five foot six, one hundred and twenty-two pounds.

Good muscle tone. Slightly hoarse from airborne allergens.
Welcome to Houston.' She smiled briefly, looking up from her
report. Jurors chuckled.

'Any prominent injuries?' Veronica called them back to order.

The nurse looked back down at her report and shook her head.
'No significant bruises or contusions.'

'What was her emotional condition?'

Edward stood. 'Objection, Your Honor. This witness isn't a
psychologist.'

'So your objection is . . .?' Judge Roberts stared at Edward,
obviously doubting Edward's competence after his stunt of
releasing the victim into the courtroom.

'Lack of foundation for expertise in this subject area,' Edward
said flatly, staring back.

Veronica rose to respond, but the judge cut her off by saying,
'Sustained.' Veronica still came to her feet, so Judge Roberts felt
compelled to add, 'Your complainant can testify to her own
mental state.'

*You don't get to paint your portrait of distraught victim with
this witness*, Edward heard, and gave Veronica a brief glimpse
of satisfaction. She sat back down very stiffly.

'Did you examine Mrs Greene internally? I don't mean stick
a needle in her, but did you—'

Veronica seemed to be having trouble with a simple question
she should have anticipated asking. The meat of her examination,
as it were.

'I examined her vaginally and anally,' the nurse answered
coolly, giving the prosecutor a look.

Edward turned to see the Greenes. Diana's head was tucked
into her husband's shoulder. Odd she'd taken the opportunity to
come watch but now didn't seem to want to be here.

Veronica had gotten very stiff in her questioning. 'What did
your vaginal exam discover?'

Edward continued to watch the Greenes, turned almost
completely around in his chair. His client whispered, 'Are you
payin' attention, man?'

He absolutely was.

'There was no semen. But there were signs of recent sexual
activity.'

At the words 'recent sexual activity,' Sterling Greene glared furiously. But not at Donald. At his wife. He pushed her away and tried to catch Diana's eye, but she kept her head turned.

Edward continued to watch. It was a rare instance of more drama in the audience than from the witness stand. Sterling Greene obviously hadn't gotten the 'don't blame the victim' sensitivity training. It was also obviously the first time he'd heard this information, even though Edward had seen the nurse's report weeks ago, as had the prosecutor and so, presumably, the victim, i.e. Diana.

Diana raised her head and held her chin up, staring defiantly outward. But not at her husband.

'Can you define "recent"?' Veronica asked.

'A vaginal exam isn't that precise,' the nurse replied in a calm, professional voice. 'There was some slight swelling. If I had to pin it down—'

Donald whispered, 'The judge is looking at you, man.'

Edward turned to find that to be true. The nurse was about to speculate, which is forbidden from a witness if anyone objects. Edward looked back at the judge and didn't.

'I would say earlier that day, hours before my examination.'

Veronica looked at the defense table, obviously hoping to draw the jurors' attention toward Donald. Edward turned and looked back at the Greenes. Sterling was still glaring at his wife. Insensitive bastard.

'Did you ask the victim about that?'

This was hearsay, but the rules of evidence in Texas said medical professionals could testify to 'medical history' information patients they'd examined had given the professional, including the name of any accused sexual assaulter. Which was ridiculous, but also the law.

'Yes, she said there'd been no sexual activity that day. It must have been with her husband the night before.'

Now Edward's attention was riveted on the nurse, even though he was dying to turn and look at the Greenes. He shot a glance at the jury box and saw some of the jurors looking up that way. It was as if someone were standing on a ledge threatening to jump while a robbery was happening in the street below. Drama all over the place.

Veronica hesitated. She was looking down at her notes like they were a treasure map and she'd lost the thread. Bridge burned out. 'Um,' she said, and Edward let her hang, now dropping his casual stare on her.

'Were there any other significant findings from your medical history, Nurse Taylor?'

The nurse shrugged. 'You might have to define "significant" for me, but no, I can't think of anything. My findings of the victim's body comported with what she reported.'

Edward almost objected to that, because it sounded so favorable to the prosecution – *Yeah, I found evidence of everything she said* – when in fact she hadn't, but he thought the jury could get that on their own.

'Pass the witness,' Veronica said. A lawyer's easy out when she got lost. Edward glanced at the prosecutor but then immediately turned his stare on the nurse.

'What does that last observation mean, Ms Taylor? Your findings comported with what Mrs Greene told you?'

The nurse's eyes widened a bit. 'I just mean I didn't find anything to contradict what she reported.'

Edward let a bit of his exasperation show. 'What could possibly have done that? Did you examine her shoes to determine whether she'd walked as far as she said through the areas she said?'

She stared. 'I'm not a detective.'

'No, you're not, are you?'

As Veronica objected to the sidebar remark and was sustained, Edward wondered briefly why he was so pissed off by the nurse's simple statement. But he realized the answer quickly and thought how to turn it to his use as a lawyer.

'Let's turn your answer around and examine it, Ms Taylor. Did you find anything to *corroborate* Mrs Greene's story?'

'I don't . . .' The poor nurse floundered now. 'I don't know what I could have found to corroborate her story.'

Edward gave her a *See what I mean?* tilt of the head. But his tone was gentle for his next question. 'For example, Mrs Greene told police she had a bag over her head part of the time. Did you find any fibers in her hair?'

'No.'

'She said she had her hands bound for a while. Did you find any rope burns on her wrists?'

'No, sir, I wasn't told to look for that.' Now the nurse sounded very defensive.

'But you said you examined her from head to toe. Note anything about her wrists?'

'No,' she said flatly, staring at him the same way.

'Did you find anything in your comprehensive examination of Mrs Diana Greene to indicate she'd had anything other than a perfectly normal day?'

The nurse's eyes actually moved now, trying to think. 'I didn't have any baseline to compare to,' she said slowly. 'I don't know her normal physical condition. So I have to say no, I didn't.'

'Looking at your chart, I see something here marked on the right side of Mrs Greene's neck. Can you tell me what that was?'

'Just a mark of some kind. Reddish mark.'

Love bite? Edward wanted to ask, but he didn't see that helping his client. Instead he asked, 'Did it look to you permanent, a birthmark, or just as you said some sort of temporary abrasion.'

'More the latter, I'd say. It wasn't a birthmark.'

'Did you take a picture of it?'

The nurse shook her head. 'It didn't seem related to the crime.'

'We won't know now, will we?'

'Objection.' Veronica was glaring down at him. Edward didn't bother to look back. After the judge sustained her objection Edward just said, 'Pass the witness.' Looking at said witness as if she couldn't be of use to anyone.

He had calmed down now, but Edward had understood why this minor witness had so pissed him off. Witnesses tailored their testimony to aid the prosecution in damned near every criminal trial. So the testimony wasn't *I didn't find any evidence to support the State's theory.* It was, *I didn't find anything to contradict the victim's account.* He saw Veronica's eyes darting as she tried to figure out how to make use of this witness and came up with nothing.

She turned to the pages in front of her and said, 'Nurse, I'll call your attention to page two of your report, about halfway down. You did observe an anomaly on the victim's left forearm, didn't you?'

'Oh. Yes. I'd forgotten that. She did have bruising on that arm.'

'As if someone had grabbed her?'

'I'm not expert on that.' Edward had made the witness gun-shy about expressing an opinion. She glanced at him as she denied her expertise. 'But there was definite bruising, more than one.'

'As if made by fingers?'

'Object to leading,' Edward said.

'Sustained,' Judge Roberts said quickly. 'Don't answer that question.'

But the question itself had planted the idea. As Edward sat down he saw the jurors' attention returned to his client. Donald sat there with his hands folded in front of him, a study in worried innocence. As much as he could pull that off. *Look at him.*

They were done with the nurse, and she was glad to leave. Veronica looked down at a list on which she'd crossed off nearly every name, and rose and said, 'The State calls Diana Greene.'

Edward turned, like nearly everyone else in the large room, to look at the happy couple. Sterling Greene, doing his best impersonation of a loving husband, put out a hand to help his wife to her feet. She gave him a worried look from under lowered lashes and hurried out to the aisle.

On the stand she answered a heartfelt, 'Absolutely,' in response to the judge's asking whether she'd tell the truth, the whole truth, etc., and turned her tight gaze on the prosecutor.

'Are you nervous, Mrs Greene?'

Diana nodded her head tightly. 'Very.'

'First time to testify?'

'Yes.'

'Well, we're going to take it very slowly, Diana, and just go through your day that this trial is about. OK?'

Diana's head bobbed in small nods again.

As Edward watched the tightly wound woman on the stand, he appeared to relax, slumping in his chair, hands folded across his abdomen. This was the crux of the trial. If Edward called his client as a witness that would be a second act highlight, but the victim testifying was the beating heart of any trial.

'I was at the drugstore on West Gray, I think it's a CVS.'

'Why West Gray, Mrs Greene? Had you just gone out to a pharmacy?'

'No, I was meeting a friend at a restaurant there. It's called Board and Bread? We'd heard about it and wanted to try it. I was early so I stopped into the drugstore.'

'Did you buy anything?'

'Some nail polish. And I think a decongestant. I have the receipt, I put it in my purse to give to Sterling.'

'We'll get to that, thank you. What time was it when you came out of the CVS, ma'am?'

'Eleven thirty? I'm not sure. I know I had time to go home before lunch.'

Veronica's slow strategy was succeeding in calming her witness. But her next question tightened her down again. 'Did you drive away from the CVS, Mrs Greene?'

'No. I had parked around on the side, and as I turned the corner of the store I was a little distracted, looking down into my purse for my keys, when I practically bumped into that man there.'

'You're looking at the defendant, Donald Willis?'

'I didn't know his name, but yes.'

'Can you please describe him and something he's wearing.'

'He's the large, uh, African-American man wearing a dark suit and a' – she squinted slightly – 'pink tie?'

'Let the record reflect the witness has identified the defendant,' Veronica said from her feet. Words Edward had heard a hundred times or more. Words he had said himself. He'd never been part of a trial where those words weren't said.

'What happened after you almost bumped into Mr Willis?'

'I said excuse me and tried to go around him, but instead he grabbed my arm and pulled me toward my car.'

'Did he say anything?'

'Maybe. I don't think so. My heart started beating so fast immediately I don't think I could have heard anything else.'

'Did you scream, call for help, anything like that?'

'I was just so startled.' Diana sounded apologetic. 'I don't think I said anything, I just let myself get dragged to my car.'

Edward turned and looked into the audience again, wanting to see Sterling Greene's reactions to his wife's testimony. Instead his attention caught on Julia Lipscomb, the district attorney, sitting up very straight on the front row and staring at her sister. Edward tried to catch her eye, but Julia appeared laser-focused on Diana. Julia's hands were tangled together in front of her. Edward turned back to see her sister's hands enfolded in the same tangle.

'What happened then, ma'am?'

'He demanded my keys, I handed them over, and he almost threw me into the back seat, then he went around and started the car and drove away.'

'Didn't you have a moment there when you could have jumped out of the car?' Veronica, a good trial lawyer, had anticipated Edward's question.

'I guess someone with sharper reflexes could have done that, but I was just petrified. I didn't even scream, I don't think.'

'So Mr Willis drove. Do you know where he went?'

'I think it's called the Third Ward. A neighborhood over near the University of Houston.'

'You can say it,' Veronica said kindly. 'How did you start to describe the neighborhood?'

'Mostly black,' Diana said softly. She glanced over at the jury with its four African-American members apologetically. *It's OK*, Edward thought. *They know they're black.*

'Did you notice the name of the street? The address?'

Diana shook her head and said quietly, 'No.' Like many victims, she sounded apologetic. *I'm so sorry for all this trouble I caused.*

Edward leaned over and whispered to his client, 'Any of this accurate so far?'

'Yeah. The CVS.' Donald answered quickly. 'That's where I picked her up. And the Third Ward.'

Edward put his hand on his client's arm. 'Take it easy, big guy. Look worried.'

Donald turned to him, his face fierce. 'You think I have to fake that, man?' he whispered.

Edward patted his arm again and sat up straighter, watching the witness intently. She inclined her head as if she felt the heat of his stare.

Veronica asked to approach the witness and did so with her lithe stride. She handed Diana a photograph already in evidence. 'Was this the house, Mrs Greene?'

Diana actually studied the picture, then nodded. 'Yes, this is the one.'

'How did you get in? Did he have a key?'

'Key? I don't remember that. It seems to me we just walked in the back door.'

'Could you see what was happening?'

'No. He had . . . he had a cloth bag he put over my head almost as soon as we got in the car. He told me to keep quiet or he'd hurt me.'

'So you went into the house. Then what happened?'

'Well, we went inside. I could feel that. Then he tied my wrists behind me and pushed me down onto a wooden chair. Told me again to keep quiet.'

'Did you?'

'No. I was babbling. Telling him he could keep my car, telling him I'd get him money, telling him anything I could think of to let me go.'

'How did Mr Willis respond?'

'He sort of slapped me, almost gently, through the bag, and he told me again to keep quiet. Just kind of showing me what he could do. After that I did shut up.'

'Could you hear?'

'Oh yes. He didn't seem to try to keep anything from me. He got my cell phone out of my purse and called my husband. He told him he had only a few hours to get a lot of money to the house where we were. Then he said Sterling had to leave for half an hour, but then he could come back and get me if he came alone. He had me say hello to Sterling to prove he had me.'

'Did your husband respond?'

'He called my name and I think he asked if I was all right, but Mr . . . Mr Willis snatched the phone away right away.'

'Then what?'

'Then we waited. For hours. I was so uncomfortable. And terrified. I asked if he could at least take the bag off my head so I could breathe and he said no. I heard Mr Willis go into another room and call someone else, an associate, it sounded like. He must have used his own phone, not mine, because I didn't have a record of the call afterwards.'

She'd headed off that line of inquiry, very smart. Edward was sitting forward now, pen in hand, still watching Diana closely. She couldn't help shooting a glance at him.

'Mrs Greene, did he – your abductor – do anything to you? Touch you?'

Diana hesitated. 'He . . . Sometimes I'd feel him close to me, just standing there, and a couple of times he touched my shoulder. Just letting me know he had me, I think. I flinched so hard. But he never . . . he never offered me violence, if that's what you're asking.'

'I'm just asking you to tell us what happened, Diana. Don't worry. So what finally happened?'

'After several hours he – Mr Willis – got a call and from what I could hear it sounded like Sterling. Mr Willis gave him the address and told him where to come, warned him he'd better come alone. Then he spoke to me for a minute. He said I'd be all right until my husband came. He was leaving, on his way out, I heard his voice receding toward the back door. Then he said – he cursed – and ran back past me again. Police had gotten there in less than a minute after he gave Sterling the address. They must have been close by already. Mr Willis clearly hadn't anticipated that.'

Edward shot a quick glance at Donald, whose brows were drawn down. He felt Edward's glance and turned to him and whispered, 'I ain't that bad a kidnapper, man. I ain't that stupid.'

Veronica's questioning continued, very gentle now. 'Were you in the chair the whole time, ma'am?'

'He let me walk around a little. And after he got the phone call I told him I needed to go to the bathroom. He said all right, and I said I couldn't do that with my hands tied. He almost balked, but then untied me. I could hear him standing outside the bathroom door while I was in there, but he did let me close the door. I took the bag off my head and I could breathe freely for the first time in a long time.'

'Was there a window in the bathroom?'

'Yes, and I tried to open it but it was painted shut or nailed shut, I couldn't tell. I thought about breaking it but there was no good way for me to climb over the broken glass, and I was sure he'd be in the bathroom faster than I could get out if he heard the glass break. So I just went about my business and walked back out.'

'With the bag back over your head?'

Diana shook her head. 'No. I just walked out. I wanted to try to connect with him on a human level. So I walked out. I kept my head turned so he could tell I wasn't trying to memorize his features, but once I did lift my head and look right into his eyes. I begged him to let me go. His money was on the way, he'd accomplished what he wanted. I said I'd just walk out of the neighborhood, he could keep my car as well as whatever money Sterling had for him.'

'How did he respond?'

'He let me talk but he was shaking his head the whole time. I started getting more frantic. I was crying. I put my hand on his arm. I told him I'd do anything if he'd let me go. But he just said no.'

Veronica was sitting, watching her star witness closely, not taking notes. Edward was by this time. Writing quite a bit. That always made witnesses nervous, to think the lawyer on the other side had found something notable in her testimony, and this time was no exception. Diana's eyes were darting at him regularly. But that also looked as if she was casting fearful glances at his client.

'But you did get away, right, Mrs Greene?'

'At the end, yes. As I said, the police arrived almost immediately after Mr Willis's last call to Sterling.'

'Inside the house, did you and Mr Willis become aware of that?'

'At some point we did. Mr Willis went to the window and looked out and cursed. Then he dragged me to the back door and looked out and saw police there too.'

'Were you tied up again at that point?'

'No. He left me untied after I came out of the bathroom. He at least did that.'

'And it sounds like you didn't have the bag over your head either?'

'No. He didn't make me put that hateful thing back on. I guess he thought – well, I don't know what he thought. I thought we were at the end and there wasn't any point in keeping me tied up or blindfolded.'

'But then he did need you as a hostage once police were there, right?'

'Objection, leading,' Edward said from his feet, to which he'd risen automatically. He was surprised to realize this was his first objection during the primary witness's testimony. 'It also calls for speculation, Your Honor.'

'Sustained, both objections. Don't answer that question, ma'am.'

Diana acknowledged the instruction with a penitent nod, as if she'd done something wrong.

Veronica raised her chin. Elegant jaw and neckline. 'How did you get out of the house, Mrs Greene?'

'There was a person – someone from the police – talking to Mr Willis from outside, just constantly negotiating with him to come out or let me out. He was hanging onto me most of the time, dragging me around the house. At one point I fell down and he didn't bother to pick me up. He was at the window looking out. I saw my chance and I just ran past him and yanked the front door open and ran out. I screamed just before I went out because I thought I felt his hand on my shoulder, but I managed to pull free and run. Thank God the police were professional enough not to shoot me.'

Edward was drawing a diagram blindly, his eyes still on the witness. She obviously felt that stare too, like a nightlight barely noticeable until the other lights are gone, when it pierces the eye. Diana kept her stare on the prosecutor, as if that connection were a lifeline.

Veronica, though, was looking down at her notes. She was at the end of her tale and clearly wondering what she'd forgotten. Edward cleared his throat.

'Did you and your husband ever recover the money he paid for your release, ma'am?'

'Objection, hearsay. She had nothing to do with that transaction, if any.'

Judge Roberts hesitated. Edward added, 'It also calls for speculation, because she doesn't know of her own knowledge whether any ransom was actually paid.'

That satisfied the judge. 'Sustained.'

Veronica didn't want to end on that loss. 'How long did you spend with the defendant all told, Mrs Greene?'

'Hours.' Diana shot a glance at Donald. 'It felt like days.'

'And how did you feel during that time? Emotionally.'

Edward found himself on his feet again. 'Objection, Your Honor, relevance.' As the judge hesitated again, drawing Edward's curious stare, Edward added, 'How she felt isn't an element of the offense, Judge.'

'I'll let her answer this one question.'

Veronica nodded to the witness and Diana immediately said, 'Terrified. The whole time. I never calmed down.'

Edward was still standing, looking at the judge, who wouldn't look back. Edward slowly sat.

'I'll pass the witness,' Veronica said.

'How do you think my client feels now?' Edward asked immediately. As Diana stared at him and Veronica was rising to object, he added, 'Never mind. Let's get to the substance of your testimony. Do you claim my client had a gun?'

'No. I never saw one.'

'Yet you never had an opportunity to get away?'

'Not that I felt I could take. He didn't need a gun to control me.' Diana pointed her chin at Donald. *Look at him.* Yes, damn it. Edward didn't even have to hear the words any more to hear everyone thinking them.

'In the car ride he hadn't tied your hands yet, had he?'

'No. I did have the bag over my head.'

'Yet you said he drove you from West Gray to the Third Ward? You knew where you were going?'

Diana hesitated, but kept her eyes on him. 'I knew where we started, and which way we set out. I could feel the turns. And you can tell whether you're riding on the city streets or the freeway. I could tell roughly where we were going.'

'Let's talk about the streets. Did he have to stop for red lights?'

'Once or twice.'

'While you were still in the West Gray area there were stop signs, weren't there?'

'Yes.' Diana saw where he was going. She swallowed.

'You had your chances to jump out of the car, didn't you?'

'Theoretically, I suppose.'

'When you exited the freeway—'

'But that takes a careful judgment and good reflexes and I just—'

'Objection, non-responsive, Your Honor. I hadn't asked a question.'

'Sustained.'

'Request the jury be instructed to disregard that response.'

'Yes, ladies and gentlemen, you are instructed not to consider that statement.'

Sure they wouldn't. Edward sat, a little wearily, and regarded the witness. Now battle had been declared. He wasn't going to be able to sneak up on Diana Greene. Nor certainly to befriend her.

He could feel her sister's stare on the back of his neck. For a moment Edward felt a sense of dislocation. It was so strange to be sitting here, from prison inmate to lawyer questioning the district attorney's sister, in a couple of years. His life track had not led here.

But on the other hand, yes it had. 'You identified that photo of the house in the Third Ward, correct, Mrs Greene?'

'Yes. I'll never forget it.'

'But in fact according to your account you never saw it, did you? Didn't you say you already had the bag over your head when you arrived there?'

She was ready for that one. 'I saw it once I was out. I was looking back at it when Mr . . . your client came out. And I saw some of the interior after I took the bag off my head.'

'Yes, after my client let you go to the bathroom, according to you. Which brings up a point. You spent hours there. Didn't *he* ever go to the bathroom?'

'I suppose. But he didn't announce it. I couldn't tell—'

'I didn't ask a question, ma'am. This isn't open mic night. You don't get to spin a narrative. You just—'

Veronica was rising hastily to her feet, but before she could get there Judge Roberts said, 'Counsel.' Very sternly.

Edward cut off his instruction, wondering why he was suddenly so furious at this mousy little victim. 'All right. Diana. You said you offered my client anything he wanted if he'd let you go. Can you be more specific?'

She suddenly blushed. 'Not . . . not anything personal. Of course I told him he could keep everything I had on me. My purse, my jewelry. The car. I even told him I'd try to get him more money than whatever Sterling had brought.'

'And what was his response?'

'Mostly he didn't answer at all. A couple of times he told me to stop talking.'

Edward stood. 'Your Honor, may we approach the bench?'

The request seemed to take Judge Roberts by surprise, but he motioned the lawyers forward. Veronica came buttoning her jacket. She stood close beside Edward looking at him curiously. Edward ignored her, leaning close to the judge and whispering, 'Your Honor, may we have the jury removed for a few minutes? I need to arrange for a demonstration.'

'Demonstration of what?' Veronica said in a normal tone of voice.

'Demonstration I will explain outside the jury's presence,' Edward said to the judge.

The judge turned to the jury and said, 'We'll take a ten-minute break. Bailiff, escort the jury.'

The bailiff did so. Edward watched them all out the door behind the judge's bench, always curious what these fascinating creatures were thinking. They gave no clues, not looking back, just shuffling to make sure they didn't step on the back of the feet of the jurors in front of them. Looking rather like prisoners on a chain, he now saw.

'Well, Mr Hall?'

'May the witness be excused for a moment, Your Honor?'

Judge Roberts remained impassive. 'Yes, please, Mrs Greene. To the hallway, if you don't mind?'

Diana scrambled down, quickly obeying. Veronica turned to Edward and said, 'Set nicely enough decorated for you yet?'

He ignored her. 'Your Honor, I want to briefly re-enact the witness's supposed escape as she described it.'

'Because . . .?'

'I'd like the jury to see how unlikely it is.' As the judge continued to hesitate, Edward turned to his client. 'Donald, stand up, please.'

That took a moment, for Donald to rise to his full height. Edward turned back to the judge. Now it was his turn to say a silent *Look at him.* What mousy little society matron, as Diana had chosen to portray herself, could dodge around that monument?

'This is the heart of my defense, Your Honor. If I'm not allowed to portray it my client will be deprived—'

'Fine.'

As both the judge and Veronica started to turn away from him, Edward said, 'There's one other thing, Your Honor. Needless to say, I don't want my client to be the one to act out her little scenario. That would be extremely prejudicial. I was hoping the court could stand in for him.'

Judge Roberts stared. 'You want *me* to play the defendant?'

'Judge, looking around the court, you're the only one of similar enough appearance to my client to make the demonstration realistic. I'm asking because you're the only person here who's . . .'

'Black and handy?'

Edward shook his head strongly, then said, 'Yes, sir.'

Judge Roberts' bailiff, a short, pudgy white guy who wouldn't do at all, had returned by this time. 'Bailiff?' the judge said.

Was Edward about to be arrested again? Always a possibility when he was in a courtroom.

Without taking his eyes off Edward, the judge said, 'Bailiff, please go down the hall to the 235th and exchange places with Bailiff Johnson for the afternoon. With his judge's permission, of course.'

The bailiff hurried to obey. The judge sat leaning forward on his forearms, continuing to stare. Edward busied himself with papers at his table.

Jurors returned to find Diana Greene back on the witness stand and a new face at the bailiff's desk. Bailiff Johnson would do nicely. He was maybe an inch shorter than Donald, but with the same solid build. He was wearing a short-sleeved uniform that showed his well-muscled forearms. His eyes moved continually, taking in everything.

'With the court's permission, Your Honor.' The judge simply nodded. 'Mrs Greene, if you could step down here, please?'

Edward approached her in case she needed assistance, but didn't touch her. That close, he had flashbacks to the glimpses he'd had of Diana in her home, moaning at the desk and naked in bed. He looked out into the audience. Sterling Greene was staring a hole into Edward.

'Look at this space between the counsel tables, please, ma'am. Is that about the width of the doorway you escaped through?'

Diana studied the space, beginning to see what was coming. 'A little narrower.'

Edward went to the far end of the table and pulled. Donald started to help and Edward shook his head at him. He didn't want Donald any closer to the supposed victim than he already was. He moved the table a few inches and Diana said, 'That's good.'

Edward strongly doubted that little house in the Third Ward had that wide a front door, but maybe the jury would see Diana was trying to cheat on the demonstration.

'Bailiff?' The other actor entered the scene.

'Now how far away from the door was your chair, ma'am?'

'It was about back here. But I wasn't in the chair when—'

'We'll get to that.' Edward placed his own chair in the space, about twenty feet behind the 'door.'

'Now, how far is the front window you said Donald was looking through when you made your move to get away?' Edward stood right next to the space between the tables, where he remembered the front window to be.

'About three feet farther to the side.'

Edward just stared at her with his hands folded. 'Ma'am, I've been in that house and the jurors have seen pictures. Wouldn't you—?'

Veronica, who'd sat fuming during this whole set-up, finally found a reason to jump to her feet. 'Object to counsel testifying, Your Honor. Also to arguing with the witness.'

'Move on, counsel,' the judge said to Edward.

'Yes, sir.' But he continued to stand there.

'You may be right,' Diana said. 'Maybe a foot closer.'

Edward waved Bailiff Johnson into that space. The sturdy bailiff took his place and looked out at the audience, unperturbed by their stares.

'Now, Mrs Greene, you said Donald was distracted, looking out the window shades when you darted out the door?'

'Yes, sir.'

'So about here where I've positioned the bailiff?'

'A little more to the left.'

'You're saying my client was standing in the middle of the window, the most vulnerable spot in the room, with a SWAT team outside?'

Veronica said, 'Argumentative again, Your Honor.'

'Sustained.'

'About there,' Diana said. Her tone was growing a tiny bit defiant, a bit of steel spine showing through her timid routine.

'All right, let's show how you escaped. Please remember there's a door there you have to open and that you said you screamed just before you jumped outside.'

'Your Honor?' Diana said, looking up at him.

'Please, ma'am.'

'And Deputy Johnson, you of course realize your role is to prevent her from getting through that space.'

'Understood, sir.'

'I was only a few feet from the door,' Diana said.

Edward waved a hand. 'Pick your spot.'

She came close, closer than any reasonable person could think a professional kidnapper would have let her get to escape. Edward let her get away with it. 'Any time you choose,' he said.

Diana took a deep breath and darted forward with surprising speed, pausing to yank open an imaginary door, giving a little shriek as she did so.

Deputy Johnson was gripping her arm tightly. No part of Diana crossed the imaginary threshold.

He gave her a couple of more tries. She didn't get close to getting through that space. After the third attempt Diana stood a little breathlessly, staring balefully at the bailiff. 'He knows what I'm about to try to do.'

'So would my client have known, Mrs Greene. Especially with the scream.'

'Objection, Your Honor!' Veronica said, obviously mad at herself for letting Edward get the whole answer out. 'Argumentative again and counsel is testifying.'

'Her answer was non-responsive, Your Honor,' Edward said calmly. 'There was no question before the witness.'

'I'll instruct the jury to disregard that entire exchange. None of it is relevant to your decision. Are we done, counsel?'

'Yes, sir.'

The courtroom resumed its normal configurations. Edward stared at Diana, back on the witness stand. Now she was glaring at him as well as her husband. Caught in the crossfire of stares. 'Had you ever seen my client before that day, ma'am?'

'Not that I recall.'

'Are you positive? Will you look closely at him, please?'

Edward hadn't prepared Donald for this, it had just come to him, but he had confidence in his client's usually mild demeanor. Donald stared back at his accuser with damp eyes and a mournful downturn to his mouth. Diana stared at him for a few seconds. That was all Edward wanted, for her to look closely at the man she was accusing, possibly see him as a human being for the first time.

'I don't remember ever seeing him before,' Diana said quietly.

Edward watched her for a moment. 'Pass the witness.'

TWENTY-THREE

As Veronica began her re-direct examination, something nagged at Edward. Something he'd forgotten, something off about the trial. It was somehow uneven. He turned and glanced back at the audience. Sterling's attention still seemed entirely focused on Edward, but a few rows behind him Edward saw Linda had come in. She smiled at him, a nice touch of home in this hostile battlefield.

Veronica was re-treading the same ground, tightening down how long Diana had spent in the house, the state of her emotions. 'How long did you have to keep the bag over your head?'

'At least three hours.'

Beside Edward, Donald shook his head. Edward put a calming hand on his arm.

After a couple more sympathy-building questions, Veronica seemed to be losing her place. 'Pass the witness,' she said, looking down at her notes.

'No more questions,' Edward said immediately.

Veronica showed him big eyes. Edward had seen quite clearly that Veronica thought she had more material for the witness in her notes; she'd just lost her place for a moment. Now she wouldn't have the chance to ask them. Veronica was looking at him as if he'd cheated. When the victim testifies, both sides are supposed to pass her back and forth multiple times, squeezing whatever they could out of her, like two dogs competing over a tennis ball until it's grown dirty and ragged.

Edward sat calmly. Veronica looked back to her notes. 'Counsel?' said Judge Roberts.

Veronica ran her finger down a checklist, then rose slowly. 'Your Honor, the State rests.'

That feeling again. Edward felt the seesaw tilt toward him, and its balance was somehow canted. There was something wrong about this trial.

Judge Roberts glanced at the clock on the far wall, then at the jurors. 'It's close enough to the end of the day to stop here. Defense, if you wish to present a case – strictly your choice – you will begin at nine o'clock tomorrow morning.'

The judge stood, the bailiff instructed everyone else to do like-wise, and they began the uneven straggle out of the courtroom. Edward felt a disturbance in the air that was Diana fleeing past him, toward the sanctuary of her husband, who stood waiting. Edward saw Julia still in her place on the front row, watching him. She'd been almost friendly when trying to talk him into taking this assignment, but that sentiment seemed used up. He tried to read her expression, and she was giving nothing back. Just evaluating him. Then she turned and hurried up the aisle to be with her sister.

Rows above them, Linda stood in her place smiling even harder at him. Now Edward was free to smile back.

Veronica was glaring at him just like Julia and the Greenes. So little love in this room. 'I'd heard about you and your "tactics." But I didn't think in a trial as important to you as this one you'd—'

'Excuse me, Veronica, I need to talk to my client.'

He led Donald up the aisle, then strode faster. Linda came out to meet him, grabbed him tightly. They kissed there in the court-room, oblivious to anyone watching.

Donald came level with them. 'Get a room, you two.'

Edward broke off the kiss but kept smiling back at Linda. 'Yes,' he said. 'We all will.'

Donald stared at him. 'Uh . . .'

*   *   *

In Edward's office in the Heights they all sat in the living room area. Edward had gotten them drinks. 'Now,' he said.

'Yes,' Linda agreed, and they both turned to look at Donald. 'What?'

'The big question, Donald. Are you going to testify?'

It was always the biggest decision for the defense in any criminal trial: whether to subject the defendant to the dangers of testifying or just have him sit quietly and rely on the presumption of innocence.

'You know how a trial works, Donald. If you don't testify the judge will instruct the jury not to hold that against you and not to presume anything from it.'

'And they always will,' Linda said. At Edward's look she spread her hands. 'I've learned that much from a few months in the system.'

Donald patted her knee comfortingly. 'We all know it, Miss. You didn't give anything away.'

The first time Edward had represented Donald he had testified very well, genuinely remorseful for his impulsive grabbing of a celebrity's son, then carefully bringing him back. It had netted him a mere eight years in prison instead of the many more he could have gotten.

But this time was different.

'I know you can do it, Donald. But this is completely unlike the last time.' The other two listened to Edward. 'Last time it wasn't something planned, it was a momentary bad decision. If you testify now the prosecution will get to bring up that other case.'

'I know.'

'And they'll use it to make you look like a career criminal and frankly a danger. If they don't convict you and put you away for a long time somebody could get killed the next time.'

Because when a defendant takes the witness stand he lays himself open. He can be 'impeached' by the prosecution with almost any past conviction. Certainly in a kidnapping trial the prosecution would be allowed to prove a past conviction for the same offense.

'Maybe I should just sit this one out,' the big man said. 'They haven't really proved anything.'

'Except every detail of the crime,' Edward said.

Donald was taken aback. 'But you made them look like such liars, man. I mean, the Greenes, there's so many holes in their story.'

Except for the crucial, intimate elements of the crime, Edward thought. Some of Diana's story might have seemed implausible, but she had come off as a frightened victim. He looked to Linda.

'He has to testify,' she said immediately. The other two turned to her, showing raised eyebrows at the forcefulness of her opinion. Linda sat forward, elbows on knees. 'He has to. The rest of your defense won't work otherwise. Donald's the only one who can provide some of the testimony that supports that.'

'What defense?' Donald asked.

'That the Greenes set you up for this. That only works if you were a good target to be set up. Someone who'd done this before and was well-known for it.'

Linda had as usual gone to the heart of the matter. Edward had nothing to say.

Donald looked at him, saw his lawyer agreed, and sighed. 'Can I sleep on it?'

'Sure,' Edward said, standing. 'And while you're waiting make sure some of those friends of yours are available to testify if necessary.' He walked his client to the door and outside. When he came back a couple of minutes later Linda was waiting eagerly.

'Were you watching the loving Mr and Mrs Greene?' she said, face alight. 'I was. I had a great seat for the whole show. We have to go back into their house tonight. There's going to be a major explosion. We can tiptoe in while they're—'

'I've created a monster.'

Linda grabbed him. 'You didn't create me. You brought me alive.'

'Isn't that what the creature said to Dr Frankenstein?'

'You are so going to pay for that. I'm going to bite you when and where you least expect it.'

'I'll look forward to that.'

'Yeah, you do.'

The next morning Linda woke, rolled over groggily, and draped herself over him. Then she opened her eyes to see he was staring into the dimness again. 'What?'

'What if he *is* a career criminal, Linda? A serial kidnapper. If

I get him off this time, isn't there a real possibility someone could get killed the next time?'

'Oh, baby.' She chuckled against his throat. 'The chance of you getting him off is so remote I wouldn't worry about it.'

'Thanks. You're always such a comfort.'

'You're completely welcome.' She kissed him, long and deep.

But she had said the perfect thing. Over breakfast at the small kitchen table he said, 'He probably is guilty, right? I mean, the vast majority of indicted people are.'

'True,' Linda said slowly. Her blue eyes were especially lively this morning. Maybe it was the light. 'But those people . . .'

She'd developed such an antipathy toward the Greenes she was not the most reliable person to evaluate them. 'I love you,' Edward said suddenly. She just smiled back.

Then, just as Linda was stepping into the shower and Edward was laying out his clothes for the day, he suddenly stood straight up. 'Oh, shit,' he said.

Moments later he stepped into the shower with Linda. 'Don't we both need to go to work?' she said, smiling as the water soaked the length of their naked bodies and she stepped close to him.

'Sorry.' Edward's eyes were hard and darting. 'I just realized I need to get to the courthouse early.'

She looked a question, but he was lathering and rinsing and stepping back out in less than a minute.

'What's wrong?' she asked, water pouring down her.

'I just realized what's wrong with this trial.'

Think like a prosecutor, he admonished himself as he hurried to dress.

TWENTY-FOUR

The first question Veronica asked Edward's first witness when he passed the witness to her was, 'Tell us about your most recent conviction, Ms Bonham.'

It seemed a mean-spirited way of asking the question, but Edward couldn't think of an objection.

His witness, Luanne Bonham, folded her arms. In a flattened voice she said, 'Theft, fifteen hundred to twenty thousand. Two years ago. Two years' probation, served out.'

Luanne was Donald's friend who'd been in his car when he'd met with Sterling Greene at the construction site. She looked like a tree branch, thin, hard, brown from sun. Her mother had given her a sweet, old-fashioned name before she'd known how her baby would turn out. Maybe thirty-five years old, maybe fifteen years more than that. The odd thing about some people who'd done prison time was they seemed to shed those years once they got out, starting back at Go.

Luanne had done fine under Edward's direct examination, stating what she'd seen very succinctly, elaborating only when asked. She even described Sterling's clothing and a ring around his neck where the sun had touched everything above and a thin ring of white showed.

'What kind of scheme did you have going on behind that theft conviction?' Veronica asked.

Edward stood. His witness knew enough about courtroom ways to keep her mouth shut until he was done. 'Objection. This very experienced prosecutor knows the rules, Your Honor.'

This particular rule was Veronica could impeach the witness with the fact of a former felony conviction but couldn't inquire into the details of the crime. Judge Roberts calmly sustained the objection. Edward remained on his feet.

'What are you doing, Mr Hall?'

'Waiting for her next objectionable question, Judge. Just saving myself exercise.'

'Take your seat, Mr Hall.'

Edward did so. Veronica said, 'You know about the defendant's criminal history too, don't you, Ms Bonham?'

Edward gave the judge a look, holding up both hands. *See?* 'Sustained,' the judge responded to the unspoken objection.

But Edward came to his feet anyway. 'I ask the jury be instructed to disregard that completely improper question.'

The judge actually turned to the jurors. 'Yes. Please put that question out of your minds. It has no foundation in the evidence before you.'

'And now I need to ask for a mistrial. May we approach?'

This was the third step in 'preserving error' for appeal, usually a matter of form, but close in front of the judge, Edward said, 'Sincerely, Judge. She's just robbed my client of the presumption of innocence. I'm genuinely asking for a mistrial.'

'I was trying to show—' Veronica began, and the judge shut her up with a glance.

'I'm going to deny that, but I'll grant the next one, Ms Salazar. Be careful.'

They resumed their seats. Veronica paused. Edward saw her picking through her mental list of questions, trying to find one that wouldn't bring the trial to a halt. 'Do you know why Mr Willis was talking to Mr Greene?'

'Donald had left the car windows down so I wouldn't suffocate. He was asking Mr Greene for a job.'

'Were you there because you and Mr Willis were planning to run some kind of scam on Sterling Greene?'

'No,' Luanne said, not taking offense. 'We're lunch buddies. We were going to lunch after that.'

Edward almost laughed. Lunch buddies. Picturing these two together looked like a crime about to happen.

Luanne did fine. He thought she sounded believable, whatever her background. She couldn't help who she was. Edward asked only one more question when she was passed back to him. 'How much time did Donald and Sterling Greene spend talking?'

'A good ten minutes. He seemed interested in Donald even though he didn't offer him a job. Mr Greene asked—'

'Object to hearsay,' Veronica said, and that ended Luanne's testimony.

Next Edward called the seventy-three-year-old African-American man who lived across the street from the supposed crime scene.

'How long had you lived there, Mr Ellington?'

'That house fifteen years. Inherited it from my mother. The Third Ward, my whole life, but for two years in the Army.'

'So you're very familiar with the neighborhood.'

'Like my own hands.' John Ellington folded those hands and sat easy in the witness stand, as if he was on his porch again.

'Why were you outside that day, sir?'

'It was a nice day, pleasant afternoon. I was just watchin' out for things. Had a book, but sometimes I'd just look around.

There's usually something going on in the street. I like to keep an eye on things.'

'What did you see unusual that afternoon?'

'Car coming down the street. Nice car, kind you don't see around there. BMW. It was comin' pretty slow down the street, as if—'

'Object to speculation,' Veronica said quickly.

Judge Roberts hesitated. Edward stared at him, willing him to overrule the objection. *As if the driver didn't know where he was going* was going to be the end of that sentence, and Edward needed it. As if Donald didn't know where he was going and was taking directions from his passenger, instead of going quickly to the stash house he had prepared.

'Sustained,' the judge said.

Damn it. 'What did the car do, Mr Ellington?'

'Swung into the driveway. Seemed like it almost drove past it, but then made a big turn into the driveway.'

'Did that driveway lead to a garage, sir?'

'Nah. Kind of a big carport sort of shed back behind the house, but the car stopped in front.'

'What happened then?'

'Two people got out. Fella sittin' next to you out of the driver's door, and that white lady back there out of the passenger side.'

'Are you referring to Mrs Greene?' Edward turned and looked into the audience, where Diana and Sterling Greene were sitting side by side holding hands. Edward looked higher and saw David Galindo, the prosecutor who'd been there when Edward got appointed on this case. David stood leaning back on the far wall of the courtroom. He returned Edward's look with a blank expression.

'Yes, sir. That lady.'

'What was she wearing?'

'Nice dress. Spring-like. Kind of floaty.'

'Anything else?'

'Not that I recall. Had a purse, I think.'

'Did she have a bag over her head?' Edward sounded ironic, like delivering the set-up for a punch line.

'Nah. If she had, how would I recognize her now?'

Good point. Except, of course, half of Houston recognized Diana Greene now, from news footage and the newspaper.

'Besides, if I'd seen a black man pulling a white woman with a bag over her head out the car I'd've called police. Believe it or not,' he added to the jurors.

'Did you ever see them come out again?'

'Not until the SWAT team came.'

'How long was that after they'd arrived?'

'Maybe an hour. Hour fifteen tops.'

Which completely contradicted Diana's claim she'd been held for hours in that house. But that depended on the jury believing Edward's witness. He glanced at that jury. There were four African-Americans on it, scattered through the mostly white assemblage. He couldn't read any of the jurors' expressions.

'Pass the witness.'

Veronica was sitting up very straight. Once she'd rested her case she'd gone on high alert to spot any flaws in Edward's and pounce on them. 'Mr Ellington, do you have any felony convictions?'

'No, ma'am. Damned lucky that, 'cause I lived through Houston in the Sixties and Seventies.'

There were chuckles throughout the courtroom. There had been a period of time when many Houston police thought dark skin equaled probable cause to arrest.

'You said you'd lived in that house for fifteen years. So are you friends with the defendant?'

'No, ma'am. I'd seen him in the neighborhood, but we hadn't ever spoken before. Still haven't, for that matter.'

'Really.' She just stared at him, still with a friendly expression but also projecting her disbelief. 'This crime happened a few months ago, sir. Have you been following its progress toward trial? In the media?'

Mr Ellington maintained his calm. He, like Edward, saw exactly where she was going. But he just gave her a slight smile in return for her own. 'Sure. Happened across the street from me, of course I'm interested.'

'Do you have an interest in the outcome of this trial?'

'Sure,' he repeated. 'Since I saw it go down I don't want to see him convicted.'

Veronica smiled and tilted her head. 'But whatever you saw, Mr Ellington, you don't know what happened before that or inside that house, do you?'

He opened his mouth to answer quickly, then closed it. Finally he said, 'No, ma'am, I don't.'

Which ended and undercut his usefulness as a witness. When she passed Mr Ellington back to Edward he couldn't think of another question either.

His next witness was a woman from a couple of houses down the block, also African-American, also above the median American age. Young people in that neighborhood moved out or went to prison.

'Mrs Hendricks, were you ever outside that afternoon?'

'Of course. We don't sit in our houses all the time there. Plus I had a neighbor across the street who was doing poorly and I went out about three or four to take her a pot of soup.'

'How nice. Did you notice the house where police came later?'

'I noticed the car. We don't get cars like that very often in the ward. Saw it sittin' in the driveway glowin' in the sun.'

Nice. 'Did you see anything else?'

'When I was comin' back across the street I saw the young man sittin' next to you come out to the car to fetch something.'

'Are you sure it was Donald here?'

'Course. When he saw me he waved.'

'Did you know him?'

'Never seen him before.'

'How long have you lived there, ma'am?'

'Years. Since I moved here from N'Awlins after Katrina.'

When he passed the nice lady to the prosecutor Veronica only established Mrs Hendricks had no idea what had been going on in the house while Donald had supposedly been outside, whether Diana Greene was tied to a chair, terrified with a bag over her head so she didn't even know her kidnapper had stepped outside briefly. In a few seconds destroying much of the value of her testimony. Possibly all of it.

When Mrs Hendricks was excused to totter up the aisle Edward stood and said, 'Now the defense has other witnesses to present, Your Honor, but in anticipation of objections from the prosecution I would like to confer with the court in chambers.'

'Why?' Judge Roberts frowned, with Veronica echoing him.

'So the court will be aware of where the defense is going and will understand the nature of the witnesses' testimony.'

Long hesitation. This was almost unheard of. But Edward could see the judge doing the calculation: *what could it hurt?* There was never a danger of reversal on appeal in giving the defense what it wanted.

'Just for the record, I object,' Veronica said. 'The defense isn't entitled to this. There's no procedure for—'

That seemed to tip Judge Roberts over the line. 'We will take a ten-minute break,' he said to the jury, all courtesy. 'Bailiff.'

All stood for the jurors to shuffle out, two or three of them looking back curiously. In trials some jurors always seemed to realize the show got better offstage, when they couldn't see it.

Veronica trailed him back into the hallway behind the judge's bench, both of them following Judge Roberts' broad back in the black robe. She followed him all the way into the court offices. Edward turned and said, 'This is the part where you don't get to come in, Veronica.'

Her eyes were very close to his, but there seemed no danger of a kiss. 'This is bullshit.'

'You won't know that yet.' He waved her away.

Judge Roberts was standing outside the door to his chamber, waiting. Edward hurried down the short corridor, glancing into the court reporter's office, the scene of the crime that had sent him to prison. The judge saw that glance but said nothing, and his expression didn't change.

In the judge's office there used to be a black leather sofa against the right-hand wall, scene of an offshoot of that infamous night. No one except Edward and one other person knew about that aspect of the crime, his unsuspected partner in that caper. He hadn't told anyone about that, not even Linda. Edward and Linda hadn't been a couple at the time, they'd barely been acquaintances. Besides, it wasn't his secret to tell.

No one knew that part. Nonetheless, the couch was gone, replaced by a treadmill.

The judge sat behind his desk and folded his hands. Edward closed the door.

TWENTY-FIVE

When he emerged he had an unexpected ally in the trial. Judge Pershing Roberts. Who knew why? Edward certainly didn't. Edward had laid out an extremely unorthodox defense to the least unorthodox judge in the building. To defend against a case by essentially prosecuting a different one. Neither of them had ever heard of it being done.

Maybe the African-American judge didn't like the scenario Edward had laid out. Or maybe he just wanted to see it as theater. Trials were generally pretty boring affairs, and Judge Roberts had been watching them for a long time from behind a bench that acted as a screen, blocking him from the fun parts.

At any rate, he'd said yes.

They took a lunch break. Edward sought out Linda, saw her taking down a hearing, and just gave her a thumbs up. Her smile made everyone in her own trial pause and look at him. Edward shrugged and hurried out.

He called as his next witness Anali Haverty, the gallery owner who didn't get involved in her clients' personal lives, but who'd let Tony Alberico use her backyard studio. She wasn't rocking Paris today. Ms Haverty wore a straight green skirt and a white blouse with only a bit of scalloping at the collar in the way of style. She had her hair pulled back and when she sat in the witness chair she leaned slightly forward with a very straight back, first acknowledging the judge then looking straight at Edward, all business.

Edward had her describe her gallery, which she did as a mini-commercial, using the phrase 'high-end' as well as 'other more casual pieces.'

'What is your relationship with the art world in Houston, ma'am?'

'I am the facilitator, one might say, between artists and patrons. And other appreciators of art.'

Veronica Salazar stood and said harshly, 'Your Honor?'

The judge looked at her blandly. 'You have a question, Ms Salazar?'

'Yes. The question would be what the hell?' As Judge Roberts opened his mouth she said, 'That is, what is the relevance of this testimony? Objection.'

'The relevance has been explained to the court *in camera*. Overruled.' As Veronica continued to stand the judge's stare became heavy enough to force her down into her seat, where she folded her arms and glared.

Edward resumed. 'Are there good local artists here?'

'Oh my, yes.' She leaned back a little. 'Of course there are in any major city, and some of my artists live in New York, even Europe. But the local art scene has been very vibrant for some time.'

'You said "my artists." What is your relationship with the artists you display?'

'I consider them clients. I buy some works to re-sell, but the majority on consignment. It's my profession to find good homes for works of art.'

She was coming off a little highfalutin and Edward thought he'd need to take her down a peg soon if she was going to connect with the jury, but then Anali apparently realized that herself. She leaned back in the chair and said, 'The painters bring me their stuff and if I like it I sell it.' Someone chuckled appreciatively. It may have come from the jury box.

Edward smiled. 'Tell me how you knew a local artist named Anthony Alberico.'

'Slowly, I'd say is the answer. I've been in this business for quite a while. I first knew Tony as an art student who brought me some of his early works. I turned down the first few but encouraged him. His gift was obvious from the beginning. But I didn't want him to trickle out with half good pieces. He needed to burst on the scene.'

'So you took him under your wing?'

She smiled. 'I don't have wings, Mr Hall. But in my calling one looks for exactly such an artist as Tony Alberico. One who isn't ready yet but with great potential. I did help him along, and he was certainly worth the nurturing. He grew into – in my opinion – the finest local artist we had. One of the best in the country, in fact.'

'We keep speaking of Mr Alberico in the past tense, Ms Haverty. What happened to him?'

She put a hand to her mouth, then removed it to say, 'He was murdered. Shot to death.'

'Have police solved that crime?'

'No one's been arrested. I follow the case closely.'

'What was the date of his murder, ma'am?'

'Months ago. April sixteenth.'

The day of the alleged kidnapping on trial here. Some jurors sat up. So did Veronica.

'Why do you remember the date so clearly, Ms Haverty?'

'I found his body,' she said, head lifted. 'Probably two days after he was killed. Police aren't sure of the time of death because no one found him for a couple of days. But at the time I had an uneasy feeling about Tony so I went to check on him and found him on the floor of his bedroom.' She sniffed.

'Where was he killed?'

'His home. A house in the Heights.'

The Heights.

Veronica shot up. 'Your Honor, this is ridiculous! Just because another offense happened in the general vicinity—'

Judge Roberts held out a hand, his broad face radiating a heat that silenced the prosecutor. 'Bailiff, take the jury out for a moment.'

Mistake on Veronica's part, Edward thought. This would only intensify the jurors' curiosity and make them pay closer attention to Edward's evidence when they returned. Theoretically.

He turned and looked into the audience. The Greenes were there, sitting next to each other again, but their body language building a wall between them. Sterling had his arms folded and Diana leaned away from him. She looked back at Edward with wide eyes. Then they narrowed.

The courtroom door had barely closed behind the last juror when Veronica resumed. 'This is ridiculous, Judge. I've heard of Mr Hall's courtroom theatrics, but this is beyond theater, it's a carnival. We're nowhere in the vicinity of relevant evidence. He's trying to distract the jury from his client's obvious guilt. Why don't we just . . .?'

The judge slammed down his gavel, a gunshot sound that not only silenced the prosecutor but made her step back.

'Ms Prosecutor, let me explain once and then we will not have this scene again. Defense counsel has explained the defense strategy to the court in chambers and I am satisfied as to the relevance. This is coming in. Do you understand?'

Edward hadn't even bothered to stand up. Donald was staring a question at him. Edward patted his arm. He'd never had this experience, of a judge being on his side against the State. On the other hand, from the judge's perspective, no judge had ever been reversed for screwing over the prosecution.

Veronica said, 'I presume it's still all right to make objections when I feel they're appropriate?'

She and the judge were backing down from their confrontation. 'Of course,' he said.

She sat slowly and turned to Edward with a curious expression. No longer angry. She looked hurt at being excluded from the very small club he had formed with the judge.

The jurors were returning. Once they were seated Edward said to his witness, 'Where did Tony do his work, Ms Haverty?'

'He started the way everyone does, in his home. But he needed more room and frankly better light. I started letting him use my studio.'

'Your studio. Where is that?'

'I have a large room in a building behind my house.'

'Where is that, ma'am?'

'West University Place.'

He thought he saw the jurors picturing that distance. We'd just moved uptown from the picturesque quaintness of the Heights to the brick estates of West U.

'May I approach, Your Honor?'

At his nod, Edward went to his witness with a small stack of photographs. 'Can you identify Defense Exhibits one through eight, ma'am?'

'Yes. That's my studio.'

'Outside and inside?'

'Yes.'

'This is where Tony worked sometimes?'

'Yes.'

Edward had the photos admitted and passed them to the jurors. From his seat he asked, 'What were Tony's subjects, Ms Haverty? What did he paint?'

Her eyes turned faraway. 'He had a wider range than most

artists. He did landscapes, still lifes. But he was known for his portraits.'

'Tell me about his work in those.'

'Yes. His portraits hung in homes and public spaces around town. The mayor—'

He cut her off before Veronica could object. 'So he painted living people?'

'Oh yes. Prominent Houstonians commissioned him.'

He got her to explain how that worked financially, then asked, 'Did he sometimes display those works in your gallery before they went to private collections?'

'Yes. It was a sort of advertising for him.' She shrugged at the jurors. Always commercial aspects even to the highest art.

'Do you know if he did a portrait of a woman named Diana Greene?'

'Yes. I'm sure it's hanging in their home now.'

Some jurors glanced up into the audience. 'What did that portrait look like, ma'am?'

'Typical society portrait. Very large, almost life-size. Mrs Greene was beautifully dressed, as if for a party, standing by a Greek-style column.'

'What was Tony's gift, Ms Haverty? Why did he get these large commissions?'

She gazed off into the distance. 'His gift was to capture a subject's best quality – humor, magnanimity, beauty – and both highlight that and amp up the volume just a bit. Not to be too obviously flattering, but capturing a person just as he or she would want to picture herself on her best day.'

Edward paused to let that good answer sink in, then said, 'Do you see Mrs Diana Greene in the courtroom today?'

'Yes. Up there on the fourth row of the spectator seats with her husband.'

Edward turned and looked, as he was sure everyone else did. The Greenes presented a portrait themselves. Captured by surprise momentarily in their icy poses, they quickly regrouped, Diana leaning on her husband's shoulder, Sterling taking her hand rather woodenly.

Edward turned back to his witness. 'Were you familiar with Tony Alberico's working methods?'

'Oh yes. Tony wasn't shy about his work. Some artists demand isolation, but Tony didn't mind a small audience. His concentration was excellent.'

'Did he have the subjects of these portraits pose for him?'

'I'm not sure I would use the word pose. He would have them come to the studio – my studio in the last couple of years – dressed as they wished to appear in the portrait, but then he'd just let them walk around, chatting, looking over his other works as he observed them from various angles. He might start the outlines of the portrait on the first day, but there was none of this business of a subject sitting or standing rigidly for hours. Tony would simply look at them, memorizing them, or at least the aspects he wished to remember.'

Edward imagined being the focus of that attention, a woman seeing a handsome young man staring at her every time she got a glimpse of him. There must have been blushes and stammering. And the occasional returned stare. The beginning of a romance right there with no one talking about anything other than light and color.

'You're saying he remembered all these people well enough to paint them from memory?'

'Oh no. He'd take pictures. It was his way of being considerate of a busy person's time. He'd take multiple pictures of the subject from a variety of angles. Then he could begin the work without them there. Of course there'd be at least a couple of other live sessions to get the final details right, but mostly he worked from the photos.'

Stop being coy, Edward thought to himself. He pulled out the other envelope and opened it. 'You and I searched your studio sometime after Tony's death, didn't we, Ms Haverty?'

'Yes.' Anali swallowed. Her memories of the young artist seemed to sneak up on her every few minutes.

'You've described his portrait of Diana Greene. Did he do another portrait of her?'

'Not that I know of. Not that I've seen.'

'But he could have painted another one of her, couldn't he? Even in your studio?'

'Of course. I didn't monitor his use of the studio. And sometimes I'm out of town for fairly extended periods on buying tours.' She shrugged again. 'She could have commissioned another portrait, for all I know.'

'Did we find in your studio certain . . . indications . . . he might have been doing that? Painting another portrait of Diana?'

'Yes.'

Edward approached her with his envelope, opening it along the way. He could feel a heat ray on his back, someone's stare. More than one person's, probably. At the witness stand he handed Anali another short stack of photographs.

'Can you identify these?'

'These are photos we found at the back of a drawer in the studio, as if they'd been hastily—'

'Object to speculation,' Veronica said quickly, sounding relieved she finally had a legal objection.

The judge turned to the witness with a kindly expression. 'Just describe how you found them, ma'am, please don't speculate about what anyone else might have done.'

'Of course. These were in the very back of a drawer behind some other things.'

'Do these photos all depict the same person?'

'Yes. They're Diana Greene.'

Edward returned slowly to his seat. 'You described how Mr Alberico would take a lot of pictures of a subject before painting her. Do these photos look like the ones he used to paint Mrs Greene's official portrait?'

'No.'

'Why not?'

'These are nudes.'

The quality of attention in the courtroom focused abruptly, like a cloud uncovering the sun on a gloomy day. Curiosity attached to the photos and to the live woman in the audience. Edward was dying to turn and look at her but needed to stay focused on his witness. Donald, though, was twisted around to stare upward.

Edward didn't offer the photos into evidence. Anali put them back in their envelope and set it on the railing in front of her. 'And you know of no painting made from those photos?'

'I don't, no.'

Edward sat musing. 'Pass the witness.'

'Are there any similar photos of you taken by Mr Alberico?' Veronica asked quickly.

'Objection,' Edward said. 'Irrelevant and an unwarranted attack on the witness's reputation.'

'I'll sustain the first objection,' said Judge Roberts. 'The second I don't recognize as a legal objection.'

'You know what I'm asking,' Veronica said to the witness. 'Were you having sex with this artist?'

Edward had wondered that himself, but he still objected that the question was irrelevant and the judge sustained him again, this time with a stern look at the prosecutor. Veronica ignored it.

Edward thought, *But thank you, Veronica, for nailing down that logic for the jury, that if Tony took nude pictures of a woman he must be screwing her too.*

'You said you went to Mr Alberico's house and found his body because you had an uneasy feeling. Was it an uneasy feeling he was having an affair with another woman?'

'No,' Anali said flatly.

'You found him. Did you have a key to his house?'

'The door was unlocked. But yes, I did have a key to Tony's house. And he had one to my studio.'

Such a pregnant answer, clearly for a moment Veronica didn't know what to do with it. Edward was putting a hand to his mouth when his client nudged his shoulder with his own. Donald leaned in and said, 'What's going on here, man?'

Edward raised a hand with all the fingers spread. 'Just spreading the guilt around at this point,' he whispered. 'Man.'

He saw Veronica regrouping. She'd charged in to discredit the witness by showing she'd been having sex with the young artist too, which didn't really lead anywhere. Now she was pondering how to go. Edward watched her closely as Veronica asked to approach the witness and did. She didn't know what she was doing here. Edward had surprised her, one of the few benefits the defense had in trial. The prosecution had to reveal its witnesses to the defense. The right was not reciprocal. Edward had used this to his advantage several times as a defense lawyer. But it was something he'd had to get used to, as a former prosecutor.

Veronica was looking through the photos of her primary witness. She picked out one and showed it to the witness. 'Doesn't it look to you in this photo as if Mrs Greene is asleep, Ms Haverty?'

Yes it did. Edward knew the one she meant. Diana asleep with a little contented smile on her face. Probably Veronica didn't want to show that one to the jury.

He saw her coming to the realization she didn't know where she was going with this cross-examination and felt a moment of sympathy for Veronica. A very short moment. She still completely had the winning hand. It was just in this moment she didn't know where the trial was going, and that was a very weird feeling for a prosecutor.

Edward said out of the side of his mouth, 'I feel that Cyclops stare, man. I'll explain at the break.' He and Donald may not have been as close as lawyer and client should be.

Veronica walked slowly back to her seat, gave Ms Haverty a long look, and said, 'Pass the witness.'

Edward asked, 'What was Tony's address, ma'am?'

'I'm not sure. You know, a familiar place, you know how to get there, but not the address. It was on 9th Street in the Heights. The 300 block, I think.'

Edward stood, asked to approach the witness, and did so with a poster-sized blow-up of a map. 'Could you pinpoint it on here?'

'Yes. Right there.'

'Will you put a pin there, please?'

She did so. 'Does this exhibit, Defendant's Exhibit one, look like an accurate representation of that neighborhood, Ms Haverty?'

Anali, a conscientious witness, studied it briefly, picking out a couple of identified locations with her finger. 'Yes.'

Edward had the exhibit admitted, then resumed his seat. 'Do you know Mr and Mrs Greene, ma'am?'

'I've met them, of course, since I had Mrs Greene's portrait on exhibit for a while. There was a reception.'

'How did they behave at that reception?'

Anali mused for a moment. 'They came in obviously angry at each other, went to far ends of the room. Mrs Greene circulated, laughing a lot, obviously having a good time. Her husband sulked. Then they drifted together. They actually went outside

for a few minutes and we could see them yelling at each other.
Then something happened and they obviously made up. They
came back inside practically rubbing against each other. It was
all rather embarrassing. Several other guests noticed.'

'Have you seen them any other times?'

'Another party, I think. That time they seemed happy together.
Whatever they were feeling, they always—'

'Objection to relevance,' Veronica finally said, and Edward
had no response.

'Thank you, ma'am. No more questions for now.'

Edward saw Veronica thinking over that questioning. She
drummed her fingers briefly on the table and admitted she had
no more questions either.

'Your next witness, Mr Hall,' the judge said. Edward turned
and looked up into the spectator seats. His eyes flickered over
Mr and Mrs Greene, back to their isolated from each other poses,
and rose to where Linda sat next to a man in a suit. She gave
him a little smile probably only Edward could see.

'The defense calls Detective Isaiah Reynolds, Your Honor.'

The man sitting next to Linda rose and walked down the aisle.
He was an athletic looking black man wearing a black suit that
fit him well. His stride was confident.

After he was sworn to tell the truth, Edward, feeling Veronica's
stare, asked quickly, 'Please identify yourself.'

'Detective Isaiah Reynolds, Houston Police Department.'

Edward established the witness's credentials and experience
in a couple of quick questions. 'Detective, were you called to
the residence of a man named Tony Alberico when Ms Anali
Haverty called police to report finding him dead?'

'I was.'

'Did you take anyone with you?'

The detective sat at ease in the witness stand, veteran of at
least a hundred trials. 'No, but a call went out and a couple of
uniformed officers met me there.'

'Did you find Mr Alberico's body?'

'Yes. On the floor of his bedroom. Shot once in the chest.'

Edward admired the witness's way of getting quickly to the
point. But of course, Edward had prepped him to do just that.
'Did you arrest a suspect?'

'No. It remains unsolved to this day.'

'What did you do to investigate?'

Detective Reynolds leaned forward, putting his hands together and looking directly at the jury. 'We searched the house, very thoroughly. We brought Ms Haverty to the station to give a detailed statement. I asked for an autopsy to establish the time of death. We ascertained that the gun beside the body, the murder weapon, was registered to the deceased. So that didn't lead anywhere.' The detective shrugged, obviously unhappy for a moment over a failed investigation.

'Detective, do you see the envelope in front of you with photos in it?'

'Yes.'

'Would you look at them, please?'

Detective Reynolds fanned through them, studying the photos. Edward finally turned and looked at Diana. Was she blushing? At any rate, she was glaring. So was her husband. But then Sterling stood abruptly and walked up the aisle toward the exit.

Edward hurried the rest of his questioning. 'Did you find in Mr Alberico's house a portrait, a drawing, that looked anything like those photos?'

'No. We found some paintings in various degrees of completion, but none of this woman.'

'Pass the witness.'

Veronica stared, obviously having no thoughts about what to ask. *So don't*, Edward thought. *Pass the witness, pass the witness, pass the witness.*

'No questions, Your Honor,' she said, as if Edward had willed the words into her mouth.

'Next witness, Mr Hall?'

'May we take a short break, Your Honor? I need to confer.'

Judge Roberts' eyebrows rose briefly. When a lawyer asked to confer with opposing counsel in the middle of a trial it usually means the lawyer has some reason to think they could agree on a plea bargain. Edward's first two witnesses had been interesting, but hardly that devastating to the prosecution's case. But a judge would favor any attempt to bring a trial to an early close. Judge Roberts tapped his gavel and the jurors were ushered out. Edward turned to Veronica. Out of the corner of his eye he saw Sterling Greene pause up by the courtroom doors, turning back to watch this development. Veronica gave Edward a questioning look and he leaned toward her.

Judge Roberts had just unzipped his robe in his chambers when there was a knock on his open door. He turned to find Edward standing there.

'I thought you were going to confer.'

'Yes, sir. I did. I made Veronica an offer so she'd need to talk it over with the so-called victim and her family. But I actually needed to confer with you, Judge.' Edward came closer, pulling a sheaf of pages out of his suit jacket. He handed them to the judge without another word. Judge Roberts gave him a curious look, then started reading. After a few seconds his eyes rose again. 'A search warrant?'

'Yes, sir. Did you hear enough from the witness stand just now to sign it?'

The judge's eyes went distant, reviewing what he'd just heard from the gallery owner and the detective. After a moment he nodded. 'I did.'

Edward held out a pen.

Sterling Greene got to his car in a parking garage a few blocks from the courthouse and drove out as quickly as he could. The defense lawyer's offer, to have his client plead guilty in exchange for only three years in prison, had been verging on ludicrous. As soon as he heard it, Sterling left his wife and her sister, the district attorney, to reject it. He drove through the streets of downtown Houston with his knuckles white on the steering wheel, his stare heavy-lidded and intense.

River Oaks wasn't far from the courthouse, not by the sprawling standards of Houston. Sterling sped up after getting out of down-town, the car seeming to gain confidence as it neared home. He drove up his long driveway and didn't bother to open the garage. Instead he jumped out and strode quickly to the back door.

Inside, he took the stairs in a few long strides. In moments he was staring around his bedroom, the unmade bed, messy dressing table, half-open closet door. He crossed quickly to the latter and went half inside. He knocked aside the empty easel leaning against the inside wall, pushed aside a half dozen of his wife's dresses, and grabbed the painting behind them. He emerged and his eyes darted quickly around the bedroom again. He shoved the painting under his arm and hurried out.

Sterling was thinking as fast as he ever had. He had a storage unit over near his office. There was the office itself, plus half a dozen construction sites with projects he had initiated. Houston was a hive of possible hiding places. He could just set fire to the damned painting, but found himself reluctant to do that. It felt warm under his arm.

He hurried out the back door and toward his car. But now another car was blocking it in the driveway. A black sedan with 'Texas exempt' plates, looking vaguely official. Its driver's door opened and a slender black man emerged.

'Mr Greene? I'm Detective Reynolds.'

'I know. I just saw you testifying.' Sterling made no attempt to hide the painting, which would have been ludicrous anyway.

'Yes, sir. But now I'm back to doing police work. I have a warrant to search your home. To find what I believe you're holding under your arm.'

The police officer held out the warrant. Behind him the other front door of the car opened and Linda stepped out. She put her arms on the roof of the car and leaned down, watching closely with no expression. But her eyes were riveted to that canvas.

Sterling hesitated. He didn't reach for the papers the detective offered, assuming they were authentic. He looked at the woman instead, wondering what her interest in this was. Their stares entwined for a moment.

Then Sterling held out the painting.

'I'll want a receipt for that,' he said.

TWENTY-SIX

During the afternoon break in trial Edward reviewed his potential other witnesses, the list Donald had compiled for him the night before. Twice-convicted thief to sponsor illegally obtained bank records of Sterling Greene's showing no large withdrawals on the day of the supposed crime. No withdrawals of any kind. Another of Donald's friends – agg assault, robbery – to say he'd seen Donald and Sterling together on another occasion.

'What next?' Donald leaned into him to ask.

'Your friends' colorful histories make them less than sterling witnesses.'

'They still saw what they saw, right? You can still call them.'

Yes, and he probably would. But the bank records, for example, had been illegally obtained and couldn't be admitted in any fashion. Edward had already issued a subpoena and gotten most of the same records legally, but what did they show? Nothing. Sterling had already testified he'd gotten the ransom money from another source. Maybe just a big pile of cash in a safe. It didn't prove or disprove anything.

He turned and saw the prosecutor in a huddle with Diana Greene and her sister Julia Lipscomb, the DA. Linda wasn't back in the courtroom yet. *Think*, Edward ordered himself. *Think like a prosecutor.* What was he missing?

Veronica broke the huddle and came down the aisle, fixing Edward with her stare the whole way, making no pretense of any other focus. He watched her with his hands getting warm. She had a remarkable stare, very physical, like a big animal on a leash.

He stood to receive her. She motioned him aside, away from his client. Edward raised an eyebrow at her. 'You want to improve on that ridiculous three-year offer?' she asked immediately.

Oh, that. Edward had just said that to slow Sterling Greene's departure from the courtroom. 'No. Do you want to improve on your offer of die in prison?'

'Yes, actually. Twenty-five.'

Edward stared at her. 'Years?'

'Yes, Edward. What else do we have to haggle over? Of course years.'

She was leaning in very close to him. There was a zone where intense antagonism edged into the same territory as lust. That was how this felt.

He stepped away. 'Let me talk to my client.'

'I will,' the prosecutor said ironically. Then she stepped toward him again. 'Edward. Don't take this as a sign of lack of confidence in my case, or that you've so cast doubt I'm afraid of not getting

a conviction. This is my client wanting to give your client a huge
break because he didn't hurt her. Also her anxiety to get this over
with. Personally, I'm sure of victory and I could go all month.'

He nodded.

'What'd she say?' Donald asked when Edward sat next to him
again. Edward was wondering the same thing.

'New offer. Twenty-five.'

Donald slumped back in his chair. 'That's the same thing as
before.'

'No, Donald. It's fifteen years fewer. It's also probably a signal
she'll drop down to twenty if I press.' An offer in the twenties
probably meant the bottom line was twenty. Any double digits
with a two in front. That was how plea-bargaining worked.

'It's the same for me,' Donald explained. 'Back to prison for
something I didn't do. Even twenty means I'd have to do ten.
You know how old I'll be in ten years?'

Edward looked at his client and realized he had no idea. 'Fifty-
three,' Donald said. 'Fifty-three and my life nearly over. No
family left, nobody waiting.' Donald shifted his stare to the jury
box. 'Tell her no.'

In Edward's head, he already had.

Now when trial resumed Edward felt the weight of his client's
life. Fifty-three and dead. 'Margaret Jeffries,' he said in response
to the judge's instruction to call his next witness.

A young woman took the stand in response. Edward knew her
to be thirty-three, nearly his own age, but she looked twenty.
Very professional, in a navy skirt suit, her blonde hair pulled
back. She carried a couple of large posters.

'Whom do you work for, Ms Jeffries?'

'You, today,' she said frankly. 'I spent five years with AT&T
and two with Verizon. Now I'm a freelance consultant.'

'In what field?'

'Cell phones. More precisely cell towers and calls. What we
call historical location data.'

'On my behalf, did you obtain cell phone records from three
known numbers?'

'I did.'

'Let's start with this number.' Edward rattled it off. 'Is there a name on that account?'

'Yes.'

'And this number.' He said another one. 'Name?'

'Yes. There's one name on both those accounts. Sterling Greene. That second number is associated with a Diana Greene. Same account.'

'And this number?' Edward said another string of digits.

She nodded in his direction. 'That's the cell phone number for your client.'

Edward felt something to his left, Veronica's table. A warmth, a focusing of attention. He kept his eyes on his witness. 'Let's start with Mrs Greene. Did we obtain the records of her cell phone's location on April sixteen of this year?'

'Yes.'

'Do cell phones pinpoint the location of the person carrying it at all times, Ms Jeffries?'

'No.' She turned to the jurors. 'They're not tracking devices. Not entirely. But when we send or receive a call or text, the phone relays that through the nearest cell tower that has line of sight.'

'So that pinpoints the user's location?' Edward was deliberately playing dumb, a trial lawyer's common tactic. Sometimes it was intentional.

'No. It places the phone within a triangular-shaped zone covered by that cell tower.'

'How big is that zone, ma'am?'

Ms Jeffries shrugged. 'It varies enormously. If you're in a sparsely populated region like west Texas and the tower is tall, as they are out there, it covers a lot of territory. In a densely populated city like Houston, a tower may cover only a few square blocks. There has to be more coverage here – more towers – so calls don't get dropped. A tower can only handle so much traffic.'

'So we're surrounded by towers?' The image was a little frightening.

Ms Jeffries smiled. 'We need to come up with another name for those. Maybe receivers. They're not just towers. They may be some equipment on an office building, disguised into a logo on the side. Or on some already existing tower such as a radio tower. We try to make them as inconspicuous as possible. But people must have their phones.' She looked again into the jury box, where one woman was frankly holding hers and another man was hastily putting his away.

During this explanation Edward had turned and looked into the audience. Diana was there, trying to look stony and instead conveying anxiety. Julia wasn't there, nor Sterling Greene. Or Linda, for that matter.

'Let's get back to Diana Greene. Do you have something showing her phone's movements on that day in April, the day she claims to have been kidnapped?'

'Object to the comment by counsel,' Veronica said, hastily on her feet.

Judge Roberts gave her an ironic look – *Really?* – but said, 'Sustained. Please ignore that remark, jurors.'

Edward had just wanted to pin down for them what they were talking about.

'I did make a chart,' Margaret Jeffries said. Veteran witness, she carried on quickly. 'A map. If I may?'

Edward waved a hand, master of the courtroom. Margaret set up her first chart on an easel facing the jury. Veronica leaned to see.

'Her first call that morning was from this location. A text from an unknown number at eight forty-five.'

'What's that location?'

'Well, it's an area that includes Mrs Greene's home in River Oaks.'

'And then?'

'Well, starting a few minutes after that her route is pretty well-defined. She travelled along here' – Margaret was tracing a path on the map with a pointer – 'and was on her phone the whole time, talking to that number that had texted her. She ended up here.'

'And what part of Houston is that?'

'It's the Heights. Portions of 8th, 9th, and 10th Streets, from to—'

'How long was she, or rather her phone, there?'

'Some time. There were occasional pings from texts or calls that went unanswered for some four hours.'

'Did any of those pings come from the phone number belonging to Sterling Greene?'

'Yes, four. Finally in the early afternoon Mrs Greene returned one of those calls.'

'Does your other chart show Mr Greene receiving that call?'

'Yes. It lasted about three minutes.'

'Let's shift to that other number, Ms Jeffries. After that call, did it travel in response?' He felt Veronica tense next to him. But this was the disappointing part.

'No. That phone stayed where it was the rest of the day.'

Damn Sterling. He'd been the smart one, doing what Edward used to advise his clients: when you go out to commit a crime, leave your phone behind.

'Let's go back to Mrs Greene's phone, then. Did she travel to another location?'

'Yes. About an hour and a half after that last call the next ping comes from a few miles away.'

'What does that location include?'

'It's known as West Gray, I believe. A commercial area that includes a CVS pharmacy, for example.'

He led her through the rest of Diana's day, from that pharmacy where she claimed Donald had grabbed her to an area in the Third Ward that included the supposed kidnap house, where it remained for less than two hours before setting out again, eventually ending up back home for the night.

Diana had a lot of friends. She got a lot of calls and texts. Some came from an unknown number. But no more from her husband after that early afternoon call.

Edward took his witness through Donald's phone record as well, a different chart showing a much less cluttered day. It started at about two o'clock in the afternoon somewhere in southwest Houston, then traveled to the vicinity of that pharmacy and from there to the crime scene where he was arrested. From there the phone disappeared from the records, presumably impounded by police, but it didn't send or receive any more calls.

'While at the house, did that phone receive any calls?'

'Yes, including three from that same unknown number that appears in Mrs Greene's records.'

It didn't seem to prove much, and the testimony had lacked drama, but Edward had a reason. A prosecutor would have introduced these records. She would have nailed down her case. That Veronica hadn't was interesting.

But then, the records wouldn't help her case. They showed a much shorter time span at the house than Diana had claimed, for example. Edward saw Veronica already planning how to argue that discrepancy.

Edward had the two maps introduced into evidence and said, 'Pass the witness.'

'No questions.'

Judge Roberts glanced at the clock, then at the jurors. They looked a little worn, as if they'd bought their clothes in antique shops. 'I think we'll stop here for today,' the judge said. At least a couple of the jurors thanked him silently.

As the lawyers stood and the jurors shuffled out, Edward turned to look into the audience again. Still no Sterling. Still no Linda.

'What next?' Veronica asked him.

Indeed. Edward just smiled at her.

Veronica leaned a little closer. 'Want to get a drink and talk about the case?'

Edward studied her for a moment. He had no idea what she was thinking. She had a little smile, which might have been about the trial and might have been about anything else.

'Thanks, no,' Edward said. 'Maybe tomorrow.' He needed to find Linda.

TWENTY-SEVEN

He called Linda, urging the call to go through.

She didn't answer.

He tried texting instead, thinking maybe she was some place where she couldn't talk. He got only a smiley face winking in reply, which anyone who had the phone could send. He wished he had his expert to tell him where it had come from. Leaving the courtroom, Edward turned toward Linda's latest courtroom, then stopped abruptly and headed for the elevators. They took forever. When he finally got to his car he headed for River Oaks.

* * *

Linda was plastered to Sterling Greene's back wall. She didn't have any way of breaking in, but didn't need to right now. Diana had come home, had only gotten as far as the kitchen where Sterling was waiting for her. Their voices were loud enough Linda could follow the conversation from the backyard.

Diana said something quiet, a meek mumble.

'No!' Sterling stormed in response. 'It doesn't matter if he goes to prison or not. They already have the painting!'

'You like the painting,' Diana said more loudly, with a chuckle she obviously intended to be sexy. This time the response was non-verbal, a little shriek from Diana. Linda couldn't tell if it was fake-scared role-playing or the real thing.

She was moving to a better eavesdropping position when her ears were assailed by the sound of a car horn. It wasn't a one-time honk, it was the sound of someone holding his palm down on the horn. Now the only sounds from the kitchen were of surprise as the Greenes rushed out to see what was happening. Linda grimaced. The sound receded. She thought about following them around the house, but there were too many windows up there. She just waited and walked out, down the driveway rather conspicuously.

She was walking down an unfamiliar River Oaks street, looking for a good corner from which to call Lyft, when a car pulled up beside her. Linda took one running step, then looked at the car. She put her hands on her hips and glared. Edward looked back, unfazed. 'If you're through with your double-naught work, Jane Bond, want a ride home?'

'After the detective and I served the subpoena, I saw an opportunity. Sterling was going back into the house, and I thought when his wife came home they might have a significant discussion. So I had Detective Reynolds drop me off at the corner and I came back.'

'I'm surprised he made himself a party to a crime. He must not be as good a detective as I thought.'

Linda stuck out her tongue at him. 'Or I'm a better liar than you give me credit for. I gave him a cover story, of course.'

They were in the kitchen by now. They'd both been in the mood for spaghetti. Oftentimes their tastes aligned that way.

Linda, barefoot, was in cut-offs and a T-shirt, Edward more conservatively wearing much the same thing but with flip-flops. The air was redolent with the smell of simmering onions and mushrooms. They brushed against each other as they worked.

'But I couldn't get in the house. You'll have to show me how to do that lockpick thing.'

'So you can be my next court case? I think not. Have you just gotten a taste for this? You know, it's Amy who was the habitual burglar, with me it's only been three times.'

Linda hit his shoulder playfully. 'No. It's just useful sometimes. I was on the verge of hearing something good when you ruined it with your horn trick.'

'Which we couldn't have used because you were trespassing when you heard it.'

'But at least now we know. It's something to do with the painting.'

He could hear Veronica Salazar's response to that. *Maybe they're just afraid of the embarrassment, as any normal couple would be.*

'Oh, it's going to be embarrassing,' he said aloud. Linda didn't even look at him strangely. She'd gotten used to the ongoing conversations in his head.

'Call your next witness,' Judge Roberts said the next morning.

Up until that moment Edward wasn't sure who that would be. Detective Reynolds waited in the hall with the painting. The gallery owner was out there too, eaten up with curiosity. Call the two of them, deflect attention from the subject matter of the actual trial?

But no, if he did that, then called Donald, the focus would be right back on him at the end of the defense case. But if he called Donald next, jurors wouldn't have the context.

The ongoing dilemmas of a trial lawyer. Veronica stared at him, waiting. 'Donald Willis.'

Because out of the corner of his eye he saw Donald poised to leap to his feet. He was ready at this moment, so let him take his turn.

Donald this morning wore a light blue suit with a white shirt and yellow tie. Edward hadn't liked the tie at first, but now thought it looked good as Donald sat in the witness chair with his hands folded. It gave him a mild, passive look. Donald looked at the jurors and nodded in greeting.

After the brief preliminaries of swearing in and introducing him, Edward said, 'Tell us how you first encountered the Greenes, Donald.'

'I wasn't doing much, moving from relative to friend, getting by on odd jobs and such. I hadn't been out long.'

'Out of where?'

'Prison. I got an eight-year stint, did six. That's when I met you.'

Edward didn't quite flinch. Yes, let's tell the jury that *I'm* an ex-con too. 'You mean when I represented you in your previous case.'

'Of course.' Donald looked innocently back and Edward wondered if he'd just been screwing with his lawyer.

There was no avoiding this part. They had to acknowledge Donald's famous case. The prosecutor could bring it out anyway, because any witness can be impeached by a felony conviction. But it was also part of the defense narrative, why Donald became a target. 'What was your conviction for, Donald?'

'Kidnapping. I kidnapped Ryan Jennings's son.'

They went through that story. Some people on the jury had admitted during jury selection they knew about that case, one of the most famous crimes in Houston history. It would have been nearly impossible to pick a jury that didn't remember that case. Donald laid it out: recognizing the boy alone, the split-second decision to snatch him, trying to arrange for payment.

'Did you know how to set up the ransom drop?'

'No, sir. I'd never done anything like that before. I came up with an idea, but . . .'

'Did you do anything to carry it out?'

'No.' Donald shrugged, gave the jury an earnest look again. 'I didn't even make a call to him, even though the boy had a cell phone with his dad's number in it. By the time I got him out of the stadium I realized what a horrible mistake I'd made. I almost turned around and went back in. Instead I waited for a couple of days, trying to figure out how to undo it without getting caught, then took him home.'

'What did you do during that time?'

'Took him to the zoo. Bought him pizza. A movie.' Donald shrugged. 'He had a good time, actually.'

Edward made notes, letting those images sink in. A few feet to his left Veronica sat back with her arms folded and a look of utter contempt on her features.

'Then I took him home. Got arrested right away. Did my time.'

'Only eight years. Not a long sentence for such a dangerous crime.'

'Objection!' Veronica said rather shrilly. Sometimes there's that adrenaline rush when a lawyer finds her feet for the first objection of the day. 'Object to the sidebar.'

'Sustained.'

It didn't matter. The jury had heard it. 'Why do you think you got a sentence on the low end of the punishment range, Donald?'

'Because I pled guilty, admitted my mistake, told the jury how sorry I was. Plus I had a good lawyer,' Donald added with a little smile. Edward didn't want to hear that. Might unreasonably raise the jurors' expectations.

'All right, back to near the present. So you decided to look for a job?'

'Yes. Try to make something of myself. Not drift back to, you know, some of the schemes my friends were tryin' to get me to pull.'

He had just acknowledged the quality of a couple of their witnesses, but no matter. 'Who did you apply to?'

'Everybody. All kinds of places. Even ones who had policies of hiring ex-cons didn't want anything to do with me. They made an exception for famous ex-cons.'

'So?'

'I saw an article in the paper about Sterling Greene, how successful he was, his companies, some great party him and Mrs Greene threw for charity. He seemed like he might have a lot of work. So I went to see him.'

'Where?'

'Tried his office, just showed up there, managed to talk my way through security, but his secretary told me he was almost never in the office, he was always at some job site or luncheon or somewhere else all over town. When I came out of the building a truck was leaving and I followed it and I got lucky, it was going to where Mr Greene was checking on a construction project. So I walked up on him.'

'Was he alone?'

'Nah, he had some guys with him. Big guys. All of them wearing hard hats and looking at some plans.'

For Donald to call somebody 'big guys,' they must have been impressive. Donald went on to describe a brief impromptu job interview in which he was brushed off. But then . . .

'So I was walkin' away, just another worthless day, when Mr Greene called me back and said give him my phone number, he might have something for me some day. So I did. Really didn't expect anything to come of it.'

'Did it?' Edward was sitting at ease, not taking notes. He'd gone over Donald's story with him so many times Edward could have testified to it himself. Probably to better dramatic effect.

'Yeah. Two or three weeks went by, and one day out of the blue my phone rang and it was him callin'. He asked if I was available for a sudden short job that would pay very well. I said of course.'

'Is that when he directed you to the CVS pharmacy we've heard about in this trial?'

'Yes, sir. They were both there. Mr and Mrs Greene. He told me his wife was going to receive some jewels, but it was in the Ward and he was worried about her. He couldn't go himself so he asked me to take her there and bodyguard her until the guy showed up with the jewels. Because she had the cash on her, see?'

'So did you?'

'Yes, sir. We left my car there and went in her car.'

Edward crossed his arms and looked at his client. He didn't glance at the jury, he didn't have to. He'd heard the story himself. Edward said, 'Donald, do you hear how crazy this sounds?'

Veronica was on her feet at the speed of passion erupting. 'Objection, objection, objection!'

'Which is what?' Judge Roberts asked mildly.

Veronica gestured at the witness stand with one arm and pointed at Edward with the other. 'He's feeding his client his lines. He's telling the story for him.'

'The court still doesn't recognize a legal objection. Something to be found in the Rules of Evidence. Over—'

'Object to counsel testifying. Sidebar. Something.'

Edward shrugged at the judge, who said, 'Both of you approach the bench.'

Suddenly Edward saw how all this would play out. You didn't, she did, that didn't happen . . . The whole back and forth of having an important witness on the stand. A decisive witness.

But there was one thing wrong.

At the bench Judge Roberts leaned forward and said, 'I still don't think your objection quite fits, Ms Salazar. I'm going to let the question stand. But no more like it, Mr Hall. Understand?'

Edward just nodded. Back in his seat, he gave his client a hard look and said, 'Pass the witness.'

Donald just stared. Beside him, Veronica's head actually swiveled toward him. Edward ignored her. But in the extending silence he felt her mind racing, felt her dilemma. That had been much too short an examination for a defendant. He hadn't even exactly denied committing the crime. Did she let it end there, with the defense's work still incomplete, or did she do what opposing counsel normally would do and try to pick holes in the story?

Edward also thought she probably wanted to repeat his question to Donald.

She turned slowly toward the witness stand. 'So this man you'd barely met entrusted you with his wife's safety, when all he knew was you were a convicted felon and she was carrying a large sum of money?'

Yep, that was another version of Edward's question.

'Why on earth would he do that?'

Objection, calls for speculation. But Edward didn't say the words. The judge looked at him.

'I don't know, ma'am. I think he thought he could trust me because of exactly who I am. I couldn't take her money and run, I wouldn't last a day. And I couldn't hurt her, same reason. I'm marked in this town. This state. And Mr Greene was looking right at me when he let me go with his wife. As soon as I walked away from him with her, he could have cops on me in half an hour wherever I was. He thought he could trust me exactly because I was a convicted felon. A well-known one.'

It was a good theory, and Donald delivered it well. Several of the jurors looked thoughtful. But it still left something out.

'Did you have a gun?'

'No, ma'am. Don't like 'em. Never owned one.'

'You were expected to guard his wife without him offering you a weapon.'

Donald just looked at her, squaring his impressive shoulders. *Look at me.* For once the size-ist thing worked. 'Yes, ma'am.'

She took him through the rest of his story, doing Edward's job. He drove at Mrs Greene's direction. No, he had no connection to that house in the Third Ward. No, he didn't touch her. Just waited for the delivery of the jewels. They each got a couple of calls from her husband. Get to know each other, Donald and Diana? Not really. Mostly just watching out the windows. He hadn't noticed the man across the street or any other potential witnesses. Donald hadn't called anyone himself, as his phone records showed. No one to back up his story. Veronica slowly and methodically narrowed the trial down to a swearing contest, Donald versus Sterling and Diana Greene. Prosecutors were usually confident of who would win such contests. But Veronica seemed nervous, continuing to ask narrower and narrower questions. Edward even objected a handful of times to asked and answered or relevance and was sustained.

Veronica finally looked weary. Also still nervous.

'Pass the witness.'

Edward hesitated. But then chose a careful question. 'Donald, did you kidnap Mrs Greene?'

'No, sir,' his client said firmly and hopefully believably.

'Did you have any intention of committing the crime you're charged with?'

This time Donald shook his head for emphasis. He looked serious as a prison sentence. 'No, sir.'

'Did you ever see this large sum of money Mrs Greene supposedly had?'

'No.'

'And of course no one showed up with jewels.'

'No, sir. Only the SWAT team.'

Edward let it lie with that, passing the witness. Veronica hesitated long enough that Judge Roberts called a recess. Edward sat staring at his client.

TWENTY-EIGHT

Judge Roberts decided it was close enough to midday to turn the recess into a lunch break, longer than usual, as if he knew Edward and his client had something to work out. Linda had shown up by then. She came through the gate in the bar into the well of the courtroom and hugged Edward, her back to Veronica, who had started to step across to say something. Veronica stepped back.

Linda looked very professional in a blue skirt suit and white blouse. But her eyes were dancing. 'Where are we going to lunch?'

'I was thinking just the Luby's in the basement. We should be able to get there and back in an hour and a half.'

'Let's go. Hi, Donald.' He had walked up and stood respectfully by.

'Not you, Linda,' Edward said as kindly as possible.

'What?'

'I may be committing a crime, and I don't want you to be part of it.'

'Over lunch? This I gotta see.'

Edward gave her his serious look. She'd seen it before. Just a hard stare, forming an almost visible tunnel between their eyes.

Linda turned and walked away. After she'd gotten a few steps she turned and looked at both of them. 'You coming?'

Yeah, the serious look had never worked on her yet.

They went down to the basement of the beautiful civil courthouse. Eventually. Those elevators. It was crowded down there in the Luby's cafeteria, but they finally got through the line and found a table. A small tile-topped table crammed among many others. Along the way, Edward kept saying, 'This was a mistake.'

Both courthouses – the lovely civil one, the criminal one that smelled like sweat and bad life choices – had once had nondescript little sandwich bars. At some point the nicer civil one had contracted that out to a chain, Luby's, which had cafeterias all over the state. Perfectly OK food – the fried fish in rectangles that disguised whatever it might have been in the sea, if those bits of flesh had ever known an ocean, were very popular.

They sat down, unloaded their trays – apparently they'd all opted for the anonymous fish, Edward with sensible spinach on the side, Donald with fried everything, okra, cauliflower. For health purposes he had added mashed potatoes with cream gravy. Donald took the space for two seats across the table, Edward and Linda sat close in two other plastic chairs. Before they'd even had a sip of their iced teas, Edward said, 'That was the biggest load of crap I've ever heard.'

Donald looked at Linda as if she'd been the offender. 'What?' He turned to Edward. 'You talkin' about me? Which part did you not believe?'

'Everything after you woke up that morning. And I only believe that because I'm sitting here looking at you.'

And then it was on. Donald set down his fork and stared at his lawyer, his brows coming together. Edward sat placidly receiving it. Finally Donald said, 'You callin' me a liar?'

'Yes, that's the clear inference when I say everything I just heard you say was a lie.'

Donald's stare remained direct. Then just slid off Edward's face. 'I need to get another lawyer right here in the middle of trial?'

'Yes, if you want one who'll suborn perjury. Look around. There are probably candidates within arm's reach.' Donald didn't survey the room. Edward leaned toward him. 'But your current lawyer already has a felony conviction and I'm not looking for another. I can't let you repeat that story. It's not just unethical, it's actually a crime. For both of us.'

Something had always bothered Edward about Donald's story of how he'd gotten involved with the Greenes in the first place. That feeling had crystallized with Donald on the witness stand. Sterling trusting this guy with his precious wife, at almost a first meeting? Maybe Sterling was furious at her. This had been shortly after Diana had been made to sign a post-nuptial agreement, obviously under threat of divorce, because she'd consulted a divorce lawyer. Maybe Sterling had caught her again. Maybe he wanted her dead. Looking at Donald, a man would think he could do such a job.

But then why had Donald waited for hours, or at least a while, at that house with Diana without doing anything? Second thoughts?

No. Edward had gotten to know Donald well enough in prison to know he was no killer. He could be violent when necessary, but he didn't seek it out. He wasn't a sociopath. He'd protected Edward.

But what else made sense?

'When does the crime happen?' Linda asked. She was following the exchange with reddened cheeks and bright green eyes.

'The crime would be if I encouraged him to commit perjury again. But I'm not going to. I'm just going to let the lie stand.' He turned back to Donald. 'Was Sterling really there when you first got to the CVS?'

Maybe Donald and Diana had been having an affair. 'Recent sexual activity' the medical examiner had said. Edward found it hard to picture, but that may have just been prejudice, which he acknowledged he carried, like everyone.

'Yes,' Donald insisted. 'I'd never seen Mrs Greene before, I wouldn't have gone there just to meet her. Mr Greene was there, he offered me a job. I wouldn't have just snatched his wife in the stupid way she said I did. Do I look like an idiot?'

The jury was still out on that. Literally.

'What was the job he offered you?'

Donald hesitated.

Linda suddenly leaned into the conversation. 'Isn't it obvious? He hired Donald to fake a kidnapping.'

Edward looked at her. Out of the corner of his eye he saw Donald stare at her.

'Tell me the clues,' Edward said sincerely to the love of his life.

Linda gestured. 'What's he known for? What would someone who barely knew Donald hire him to do? And Sterling would certainly think Donald wouldn't have any moral objections. Not that I think Sterling would recognize such a thing anyway.'

'Is that right?' Edward said to his client. 'Why?'

'So Sterling could hide some money losses,' Linda said. When Edward turned back to her she said, 'What? What do we know about Sterling? He was constantly on the financial edge. He'd probably stolen from some account he wasn't supposed to touch, client trust funds or something, money he was supposed to hold until a job was finished but it had fallen through. Something. We know from Donald's friend hacking into Sterling's records—'

'Illegally.'

'Yes, but we still know it. Sterling didn't remove any large sums from any known account for ransom money. He was just going to say he'd pulled the ransom money to cover the losses.'

Edward turned back to his client. 'Is that true?'

'No,' Donald said firmly, looking him in the eye. He leaned across the table. 'Nah, man, it went down the way I said. He hired me to bodyguard.'

'But Linda's story makes sense,' Edward said, thinking out loud. 'You thinking the three of you were in on this together when in fact you were the fall guy. And you not holding Diana for the hours she said, but only long enough for Sterling to fake something financially, call a few people to act frantic, then get the SWAT team on their way. Then he could tell whoever he stole from the ransom money just disappeared. This one I believe.'

After a long pause Donald said, 'But that's not what happened. I told you what happened.'

He sounded believable. Edward folded his arms and stared off across the room. Next to him, Linda ate with a good appetite. Donald popped an okra.

'What you thinkin'?' Donald asked quietly.

Linda glanced at her lover. 'He's wondering how he can use this information without putting it on in evidence.'

'Really? Is that true, Edward?'

Edward frowned. 'No, I was wondering if that food you just ate is an okra, or is the whole collection okra, plural. Like rice, you know? You don't say I ate a rice.'

Linda chuckled. Donald stared. 'Really?'

'No, of course not. I was thinking what she said.' And he

imagined Linda's increasing ability to read his mind could be a problem one of these days. She smiled, obviously doing it again.

'So did you come up with something?' she asked.

'Just Sterling and Diana. I need to let them think I know something I shouldn't. Put the fear of God into them. So maybe they'll be receptive to a deal.'

'Even though they know you can't prove the truth?'

'I can get close. I can bring out enough to make Sterling very afraid of someone looking into his business activities.'

'Then what?' Donald asked.

Edward shrugged. His food was cold and looked completely unappetizing. 'Then I figure out what to do with that.'

'Sounds like a plan,' Linda said. 'It's not, but it sounds like one. Maybe a half-assed plan.'

'Half an ass is all I got at this point.'

Donald put out one hand palm upward in supplication. Linda began eating Edward's spinach.

TWENTY-NINE

Back in the courtroom, Edward found Veronica already in her place, looking through her notes. Her eyebrows, partially drawn in, curved seductively around her deep brown eyes. Was it his imagination, or had she been getting prettier during trial? Maybe using every tool she had to get the jury on her side? No, that was ridiculous. At any rate, she looked good in a deep green suit and a yellow blouse to which his eyes refused to wander.

'What?' she said without glancing up.

'Be thinking about a better plea bargain offer,' Edward said. 'Maybe something closer to the eight Donald pled for the last time.'

Now she did look at him. 'Are you crazy? What's gotten worse with my case or better with yours?'

'Ask your clients.' Edward looked out into the audience, where Mr and Mrs Greene weren't even sitting together. Sterling remained in his usual seat while Diana was closer down with her sister, the district attorney.

Veronica didn't even glance back. 'My only client is the State of Texas.'

'Right. I forgot. Justice and all.' Edward took his seat.

When the judge asked Veronica if she had further cross-examination she curtly said no. Edward had already decided to ask nothing else of his client. Donald stood up from the witness stand and walked slowly to his place, looking everywhere but at the jury. For one long moment he stared out into the audience.

Edward called Detective Reynolds as his next witness. He came in from the hall carrying a package now wrapped in brown paper, and took that into the witness stand with him. Edward really wanted to turn around and see the effect on the Greenes, but refrained. Isaiah Reynolds stood to take the oath, then sat at ease.

'Good afternoon, Detective. Please remind the jury of your profession.'

'I'm a detective with the Houston Police Department.'

'Yesterday did you do something in that capacity relevant to this trial?'

'Yes, sir. I obtained and executed a search warrant.'

'Where?'

The detective said an address, then clarified, 'The home of Sterling and Diana Greene.'

'What were you authorized to search for?'

'A painting. A portrait of Mrs Greene.'

'Did you find it?'

'It turned out to be surprisingly easy. Mr Greene came out of the house carrying it just as I arrived.'

'As if bringing it to you? Had you called him in advance?'

'Oh, no. Carrying it as if taking—'

'Object to speculation, Your Honor.' Veronica had found her feet and her voice. She no longer sounded hostile, just very professional.

Edward stood slowly and said, 'He's a veteran detective, Your Honor. I believe he can testify to what his observations led him to believe.'

The judge hesitated, one finger on his lips. He was a good judge, Judge Roberts, he didn't make snap judgments. 'That will be sustained,' he said slowly. Then he added: 'Ask a different question, Mr Hall.'

Good instruction. 'How did Mr Greene look when you saw him coming out of his house, Detective?'

Isaiah Reynolds raised his gaze, remembering. 'Hurried. Furtive. Obviously surprised to see me. His eyebrows shot up, he tried to thrust the painting behind him, realized that wasn't going to work, and started back toward the house until I stopped him and said I had a search warrant for that very object.'

'Did he say anything then?'

'Only that he wanted a receipt for the painting.'

'Well, no reason to keep the jury in suspense any longer' – Veronica rose quickly and objected to sidebar remark. Edward ignored her, as did the judge. She stood looking uncertain, then slowly sank back into her chair – 'Detective. Do you have the painting with you?'

'I do.' He held up the wrapped package.

Edward established this was the same object the witness had seized from Sterling Greene at his home, how he knew, so forth, the few crucial sentences, then said, 'Move to admit Defense Exhibit Three, Your Honor.'

Veronica stood next to him. 'We are so far from relevance I can't even see it from here, Judge. What does this portrait have to do with anything?'

The judge gestured them forward with a bending finger. At the bench he leaned toward them, looking directly at Veronica and said, 'As we've already established, counselor, Mr Hall has explained to the court's satisfaction the relevance of this line of inquiry. In answer to your question, as we used to say when I was a child, that's for me to know and you to find out.'

In a louder voice he said to the jury. 'The exhibit is admitted.'

Back in his seat, Edward said, 'Did you look at the portrait, Detective?'

'I didn't study it. But of course I looked closely enough to make sure it was what I was sent to find.'

'Can you describe it? Generally.'

'It's a portrait of a woman. Nude. Reclining.'

Edward felt Veronica's stare on the side of his face. Why was he being so coy? Why not just show it to the jury?

'Do you know the subject of the painting, Detective Reynolds?'

'I'd never seen her before yesterday. But I see her sitting in the audience.'

'Can you point her out and describe her?'

'The woman there next to the district attorney. Fortyish, mid-length brown hair that flips up at the ends, wearing a blue blouse.'

Edward had heard a lot of testimony in his life, some of it excruciating in its gory details, but he had rarely heard anything as brutal as that brief description of a woman trying very hard to be beautiful and largely succeeding, but the brief description reducing her to a nondescript white woman verging on middle age. He turned and looked at Diana. Yep, the detective had gotten it right. Except he might have mentioned she was blushing.

'Pass the witness.'

Veronica looked at the police detective, opened her mouth, closed it, and shrugged. 'Since I have no idea what relevance all this has to this trial, I have no questions.'

'Do you have any other witnesses, Mr Hall?'

'I'll re-call Anali Haverty, Your Honor.'

The gallery owner came down the aisle moments later. Today she wore a sheath dress in thin vertical black and white stripes, black high heels, and another scarf, this one a muted red. She walked carefully but casually, eyes on the jury. She was not smiling. No smile was even hovering in the vicinity.

The judge reminded her she was under oath. Edward started in quickly. 'Ms Haverty, there's a wrapped painting there in the witness stand with you. Will you unwrap it, please?'

She did so, expertly, then sat looking at the painting in her lap. Her expression was hard to read. Appraisal of the painting's value, laced with a hint of jealousy? He may have been reading in that last part.

'Can you identify the subject of the painting, ma'am?'

Her eyes went up into the audience. 'Diana Greene.'

'The same woman of whom Anthony Alberico painted an official sort of portrait?'

'Yes.'

'The same woman whose portrait he was painting in the studio behind your house?'

'Yes.' Her voice was flat.

'The same woman who was the subject of the nude photos we saw?'

'Yes.'

Edward shifted, edging into this. 'Ms Haverty, you were Tony's exclusive dealer, weren't you? The only art dealer who sold his works?'

'As far as I know. I certainly thought so.' She was still looking out into the audience. So were a few of the jurors.

'Did you sell that portrait you're holding to anyone?'

'No. I've never seen it before this minute.'

Edward asked to approach the witness and did, treading through her stony gaze. He found on the bench the collection of nude photos that had been previously admitted, handed them to the witness, and said over his shoulder as he returned to his seat, 'Ms Haverty, will you please look closely at both those photos that have been previously admitted and the painting you're holding?'

As Anali started doing so, Veronica said, 'Your Honor, I object to this. Whatever he's asking her to point out, the jury can see for themselves.'

Edward responded, 'Do I have to establish her credentials as an art expert, Your Honor? Haven't we already—'

The judge said flatly, 'No, Mr Hall, you don't. The objection is overruled.' He seemed to be regretting having let the trial go down this path.

In the meantime, Anali Haverty was following Edward's instruction, eyes going back and forth between the painting and the photos, at first angrily, then leaning closer, eyes intent.

'Do you see any differences between the painting and the photos, ma'am?'

'Yes. In the portrait there's a mark on the subject's neck that doesn't appear in the photos.'

Edward made an elaborate note of that, letting it sink in with the jurors. She had a good eye, Ms Haverty.

'You were familiar with Mr Alberico's work?'

She looked up from her study. 'Very. I followed Tony's work for years, since he was a student.'

'Did you ever know him to do a follow-up nude portrait like this after doing a commissioned painting of the subject?'

'No. I never knew him to paint a nude at all. This is the first one I've seen.'

There was that hint again. Edward said, 'I pass the witness, Your Honor.'

Veronica looked exasperated, even made a gesture as if to say, *What am I supposed to do with this?* Then she said to the witness, 'But you have no way of knowing, do you, ma'am? For all you know he painted naked pictures of every woman he ever painted, right?'

Anali waggled her head. 'That's true. If he sold such a painting privately, or gave it away, I'd have no way of knowing.'

Veronica walked up to the witness stand. 'May I see the painting, ma'am?' She took it and studied it closely. She showed it to Anali again. 'How do you know this is Mr Alberico's work?'

Anali looked at the painting as if asking herself the same question. 'It's his signature, for one thing, the way he signed all his work, that short squiggle followed by his readable last name. Plus it's just Tony. I know his style when I see it. That direct stare out of the canvas, for example. That's a Tony touch. He got a woman's stare better than anyone I've ever seen. Not sleepy like the Mona Lisa. Not coy. A woman looking at something she wants. That's Tony.'

Veronica looked at her, taken aback. She handed the painting back to the witness and walked to her seat. Just before sitting she looked at Edward, studying him briefly. Then she said, 'But there are imitators, aren't there, Ms Haverty? Other painters who make a living copying the style of more successful artists?'

'Of course. There always have been. Some of them are good enough that I sell their regular work.'

'Had Mr Alberico become well-known enough to have such an imitator?'

Anali shrugged. 'I suppose so. Of course.'

Veronica looked back into the audience. 'So if Mr and Mrs Greene liked her official portrait, as Mr Hall called it, aren't there local artists they could have hired to replicate the style but this time a nude of Mrs Greene? Because they wanted one for their own private reasons?'

She seemed to be suggesting a story line to her clients. Nothing Edward could do about that. But he did stand to say, 'Objection, Your Honor, calls for speculation. That's based on absolutely no evidence at all and the witness has no way of—'

'Sustained,' the judge interrupted him, with a strong subtext of *Shut up.*

But the story had already been unleashed in the courtroom. 'Pass the witness,' Veronica said, and Edward wasn't imagining the smugness. He asked, quickly, 'Ms Haverty, you knew Tony Alberico well?'

'Very well.' She was holding herself very upright.

'We've heard in this trial, and I suppose you knew, he was killed with his own gun? Did you have a reaction to that news?'

'I was very surprised. Tony wasn't the kind to own a gun. He was always caustic about Texans and their guns.' She shrugged, Gallically. 'People can change, I suppose.'

Edward sat thinking, then asked to approach the witness again.

'Knowing Tony as well as you did, have you been to his house?'

'Many times.'

There was an edge to that answer as she looked out into the audience.

'Would you please study the background of that painting and see if you recognize where it was painted?'

She drew glasses from her purse and did as Edward had asked, studied the painting closely. 'Oh,' she said after a moment.

'Do you recognize the locale?'

'It's Tony's house. Specifically his bedroom.' Her voice had flattened again.

'Are you sure?'

'Absolutely. That small corner of wood behind her, that's the edge of his desk. And the thing she's lying on, it's a small divan Tony had next to the desk. I hadn't noticed.' She took one more close look and put away her glasses. 'I'm sure,' she said, looking at Edward.

'Your Honor, I offer Defense Exhibit Three.'

'Object to relevance,' Veronica said, obviously with no hope of being sustained. She was correct. Edward took the painting from the gallery owner's hands and handed it to the jurors, who passed it slowly among themselves. It was interesting to watch their reactions. Some took it as if contact was going to stain their hands and passed it on quickly. A couple of the men pretended to do that but let it pass slowly across their fields of vision as it moved on. Two or three of the men and at least as many of the women gave it a long gaze.

'Where was that house, Ms Haverty?'

'In the Heights. Ninth Street, a block or two off Studewood.'

Edward took a photograph off his table and carried it to her. 'Is this the house, ma'am?'

'Yes.' She said it quickly but then continued to stare at the picture. Her expression projected melancholy, nostalgia, and some other emotion. A portrait in herself.

'Offer Defense Exhibit Four, Your Honor.'

While the inevitable objection was overruled and the photo admitted, Edward studied it himself. A little white house with blue trim and nice decorative touches like a porch railing painted to duplicate the house. Flowers in a permanent holder. A porch swing on chains, padded with cushions. A pretty little house reflecting a nice life. Very inviting. But also very private. The windows were shaded, the door without glass. Edward looked at it closely, feeling he was there.

It all came down to that little house in the Heights.

THIRTY

Edward could think of nothing else to be wrung from Anali Haverty. She slumped in the witness stand, no longer quite so elegant. He felt he owed her an apology. But all he could say in court was, 'Pass the witness.'

Veronica had no more questions either. As the gallery owner stood and walked slowly past them, Edward stared at the empty witness stand. Who else could he put there? His defense seemed to be nothing. He felt Donald's stare.

Then he stood and said the words he always hated. 'The defense rests, Your Honor.'

Veronica turned and looked out into the audience.

She was obviously wondering which of the Greenes would be more likely to lie for her. Edward wondered the same thing. Sterling seemed completely amoral, given what Edward knew about him that the jurors didn't. He'd say whatever was needed, and Veronica had already laid out the script for him. But he also looked like an obvious liar, at least to Edward.

But Diana, she was a case study. What did he know about her? The divorce lawyer, for one thing. She'd been trying to find a safe way out of her marriage and failing. She was going to be cast out. Instead she and her husband were tighter than ever, bound by the events presented in this trial. And she . . .

'Do you have any rebuttal to present, Prosecutor?' Judge Roberts asked.

Veronica was standing, her eyes sweeping the spectators as if looking for a witness who would be a surprise even to her. Her eyes fastened on Julia Lipscomb for a moment. The district attorney, the boss who'd fired her. Julia's own eyes widened.

What could the DA possibly have to contribute? Edward wondered.

'Diana Greene, Your Honor.'

Diana stood, pulling her hand away from her sister's. She made her way through the row and down the aisle stepping delicately, an invalid, sick with the truth. When she sat in the witness stand and the judge reminded her she was under oath she nodded, shoulders slumped with the solemnity of it all.

Bullshit, Edward thought, trying hard to catch her gaze and failing.

'Mrs Greene' – Veronica stood and walked to the jury box – 'may I?' she said to the man at the end of the back row holding the painting on his lap facing him. He handed it over sheepishly. Veronica in turn passed it to Diana. 'Do you recognize this painting, ma'am? Is that you?'

Diana blushed. She wasn't faking that. 'Most embarrassing thing in my life. Yes, that's me. Sterling wanted it. After my official portrait—'

'Object to narrative,' Edward said.

A witness wasn't allowed just to spin the tale. She had to respond to individual questions. Diana looked chastened.

'Who painted this?' Veronica asked.

Diana opened her mouth and hesitated, obviously wondering whether to follow the storyline Veronica had suggested, of a different local artist copying the style of the much better-known portrait painter. But then Diana said, 'Tony did. Mr Alberico.'

Veronica exhaled a small gust of exasperation. Witnesses, they made lawyers' jobs so difficult. The lawyer knew just what they should say but the witness often didn't.

'How did that come about?'

Diana shifted in her chair, looking at no one but the prosecutor. 'It was Sterling's idea, like I said. He really loved the portrait, the big one. Sterling also . . . he's very complimentary about my appearance.' She looked out into the audience as if for encouragement but didn't seem to find any. 'So he had the idea of asking Mr Alberico to paint a nude of me.'

Edward turned and looked at Sterling, who sat there with hooded eyes and a hand covering his mouth.

'That seems like sort of an intimate request,' Veronica said.

Diana brightened. 'Well, Sterling really wanted a good quality painting and we knew Tony's work. Plus Tony and Sterling had become great friends after Tony painted my first portrait.'

Edward's head swiveled back to the witness. The elegant and refined artist and Sterling the boor had become great friends? What horseshit.

What was Diana trying to prove?

'Really,' Veronica said, sounding surprised herself. 'How did that come about?'

Diana gave a little shrug involving her face. 'How does anybody become friends? Of course the three of us spent some time together while Tony was painting my portrait. He didn't mind an audience, he rather seemed to enjoy it. Then after it was done and we'd had the big unveiling reception and all Sterling came home one day and said Tony had called his office to invite him to lunch. Then we'd see him at social occasions, parties and so forth. Sometimes we'd invite Tony, sometimes he'd invite us.'

'What did Mr Alberico and your husband have in common? What did they bond over?'

They'd gotten rather off topic, but Edward wanted to hear the answer to that one too.

'I wasn't there for a lot of their meetings. Sports, I guess. Guy stuff.'

Tony didn't care anything about sports. Edward remembered Anali Haverty's describing him. But now Edward also remembered what his old friend from River Oaks had told him, that Tony Alberico was seen regularly with the Greenes after he'd painted her portrait.

'All right, let's get back to the painting,' Veronica said. 'The second one. So are you saying Sterling felt comfortable enough with Mr Alberico to ask him to paint a nude portrait of his wife?'

'I suppose so. He did.'

'Did you yourself stay close with Mr Alberico?'

Diana shook her head. 'He was Sterling's friend. I only saw him when we were all together.'

Well, except when Tony was painting her naked.

Veronica switched back. 'Did you see Mr Alberico the day he was killed?'

'I doubt it. What day was that?'

'The day you were kidnapped.'

'Oh. Well then no, of course not. I was being kidnapped and held hostage. It was terrifying, I thought—'

Veronica cut her off before Edward could even rise to object. 'Had you seen Tony in the days before that?'

'No. Not for some time before that day. I didn't even hear about his death for quite a while, because of all the things happening with me after I was kidnapped and rescued and started all that process of working with the nurse and police and you.'

She made it sound arduous, and Edward knew from experience it could be. Victimization didn't end the day of the crime. He turned and looked at his client. Donald was staring at Diana with a look that held no anger at all, just bafflement and sorrow. Edward coughed, hoping to draw the jurors' attention to his client.

Veronica was looking closely at Diana, assessing her, wondering what else she could draw from her. 'Pass the witness,' she finally said, obviously having decided the answer was nothing.

Edward sat silent for a few moments himself. He hadn't believed a word of this testimony, but where to begin attacking it when it actually seemed to hold together?

'So you posed naked for Mr Alberico?'

Diana actually gave a little shudder. 'Yes. A very few times. Three, I think. I couldn't do it any more than that.'

'Just the two of you?'

She hesitated. 'Sterling was actually there at least one of those times. In some ways that was even more uncomfortable. But Mr Alberico was very professional. Even when it was just the two of us he acted strictly as if we were working. Even though we'd become friends by then he never called me Diana when he was painting. Always Mrs Greene. As if putting a distance between us. And whenever we took a break he had a robe handy for me immediately. If anyone could make a woman feel more at ease in that horribly awkward situation, it was Mr Alberico.'

Edward stood and asked to approach the witness. On his way he said, 'Sometimes in a situation like this I might pull some theatrical stunt, as Ms Salazar has suggested—'

'Object to sidebar.'

'Sustained.'

'Such as asking you to disrobe so we could check the accuracy of the portrait, but in this case it's not necessary,' Edward finished smoothly. Veronica sat and gave a rather theatrical sigh herself.

'We have the photos,' Edward continued. He handed Diana the nude photos of herself. 'Where were these taken, Mrs Greene?'

'Tony's studio.' She wouldn't look at them. 'The studio behind Ms Haverty's house that she mentioned. It was just one day. I was so embarrassed I made him hurry through it.'

She didn't look embarrassed in the photos. Edward picked out one. 'In this one you appear to be sleeping. Is that the case?'

Diana barely glanced at it. 'No. I had my eyes closed pretending I wasn't there. Sort of trying to hide behind my eyelids, like children do.'

'Then there's the portrait itself.' Edward held it to face her. 'Is this an accurate portrayal of you?'

She was blushing, the scarlet tinge going all the way down to her neck. 'Yes, I suppose so. I haven't studied myself without my clothes on.'

'Do you see any differences between the photos and the painting?'

Now she had to look, back and forth between them. She shook her head.

'What about the backgrounds? They're different, aren't they?'

'Oh. Yes. I heard what Ms Haverty said about the portrait background looking like Mr Alberico's bedroom. I wouldn't know. I guess he just decided to put in some background details of his own house to make it look less like a studio painting.'

Uh huh. 'More intimate?' Edward suggested.

Diana shook her head again and repeated, 'I wouldn't know.'

'Pass the witness,' he said. He didn't think anyone else in the courtroom realized it, but he'd gotten what he needed.

'No more questions,' Veronica said. Edward looked at her as he walked back to his seat. She seemed to be regretting having called Diana.

'Call your next witness.'

Then Veronica made that same long pause Edward had before resting his case. 'I have no more witnesses, Your Honor. The State closes.'

Judge Roberts looked at Edward. 'Defense?'

Edward was thinking. He could re-call Anali Haverty to say Tony didn't give a damn about sports and didn't have any friends like Sterling Greene. But then Veronica would put Sterling on the stand to say no, they'd talked about other things, Houston life, Tony interested in Sterling's work and Sterling learning more about the art world and so on and on. At some point the game of *Uh huh, Nyuh uh* had to end. 'We close, Your Honor.'

The judge looked at the jurors rather closely. They mostly seemed attentive, but one was looking at his watch. 'Attorneys, approach the bench, please.'

When they did the judge leaned forward and said softly, 'It's only mid-afternoon, but if we have the charge conference and final arguments now I may have to sequester these jurors over-night and I don't want to do that. Any objections to arguing in the morning?'

No. Lawyers seldom object to postponing. The judge looked up and said, 'Ladies and gentlemen, the lawyers and I have some work to do to prepare the court's jury instructions. I'll ask you to be back here at nine o'clock tomorrow morning for final arguments, then it will be your time to deliberate.'

As Judge Roberts continued to give them the usual instructions not to watch any television or any other accounts of the trial overnight, Edward and Veronica looked at each other. It had been a hard-fought trial and it wasn't over yet. Neither of their stares was hostile. Veronica held out her hand. She may have just wanted to look nice in front of the jury, but Edward took it.

Then he turned to the audience, where Diana was rejoining her sister. Julia held out her arms to her and Diana went into them. At the defense table, Donald was just shaking his head.

THIRTY-ONE

'It kind of looked like you were just trying to embarrass Diana,' Linda said that evening in her kitchen.

'You were there?' Immediately after the jurors left Edward and Veronica had gone into the judge's chambers to discuss the jury charge. It was going to be pretty standard. No subtle legal theories were going to help either side win this case. It was all about whom the jury believed.

'Yeah. You only had eyes for other people apparently.' She put her hand on his to soften the statement, and smiled. 'But was there some other point to showing Diana naked pictures of herself?'

Edward thought about that for a minute. As with so many things lawyers do, it had just been something sprung in the moment. 'I guess I was trying to say her story was ridiculous that it was her husband who was close to Tony.'

'What are you going to say to the jury tomorrow morning? Want to practice?'

'Not with you. You're too good at picking my arguments apart.' But he smiled at her as he said it.

She smiled back. 'Don't you need that?'

'No. I need support.'

Linda moved quickly next to him and put one arm around him, the other on his leg. 'Oh, Edward, you'll do great. You're so brilliant. You're the best.'

That was as far as she could go. They both burst out laughing.

The next morning, last day of the guilty-or-innocent part of trial. Edward parked four blocks away, because that was the best parking spot he could find in downtown Houston. Walking toward the courthouse, looking down at his feet. Lawyer shoes. Nice tassels. He didn't have the law license any more, but he still had the shoes.

Closing argument, when he didn't know what his defense was, didn't even know if he believed his client. Donald's story didn't make any sense. Even Linda's version. Nobody in the Greenes' position would hire Donald to do anything. Even if they thought he might be useful as muscle, or as . . .

Oh, shit.

He stood there on the sidewalk and got it. Or at least a story he might be able to sell. A story he actually believed. Not that that mattered. As he hurried toward the courthouse he was rewriting his closing argument in his head.

In the courtroom Edward put his arm around Donald's broad shoulders. They hadn't been very close during this trial, Edward caught up in his own job, Donald just a swamp of worry it wouldn't help his lawyer to step into. 'It'll be all right, big guy.'

Donald's brown eyes begged him for something he could believe. 'How will it?'

Edward smiled at him, projecting confidence he didn't feel.

In closing arguments the prosecution got to go both first and last, ostensibly because they had the burden of proof but really just because the system made almost everything better for the State in trial. But when a trial was conducted by just one prosecutor, like this one, she would often waive opening argument and save all her time for making a final pitch to the jury. This tactic was designed to catch the defense lawyer by surprise, thrusting him onstage immediately when he thought he'd have a few minutes to gather his thoughts. It had probably last caught a defense lawyer by surprise some time in the 1700s.

When Judge Roberts prompted Veronica to begin, she stood and said, 'The State will waive opening, Your Honor.' She sat with her eyes on her desk, lost in thought.

Edward rose and got his first good look at the jury since

selecting them. Some were watching him closely. At least a couple looked bored, waiting for him to get it over with. They'd already made up their minds, but there was no telling which way.

'Finally you get to do your parts,' he began. 'This is the part that's hardest on everyone. Certainly hard on the lawyers, waiting to hear your verdict. Certainly hard on the supposed victim. But most of all on him.' He pointed. 'The defendant. Because he's going to be waiting to hear how twelve strangers have decided the rest of his life will go.

'And I know it's going to be hard on you too, because you take your jobs seriously, you know this is one of the most important decisions of your life, and you want to get it right.'

He talked about the State having the burden of proof, that if the jurors couldn't make up their minds one way or another then they were honor bound to find the defendant not guilty.

'The prosecutor is going to tell you this is an easy decision. Woman says she was kidnapped, police find her in a house with a large black man, she runs out screaming. Oh, and by the way, he's the best-known kidnapper in Houston, ever. Easy.

'But it's only easy if you don't do your job. If you don't think. It's only easy if you buy the Greenes' story from the beginning. And you have to buy every part of it. The State wanted to give you a simple story, very straight storyline. But let's see what they left out. Remember the State has that burden of proof and every prosecutor tries to nail down his case as tightly as possible.'

He began ticking them off. 'The cell tower records. The prosecution didn't bring you those, I did. They show that Donald went straight from a location across town to the area of that CVS where Diana says he kidnapped her. Seems to support her story. But how did he know where she was? How did he drive straight to that drugstore where she said she'd gone rather spontaneously because she was early for lunch with a friend? How did he anticipate her schedule like that when even she didn't know?

'What those records should show is first Donald going to River Oaks, to the Greenes' house. If this was the carefully plotted kidnapping they want you to think, wouldn't he have had to stake her out and find her first, then follow her to that CVS?'

Edward looked across their faces. They were thinking. They may have been thinking he was an asshole, there was no way of knowing. 'That's one. And that's one piece of evidence the State should have brought you and didn't. Cell phone records get admitted by the prosecution in so many trials now—'

'Objection. What happens in other trials is irrelevant and not in evidence.'

'Sustained,' said the judge's deep voice. 'The jury will disregard that argument.'

Sure they would. Edward hadn't even turned away from the jurors. 'But she didn't bring those records to you because they don't support her case. Even the timing of the calls. Diana says this happened just before noon. But one of her early morning calls came from the Heights, to her husband. The next call from her phone to Sterling's is much later, almost three o'clock. Why would the kidnapper wait that long, risking exposure all the time, before setting in motion his plan to get the ransom?

'Next evidence I brought you and the State didn't. People in the neighborhood who saw the two of them go into that house in the Third Ward. Only two, but that's two more than the State found. And they both said it didn't happen the way Diana said it did, she didn't have any bag on her head and she seemed to go in the house of her own free will. Only two, but police have an army to scour that neighborhood. Why didn't they find anyone to say yes, she'd seen Mrs Greene being dragged into the house with her head covered? Little thing but another way the State's case doesn't add up.'

He walked a few steps to look at another batch of jurors. This included one of the African-Americans, the only man. He was staring at Edward attentively doing his best, Edward thought, to look objective. And Edward couldn't take his vote for granted. Sometimes black people were even more offended than others when a black man committed a crime. Edward looked at all the jurors, who all looked back.

'And what about that house? That little ramshackle house in the Ward. Who owned that house? How did Donald have access to it? Another small detail with which the State could have strengthened their case but didn't. If they could have shown Donald had some ownership interest in that house that would have really nailed it down. Or a relative or friend of his. That's left unknown. For all you know from this trial he just chose a stranger's house and was lucky enough to find it empty, so he could hold his hostage there for hours, as she said.

'Finally, where's the ransom money? If Donald had already had an accomplice pick it up, why was he still lingering in that house in danger of getting arrested? Why was it never found? Did it exist?'

He was running out of fingers. 'All those details are missing. Ms Salazar will tell you they weren't presented to you by the State because they're not important, because the story is so straightforward. But it's only straightforward if you believe everything Diana Greene said and don't believe a word of Donald's story.

'So let's talk about that. Donald's version of events.' Edward went and stood behind his client, so jurors couldn't help but look at him, and trusted Donald's face to do its job. 'He got out of prison, couldn't find anyone who'd give him a job, notorious as he was. He approached Sterling Greene because he'd seen something about how successful he was, how many projects he had going on. But Sterling wanted nothing to do with him either. Donald was known for only one thing, being a kidnapper.'

He'd moved over to the side, and felt Donald crane to look at him. Did we want to emphasize that?

Yes. 'Then one day, out of the blue, Donald gets a call from that man. Asking him to do a job. Asking him to guard his wife while she met a man who wanted to sell her jewelry.' Edward stepped back closer to the jury. 'Would anyone believe that story? Donald did, because he was so desperate for work. But would anyone else? Particularly twelve strangers like you? Why choose Donald for that job? What skills did you know he had? And if you wanted him to bodyguard, give him a gun. Yes, I know what everybody says about that. Look at him. But he can't stop a bullet.'

He stepped closer to them. 'We'll come back to that. Now I want to talk to you about something else. About why all this started in the Heights. That sweet little neighborhood. I have an office there myself. My girlfriend lives there. Nice area. But why did this case start there? What did it have to do with anything?

Diana says she was meeting a friend for lunch in a different part of town a few miles away, but she didn't explain why her earlier call was from the Heights. And where was the friend to say yes, we were supposed to meet, I waited for her for an hour, I kept calling her phone?

'She's nowhere, that's where that imaginary friend is. Because she wasn't the reason Diana was in the Heights. She was there in another nice little house.' He put the photo up on the screen. 'Tony Alberico's house. The artist who'd painted her. Twice. One officially and one secretly. He didn't do that with any other subject we know about. His exclusive dealer was very surprised to see it. He didn't just—'

'Object to relevance,' Veronica said, rather tonelessly.

Judge Roberts overruled that without any response from Edward. Edward continued as if it hadn't happened. 'This wasn't Tony's pattern. To take the nude photos, to spend hours alone with a woman who'd only paid for his work. No, there was something else going on there. Look at Diana's face in some of these photos. She closed her eyes to distance herself from the surroundings because it was so embarrassing, she said.' He held up one of the photos. 'Is that what this looks like?'

No, it looked like a woman with a contented little smile on her face, sleeping after a pleasant interlude.

'So this was going on. Tony and Diana. And what do we know about the Greenes' marriage? Sterling was suspicious, he was jealous. He was a volatile man with a temper.'

Veronica was more forceful this time. 'Your Honor, I have to renew my objection. This is typical Edward Hall, dragging the reputations of two innocent people through the mud just to distract from the real story of the trial. This is nothing but—'

'Sounds like she just attacked *my* reputation,' Edward mused aloud. He wasn't offended.

'The objection is still overruled. Continue, counselor.'

'We're not sure where Sterling was all this time because he was smart, he left his cell phone in his office. At a time when his secretary testified he was out of that office. But is it too much to imagine that he finally followed his wife one morning, suspecting her? She must have been dropping clues, this was too intense an affair, it had been going on too long.

'And Sterling Greene burst into that sweet little house in the Heights, found Tony Alberico with his wife, and shot him to death.'

Edward took a turn around the front of the room. 'Then the Greenes had a problem. Imagine them there in the room with the rapidly cooling body. Diana terrified, probably claiming nothing had happened, Sterling starting to wonder if he'd made a mistake, deciding quickly he wasn't going to kill her too, but only if she helped him. Diana must have immediately told him she'd help, that's how she survived, that's how she got herself out of that house.

'They were obvious suspects in the murder and they must have left clues to themselves in that house, particularly Diana, who'd spent who knows how many hours there, shedding DNA everywhere. They had to give themselves an alibi and they had to distract attention from the murder. Tony Alberico lived alone, he was known to disappear from public view for days at a time sometimes if he was working. No one might find his body for days if they were lucky. Time of death would be muddied. If they could just distract police away from them, or in another direction, they'd be fine.

'They're dramatic people, Mr and Mrs Greene. They love playing out their lives in public. You heard that from Anali Haverty. So instead of just saying go about our lives, Sterling to a construction site, Diana to lunch and a gallery, they decided to make a much splashier record of something else they were doing. Instead of murderers they'd be victims.'

Edward was pacing back and forth now, like a trapped conspirator trying to find a way out of the room. At one turn he saw Sterling Greene sitting in the audience with his fists clenched, pinstriped suit strained by his shoulders.

'But it needed to be something big and public. If they went home and staged a burglary police would come and note the time, but it would be commonplace. No witnesses. They needed not only a crime, they needed a quick solve.

'Then Sterling remembered Donald Willis. The ex-con who'd asked him for a job, who was clearly desperate for any kind of employment after getting out of prison. And who was known throughout Houston for only one thing.'

He stopped and looked out into the audience again. The Greenes remained separated, Diana huddling into her sister's embrace, trying to look the tiny little victim. 'However real or illusory Sterling Greene's success may be, we know he's shrewd. He can think quickly, and he never thought faster in his life than there in that house with the smell of blood starting to fill it. He could get Donald there on some pretext, hire him for some fake job, it had to involve his wife, guarding her, taking her somewhere, something. So they drove a few miles away, distancing themselves from the crime, and got Donald there. Then after he and Diana were gone Sterling could set up the fraudulent kidnapping. Long before anyone even found Tony Alberico's body and started trying to pin down his time of death, all of Houston would know what Diana and Sterling Greene were doing that day. How they couldn't possibly have been involved in the murder.

'It's crazy, isn't it?' Edward spread his hands to the jurors. 'Remember when I asked Donald that question? It's a crazy story.' He lowered his hands to the jury box rail and stared closely at them. 'It's deliberately crazy. They wanted to stick Donald with a ridiculous story, for when police questioned him and when this day came, so nobody would believe it.'

He grew more casual. 'And it remains crazy, I grant you that. I can't help that. That's what Mr and Mrs Greene left me. Left all of us. But their kidnapping story doesn't make sense either. Not in the broad picture, not in the details. I've already pointed out some of the things wrong with it. Here are others. Remember the officer who inventoried what Donald had when he was arrested? It included some eight hundred dollars in cash. Where did an out-of-work ex-con, so desperate for money he decided to try to pull off this very risky crime, get that kind of money? He got it from Sterling Greene, that's where. Sterling must have given him every bit of cash he had on him to hire him for this supposed job.

'But he didn't equip him very well. No gun, remember? The only gun the Greenes had handy was the one Sterling had used to kill Tony, the artist's own gun. They couldn't use that one. Sterling certainly wasn't going to hand over the murder weapon to Donald, that could be traced to the murder by ballistics. So they just trusted the image to work for them.'

He turned, enticing their gazes to his client. '*Look at him.* That's what everybody says about Donald. Stand up, Donald.' Donald started to rise and kept going, to his full six foot four inches or so, his shoulders spanning the courtroom. 'Look at him.' Turning back to the jurors, Edward motioned Donald back down. 'What kidnapper doesn't have a gun? Even if he thinks sure, he can control little Diana Greene without one, what if a bystander gets in the way? What if cops show up? Anybody would have a gun just in case, if he was such a hardened criminal.'

Edward looked thoughtful. He could do that in public. 'Before I finish with the Greenes setting up the fake kidnapping, let me go back to the murder. How do we know it was the Greenes who killed Tony Alberico?' He went back to his fingers. 'First, it still hasn't been solved. Well-known local artist murdered, police should have solved that by now. Right? No signs of a burglary, must have been someone he knew. Police would have devoted hours and days to that. The detective told you they did. And they came up with nobody.

'Because Diana and then Sterling were the secret suspects. Diana certainly tried to keep the affair unknown, from everybody including her husband. And if you don't know about Diana you don't guess Sterling. Once they fled that house they were half-safe already. So how do I know they killed Tony?

'Several things. First, that painting. They didn't buy that painting. Sterling stole it. That painting wasn't a commercial object, it was an act of love. Tony did that for himself. Himself and Diana. Study that painting when you go back into the jury room. That's not a portrait an artist painted of a woman to sell to her husband. That was going to be Tony's keepsake when the affair inevitably ended. They didn't go through his usual broker because there was no sale. When Sterling saw it the day of the murder he couldn't keep himself from taking it. It was part of his proof that Diana had been having an affair. Maybe he wanted to hold it over her head for the rest of their lives. For whatever reason, he stole it. He didn't buy it. He didn't produce a receipt because he doesn't have one.

'That's one thing. Minor, you might say, but I disagree. It's what proves the affair and therefore the murder. Tony tried to

put it all in that painting. First because he was in love but also
because he was trying to say something. Tony knew about
Sterling's reputation. His jealousy, his rages. Tony did his best
to protect himself from that by pretending to befriend Sterling
and by buying a gun. He also tried to send a message about who
his killer was if he didn't make it. He sent me – he sent us – a
couple of messages from the grave.'

Edward took the now-unwrapped nude painting from its place
with the other evidence in front of the judge's bench, gave it a
close, blank-faced study himself, then turned it toward the jurors.
'He marked his killer. He marked Diana as being involved, being
the reason. See the neck in this portrait? The mark, maybe a love
bite, something? It's there. Diana also had that mark on her neck
after she was freed by the SWAT team. The nurse noted it in her
report, the day of the fake kidnapping, the day of the murder.
Some kind of actual mark on her very real neck.'

With his other hand he picked up the batch of nude photos.
'But it wasn't there before. Look at these pictures. They detail
every inch of Diana. No mark on her neck. And none when she
testified. It had healed by then.

'Infatuated as he was, Tony was afraid of what might be
coming. So when he painted his lover he painted that non-existent
mark on her neck. So tiny no one might notice. But when the
time came, when he sensed his murder coming, he gave the real
Diana that same mark on her actual neck. As clear a sign as he
could send. "This is the one."' He shrugged. 'You may think
that's fanciful, but I think that's how his artist mind worked.' He
looked out into the audience. 'But if he marked Diana, he also
marked Sterling. Maybe not as deliberately, but certainly. How?
Tony marked Sterling with his friendship. His pretend friendship.
You heard that in his last weeks Tony spent a lot of time with
Sterling Greene. "They became great friends," Diana said. They
were seen at a lot of public events together. Why? Because
Sterling and Tony had so much in common? Please. They had
nothing in common. Tony would never be friends with someone
like Sterling. A boorish clod with no taste in anything except
perhaps women. No, Tony tried desperately to befriend him so
Sterling wouldn't suspect him as his wife's secret lover. It didn't
work in the end, but he tried.'

Edward bent his neck and blinked rapidly. Then he took a deep breath and lifted his gaze to the jurors. 'There's other evidence of the affair, and it happened right here in front of you. I released Mr and Mrs Greene from The Rule so they could be here in the courtroom. You all don't know about the Rule, this is your first trial, but believe me that's very unusual. I did it because I wanted to see Sterling's reaction to certain pieces of evidence and testimony, and I wanted if possible for you to see it too.'

That's why Edward had made such a point of turning and looking at Sterling during some of the testimony. He'd wanted to direct the jurors' attention towards him. He didn't know whether he'd succeeded or not. And sometimes he'd been paying attention to the witness and couldn't observe them.

'Did you see him when the SANE nurse mentioned his wife's "recent sexual activity?" He was surprised. And furious. Did you see Sterling's face when he heard that news? "Recent sexual activity." He knew that hadn't been with him, and he knew it hadn't been with Donald. Diana certainly would have shared that detail with police, if they had that against the supposed kidnapper. No, the recent sexual activity had been with someone else, and Sterling knew exactly whom. Tony Alberico. Maybe Diana had convinced her husband she'd gone there to break up with her lover, or that he wasn't her lover at all, he'd just been stalking her. Whatever. When Sterling heard about the recent sexual activity, all that story went to hell. No, she'd had sex with Tony Alberico before Sterling got there. It was still on between the two of them. And if you saw Sterling's face at that moment, you know he realized it too.' He looked out into the audience again. This time Sterling was maintaining control of his face, but he was smoldering. 'I would love to have been at the Greenes' house that night.'

He really would have. Linda had tried it, in fact. He saw her sitting out in that audience too, about halfway up, an interesting smile on her face. She nodded.

Edward went back to stand behind his client again. 'So the Greenes were trapped with a dead body and needed a story.

'This is the most cynical thing the Greenes did. The most disgusting. The casting. When they picked who to cast as the

kidnapper they knew this day would come. This trial. They probably hoped with Donald's record he'd roll over and plead guilty,
but they knew most likely whoever they chose would fight the
case because it wasn't true. So they needed to pick somebody
who'd naturally be disbelieved as compared to them. Sterling
thought quickly and quickly settled on cliché. Big black guy. "Who
was the suspect, sir?" "It was a big black guy, Officer. That's all
I really remember." Cynical. Big black ex-con, even better, famous
for just what they were going to charge him with. He was perfect.
Perfect for a certain kind of thinker. A certain kind of criminal.'
Edward continued to stand there with his hands on his client's
shoulders. 'They're counting on that with you. That racism. That
limited thinking. Be better than that. Be better than them.'

He had more to say. He always did. But that sounded like an
end line, and Edward took it. He circled Donald and sat.

Silence extended. It fed on itself and grew. Edward sat there
with his eyes down, thinking of things he should have said and
hadn't. No point in concentrating on his adversary, because he
wouldn't get to respond to her arguments anyway.

But finally the silence tapped him on the shoulder and made
him look up. Veronica sat there staring into nothing. Then she
obviously felt the weight of the silence too. She rose slowly,
using the arms of her chair, and walked toward the jury. As she
did her back stiffened and her cheekbones became prominent.
'That's a hell of a story,' she said icily. 'Something we can always
expect from Edward Hall. He had to come up with something
to divert attention from his client, because he's so obviously
guilty. And yes, the real story is a common one, with no twists.
A criminal commits a crime. A kidnapper kidnaps. There's a
reason some stories are obvious. Because they follow logic.
They're the way we all know things happen.'

She turned to look at Edward. Not his client, Edward. There
was something odd in Veronica's expression, with her back to
the jury. Edward thought there was some desire mixed in there
with whatever else, but that might have been his ego whispering
in his ear. He looked back at her flatly.

'But here's what you need to ask yourselves,' Veronica said
to him, before turning back to the jurors. 'It's an interesting
theory, it's a fun story, but if Mr Hall had any evidence at all

that Mr and Mrs Greene, the obvious victims in this case, had committed some crime that had nothing to do with this kidnapping, why didn't he take that evidence to police? It's an unsolved murder, police would be very—'

'I did.'

Edward almost didn't recognize his own voice. He didn't have a voice during his adversary's argument, he wasn't allowed to speak. But that was definitely him talking.

Veronica whirled. 'Damn you, you don't get to talk dur—' Then she stopped, looking up into the audience. Edward didn't have to turn and look over his own shoulder. He knew what she was seeing. Detective Reynolds, the homicide detective, sitting up there high in the audience, impeccably dressed again, probably with his long fingers steepled together. And this time he wasn't alone. There was a uniformed cop beside each exit door, standing at ease as if just watching an interesting trial.

Veronica just stared. Probably bad move, that, because it invited jurors to do the same. Edward finally did turn and look. At Linda. This time he returned her smile.

THIRTY-TWO

The jury wasn't out long after that. The drama didn't happen in the jury room, it continued in the courtroom. Veronica stood so stiffly while the jurors trailed out it looked as if her spine would snap. 'You!' she said quickly as soon as the door closed behind them. 'You with your . . .'

Edward ignored her. He hurried to the gate in the rail and up the first few steps. Sterling Greene was faster. He was already hurtling up that aisle. Detective Reynolds stepped out to intercept him. It looked like Sterling would barrel through him, or try, but then he stopped, they exchanged a few words, and walked out together, Sterling turning to direct one last glare at Edward before the detective led him away.

Edward shrugged it off and went to Linda. 'Thanks.'

She stood and put her hands on him. 'Just made a call, like any concerned citizen would.'

He chuckled. It was weird when a trial ended, like a soldier being home on unexpected leave, feeling the war still going on. Edward needed to decompress from the constant pressure he'd felt for weeks, leading up to this trial. It was going to be difficult to do the ordinary things in life without being poised to object or react. He kissed Linda right there in the courtroom, but very chastely. At least he hoped so. They walked out holding hands.

But couldn't go very far. Donald joined them in the basement at Luby's. Having coffee in cracked ceramic cups. Edward's just sat there.

'Now what?' Donald asked.

But there was no now. There was just then, the future, after whatever was about to happen happened. They couldn't do anything until then.

Edward's cell phone finally beeped. Damned jurors, they'd been out an hour. Only an hour. A long, long hour.

When they reassembled in the courtroom the cast had some disappearances, notably the Greenes. And the cops. But the district attorney was there, looking bleak. 'Good job,' she said to Edward as he walked by. Her stare saying something else entirely. Her sister possibly charged as an accomplice to murder. It was clear Julia had expected something else as the outcome to this trial.

Judge Roberts looked at the lawyers and at Donald. Veronica hadn't done the same. She remained rigid, gaze directed only at the judge. She hadn't met eyes with Edward since he'd turned away from her after the jurors went out.

When the jurors filed in like baby ducks they bore the usual scrutiny with equanimity, most of them with eyes downcast. Jurors always seemed to hate their few moments of trial stardom. But they clearly knew all eyes were on them.

'I'm told you have a verdict,' Judge Roberts said. 'Which of you is the presiding juror?' The word 'foreman' had been replaced. Sexist. A thirtyish Hispanic man at one end of the front row raised his hand. 'Is your verdict unanimous?' the judge asked.

The presiding juror rose to nod. 'Yes, sir.'

'Why don't you read it to us then?' Judge Roberts asked gently. Most judges preferred to do that themselves, or at least read it before anyone else got to hear. It was nicely old school when a judge asked the juror to do it.

Edward stood and urged Donald up too. The presiding juror cleared his throat and, looking nowhere but at the paper, said, 'We the jury on the charge of kidnapping in the first degree find the defendant not guilty.'

He folded the paper and handed it to the bailiff. There was no sound. Edward was gripping his client's arm, feeling Donald's intended scream of joy. Veronica just sat.

Then a rustle started from the audience, as if the words had taken that long to reach them. Somebody clapped, just two or three times. Whispered comments began to reach the lawyers. Edward turned and accepted Donald's hug, looking past him. Veronica just sat. She declined the judge's offer to poll the jury, and the judge said, 'Since that is your verdict, ladies and gentlemen, your service is now concluded and you are free to go.'

Most judges made the jurors return to the jury room one last time and went back there to talk to them, thank them for their service, so forth, because after all they were voters. Judge Roberts just released them on the spot. Two as they filed out stopped to shake hands with Donald. Veronica just sat, not looking at them. But Edward stared thoughtfully at her.

Minutes passed, and the world turned gradually into one in which no trial was looming. It wasn't until these moments that Edward always realized what a different world that was, Trial World, going to sleep and waking up knowing exactly where he'd be at nine a.m. He looked around for Linda and didn't see her as he walked out into the hall with his client. The judge didn't detain them for any post-trial conference, either, though he might call the lawyers and ask them to come in in a couple of days from now. Normally Edward and his opposing counsel would shake hands and murmur congratulations, but clearly Veronica wasn't in the mood. She'd already gathered up her few things and fled in long, brisk strides.

After Edward accepted Donald's effusive thanks with a pat on the shoulder, he said, 'Go celebrate, big guy,' and went looking for his own celebration, but he found Linda working in another courtroom, her fingers moving quickly while she smiled without looking at him. He gave her a thumbs up and walked out.

Edward didn't carry a briefcase this morning, his hands were empty. He waited patiently for the elevator and didn't mind the stops on nearly every floor on the way down. The elevator looked very pretty this afternoon. So did the people in it.

Edward was clothed in a quiet little smile without knowing it. Down on the sidewalk, halfway back to his car, he finally let out a whoop, pumping his fist. A Not Guilty was rare enough for a defense lawyer. Under the circumstances of this case it was huge. The DA was clearly pissed off, but she couldn't deny he'd done his job. Neither could the State Bar. Edward grew more somber and thoughtful as he resumed his walk. Now he had to decide whether he really wanted to continue to try to be a lawyer. There'd be a certain satisfaction in walking away on a win. Certainly a mic drop moment. He'd be hearing congratulations on this for days if he remained in the courthouse world. The legend continues. He'd . . .

'Asshole.'

The world wasn't supposed to revert to reality that quickly. Edward turned and saw Sterling Greene around the corner he'd just passed. Sterling no longer wore his suit jacket. His shoulders strained his white shirt. Edward thought he could probably outrun Sterling Greene on a given day, but the tire iron in Sterling's hand added several angles to that problem. It could be a hurled weapon as well as a club.

'How did you—?'

'They didn't arrest me, asshole, they just wanted to question me, and I told them to fuck off, see my lawyer.'

Edward closely studied his red face, wondering if he could goad the big man into a stroke before Sterling killed him.

'So you want to hire me?'

Inappropriate humor had gotten Edward in trouble before, and this occasion was no exception. Sterling screamed and rushed him. Edward ducked his shoulder. They were too close, if he turned to run Sterling would bash the back of his skull. He could feel the blow coming. If Edward got low enough he might be able to flip the charging titan over his back, but Sterling probably didn't have enough speed for that. So Edward moved sideways, hoping to dodge his initial rush and slip to the side. But the tire iron was already descending. Edward wondered if it would hurt or if darkness would just overwhelm him suddenly. At that moment, the latter sounded great.

He was screaming himself, he knew. The clash of sounds were dueling if the men were not. Edward waited for the blow.

And something happened. What happened was nothing happened. Edward continued his slide out of the way and looked up. A hand even bigger than Sterling's had closed over Sterling's, holding the tire iron in place. A dark brown hand.

Sterling was straining, but Donald just held him easily in place. Then Donald pushed his face forward, only an inch from Sterling's. The businessman flinched. He released his grip on the iron, and Donald let him. It clattered to the sidewalk.

'And I'm going to get you charged with that drive-by too,' Edward said. 'You're the only one who wanted him dead so he couldn't testify, then wanted both of us dead so this trial would never happen.'

He waited for some denial, but Sterling only shook a finger at both of them and didn't have to say, *This isn't over.* Then he stalked away, trying to maintain his dignity. Edward stifled his urge to laugh. He called after his departing attacker, 'And I am pressing assault charges.' Sterling raised one finger without looking back.

Then Edward did laugh. 'Thanks, Donald.' He held out his hand.

Donald took it. 'Thought he might try somethin'. I owe you more than that, man. Thank you.'

Edward waited for the manly moment to end. He was grateful when his cell phone squalled for his attention.

It was David Galindo's voice on the other end, the assistant DA and Edward's former colleague and adversary. 'The DA wants to see you,' David said without preamble.

'Of course she does,' Edward said.

THIRTY-THREE

They were all there in the conference room a few feet from Julia's office. David lounging against the wall, his boss seated and glowering, but only at the tabletop, as if she didn't want to give away her feelings about Edward yet. As if anyone needed a clue.

This time Veronica was there too. And very oddly, Diana Greene. The group was rounded out by the nice young woman from the State Bar, Ms Swan.

'You're all supposed to shout "Surprise",' Edward said.

'Shut up for once.' Julia barely moved her mouth. Then her face did lift to him. Her eyes were rather deadened instead of blazing, as if she was remembering an old tragedy.

She said, 'Congratulations, you found a murderer and got a kidnapper off.'

'An accused kidnapper. And accused no longer. Your sister's lie got found out.'

Edward looked at the sister. Diana didn't look back. Edward had never seen anyone so white, up to the roots of her dark hair. Her fingers trembled as she raised them to her lips.

'Has Sterling been arrested?' Julia asked.

'He has been now. But for assaulting me, not for murder. Police are still investigating that. But they've got fresh clues now. Once they started looking at Mr and Mrs Greene as suspects other leads turned up.'

Now Diana's eyes fastened on him. Edward nodded to her.

'I thought Sterling came to Tony's house, caught him in bed with Diana, and shot him. The classic scene. Should've been in *Hamlet*. But I've had time to think about it now, and that's not how it was.'

'What makes you think you know this?' Julia asked.

'A few things. But mainly this. Tony was killed with his own gun. He'd only bought it a few weeks before his death and it was completely out of character for him according to his friends. Once he'd started banging Diana' – Edward was deliberately as harsh as possible. Diana put a hand to her lips – 'he was terrified of Sterling. He would never have opened his door to Sterling with Mrs Greene naked in the bedroom. He certainly wouldn't have let Sterling get close enough to use Tony's own gun on him. If anything, if Sterling had burst in Tony would have shot him, with perfect justification. Plus Sterling had no motive.'

'What?' This from Julia, while her sister stayed silent, eyes downcast. 'You just laid out the classic motive.'

Interesting she used the word 'laid.' Edward shook his head. 'I don't think so. Maybe actually seeing his wife physically in another man's bed might have made Sterling mad enough to shoot the man on the spot, but how'd he get the gun? How did he get into the bedroom? No, Sterling's only motive would have been to walk away. He'd already had Diana sign a post-nup, he'd already consulted a divorce lawyer. She was on marital probation. He'd told her if he caught her once more he was done.'

This time Diana did look up. Her eyes looked like marbles, cold glass. Edward said to her, 'No, the one who had a big motive was Diana, and the motive was to save her marriage. I think she felt a little too post-debutante to start looking for another husband. Maybe she could have found one just as rich, but I have it on good authority she'd already tried once and failed. No, I think Sterling must have found out about the affair – it would have been easy, just have his wife followed to that studio in West U – and was ready to pull the trigger on the divorce. And Diana knew it, she could sense his changed attitude, maybe Sterling had actually told her. In any event, she needed to prove her devotion. She went to Tony's for a tearful goodbye that did end in bed. That's when he realized what was coming, at least that's what I think, and gave her that love bite on the neck that he'd anticipated weeks in advance. That was him sending a message from the grave: she's the one.'

Edward looked around the room. No one interrupted him. 'By the time Sterling arrived Tony was already dead. Your sister had killed him. She was dressed and so was the corpse. She presented the body to her husband like an anniversary present. "Look how much I love you." She'd removed the man who threatened to break up her marriage. She didn't tell Sterling about the sexy goodbye, because he was clearly surprised by that testimony at trial. "Recent sexual activity." My God, that's cold,' he said to

Diana, who wouldn't look at him. 'But here's the beauty part. Her killing the artist, her lover, actually did make Sterling want her. Want to keep her. He started helping her immediately. They were the natural suspects. Someone might have seen either of them, if police came immediately and could pin down the time of death. They had to do something to throw attention elsewhere. Throw together a plot where they were somewhere else.

'It wasn't Sterling who killed Tony Alberico, Julia. It was your sister.'

Diana was softly sobbing, head down. Everyone else looked at Edward skeptically. The district attorney, her arms folded, was more than skeptical. She was furious.

Edward looked straight at her. 'And what's more, Julia, you knew it.'

'What?!' Now she leapt to her feet.

Edward didn't take a step back. 'Yes. Either Diana told you what she'd done, some version of it, maybe because you already knew about the affair. You two are very close, she probably shares with you, maybe more than she knows. Yes. You intuited the truth, or she outright told you. Because you did two unusual things. No, three. You got me appointed to defend Donald, thinking you'd have a hold over me to talk him into pleading guilty and making the whole thing go away quietly. Then, between the events and when Donald needed to have a lawyer appointed, you fired one of your best prosecutors.' He pointed at Veronica, who was looking at her former boss, not at Edward. 'Certainly your most ruthless prosecutor, one you wouldn't even have to tell to come after me as hard as she could. With either the outright promise of getting her job back or an unspoken agreement.'

Ms Swan, the woman from the State Bar, said, 'How do you get there?'

'Veronica wasn't even trying to establish a practice. She was officing out of her house, making only minimal efforts to get appointed on other cases. Some firm would have hired her, such a good trial lawyer, but Veronica didn't even try. No, she anticipated coming back into the DA's office after this trial. Right, Julia?'

She was back to the folded arms. It somehow made her look vulnerable. Defensive. 'Absolutely not. I'd never have her back in my office.'

'Ouch.' Edward looked down at Veronica, who had now turned her gaze on him, giving him a slow third-degree burn. Edward had just screwed up her life plan, he felt pretty sure.

'It's debatable whether she'll have a license to practice law anyway,' Mrs Swan interjected.

'What?' That came from both Julia and Veronica, the latter swiveling to stare at her. 'I never—'

Ms Swan silenced her with a small hand. She spoke only to Julia. 'I noticed the defense case in this trial looked very much like a prosecution case. The defense was presenting evidence the prosecutor should have presented. Just out of curiosity, I contacted the cell phone providers Edward used as witnesses. They confirmed Ms Salazar here had obtained the same records much earlier. Records she hadn't turned over to the defense as required by *Brady*.'

Brady v. Maryland, a long-time Supreme Court precedent that required prosecutors to give evidence favorable to the defendant to the defense. Edward watched the slender young woman from behind a hand that hid his smile. She knew more about trials than he'd expected.

'Because of that, I obtained a search warrant of my own, to search Ms Salazar's home.'

'What?' Veronica leaped to her feet. 'The State Bar? You can't do that.'

Ms Swan shrugged. 'You can challenge the search, but our hearings aren't bound by the rules of evidence.'

'Anyway . . .' Edward waved Veronica to silence.

'This morning while you two were in trial, a detective found in Ms Salazar's home office a whole other file on the case, including statements from two other witnesses in the neighborhood who saw Mrs Greene walking into that house apparently completely willingly, leading the way in fact, with her head uncovered. More evidence that should have been turned over to the defense.'

Edward said, 'It doesn't sting as much as you'd think to get disbarred, Veronica. Beats the hell out of going to prison.'

Ms Swan turned to Edward with the slight beginning of a smile. So faint he could have been imagining it. But he was starting to like her. 'You said there was a third odd thing the district attorney did,' she said.

'Oh. Yes. She got the case landed initially in the court of a judge who was one of Veronica's best friends. Oh, stop, Julia, everyone knows a DA can manipulate where a case gets filed. Anyway, you send me to a judge you knew and I didn't who liked Veronica and wanted to help her out. Were you in on that, David? You must have been. You were the one who suggested I go to that judge to appoint the DA *pro tem.*'

David Galindo looked at him and didn't respond. Edward shrugged. 'At any rate, Mrs Greene, you should probably go turn yourself in to police as soon as possible. Because your husband's in their custody already, trying to talk his way out of a murder charge, and you're the only person he has to throw under that particular bus.'

Nearly everyone in the room started talking, except Edward. He turned and walked out, leaving everyone else in the room to sweep up the shards. It was very satisfying.

He was happy to find Linda was also through for the day, and the two of them went to their favorite restaurant, Linda's kitchen, picking up Thai food on the way. A while later, both of them down to shorts and T-shirts and with cardboard cartons mostly empty, Edward through telling her the rest of the story, Linda finished with telling him about her day. Linda summarized, 'So maybe you can start practicing law again.'

He nodded. 'Yeah. In a jurisdiction where the DA hates my guts.'

'No, hates that you have guts.'

Edward smiled at the remains of the feast. 'Nice celebration.'

'That wasn't the celebration, idiot,' Linda said, her smile erasing the insult. 'Come here.'

Two of the finest words one person can say to another, especially with that slow smile of Linda's drawing him in as she leaned back in her seat.

Edward went there.

ACKNOWLEDGMENTS

Thanks to my agent Ann Collette for her editorial advice and encouragement.

Everyone at Severn House has been wonderful to work with: Kate Lyall Grant, Carl Smith, Anna Harrisson, and Natasha Bell.

And as usual thanks to my old friend Robert Morrow for continuing advice on life in the Harris County Justice Center and Houston in general.